The Rare Pearl

Broken Water Series

Book 1

Wentworth-by-the-Sea

Jennifer W. Smith

Published by Ö Apple House Publishing
ISBN: 978-0-9966954-3-5

Visit Jennifer W Smith's official website at
www.jenniferwsmith.com for the latest news,
book details, and other information

Editing by Sue Ducharme of Textworks

Printed in the U.S.A

DEDICATION

For you, my husband, who stands by my side — a solid citadel, or shield when needed. Thank you for supporting my passions and sharing in the family life we've built together.

1

The thick fog came out of nowhere. It rolled in, consuming daylight, extinguishing the shimmer that gleamed off the ocean's surface. Dense fog pressed the waves flat, the sea still as glass. The thirty-five-foot cruising vessel was cradled in silence, until its three passengers anxiously discussed their concerns over the unexpected weather.

"I heard it was supposed to be a nice sunny day. Where on earth is this fog coming from?" Margaret asked Harry. She slid her sunglasses down her nose.

Harry, the boat owner, stepped onto the bridge of his Pilothouse boat and tried the radio, but it crackled and fuzzed in reply. "I dunno. I've lost radio contact."

In minutes, the boat was enclosed in compressed, moist mist. Margaret could barely see Harry's wife sitting next to her.

"Curse this New England weather! Harry, maybe we should cut our pleasure cruise short. It's not so pleasurable if you can't see anything," Harry's wife complained before she moved to the helm to switch on the cabin's interior lamp. Lighting the fixture didn't help; the glare seemed to make the fog opaque.

Suddenly, something solid bumped the side of the boat. The two ladies squealed.

"What was that? It can't be another boat!" Harry's wife cried as she peered out the window over the bow.

Harry grumbled at his wife's frantic voice. "No, it can't be a boat. I don't hear any motor. I dunno..." he said, his voice trailing away in the mist.

"Maybe it's a shark?" his wife whispered to her

best friend Margaret, who stood at her elbow to join her friend's investigation. Nothing could be seen over the bow; only a splash revealed something big was out there. The boaters strained their ears, listening.

Before anyone could propose further theories, the water seemed to boil like a lobster pot. Something was rising to the surface. *No shark makes this commotion or that glugging noise,* Margaret thought.

"Maybe it's a whale?" Margaret said, knowing the whale-watching tour boats passed through these waters during tourist season. Something large was surfacing, and her mind screamed, *That is no whale!* Her gut twisted, and all the hairs on her arms stood on end. With rising panic, Margaret recalled the stories her grandmother had told her about the ancient water god and how he would send his sirens and sea monsters to collect the souls of his victims. Her heart rammed against her ribcage, and she placed a sun-spotted hand over it. In an attempt to control her rising fear, Margaret murmured a silent prayer to the ancient water god. "Give us safe passage. Give us safe passage."

"What the hell is that? Sounds like a submarine broaching!" said Harry, a World War II navy veteran. The sound, like steel banging against steel, rang in their ears. Harry opened a storage compartment and yanked out orange vests. "Ladies! Put these on!" He locked eyes with this wife of forty-four years, the flotation device between them, and he saw her confusion. Abruptly the blanket of turbulent water made the boat dip and spin, and something thrust upward with tremendous force. From far above they were showered in sea spray, as if from a surrogate rain cloud. The boat rocked dangerously, and Margaret, Harry, and his wife each grabbed on to something solid, trying to maintain their footing. The spray hissed around them. Another unearthly sound was soon unleashed, like the blast of a

fog horn. The passengers fell to their knees, h
pressed to their ears.

Margaret squinted at the orange vest on the deck
her knee. With a trembling hand she snatched for it,
the rolling vessel sent her crashing into the bench se
Slumped to the deck, she could just see her dear frienc
clinging together. Her eyes searched up into the fog. Th
blast rolled out over the open sea like a fading echo until
she heard only the fear pounding in her ears.

Through the impenetrable fog, they never saw what
capsized the boat and sent them to their watery graves.
The water god looked on. His sea serpent collected one
very important soul that day.

***

1989

The waning moon winked behind fast-moving clouds.
The silhouette of the enormous, decaying hotel sprawled
before her. It had been in a state of hibernation for
almost seven years. Originally built in 1874, it had
undergone various architectural changes over the last
one hundred years. Today the main portico and three
iconic towers loomed in the darkness. The Victorian
section gave the hotel a hulking dominance over the
hillside on the tiny island. The island town of New
Castle, New Hampshire, encompassed about five
hundred acres, and the hotel and grounds occupied three
hundred of those acres. This snip of land tucked into the
protective cove of coastline was connected to the
mainland by two squat bridges, one just below the hotel
and the other off the tip of its cape.

Harmony Parker lived on the other side of the island,
up the road to the end and then left at the water's edge,

ands

by
but
it.
s
e

thing about this building that always
. to it. Its vacant shell haunted her
.ne hotel, the Wentworth-by-the-Sea, sat
.ne ocean at its face and a bay at its back
.ft Piscataqua River hugged the far side of
n a clear day it was said that visitors could
.k of Mt. Washington and three states—New
.e, Maine, and Massachusetts—from their
.m windows.

.nony stashed her bicycle behind an overgrown
.t the base of the hill, out of sight of the cars that
.sed the bridges to pass through the small
.nmunity. Her Reeboks crunched along the sparse
.ass, dirt, and gravel beneath her feet. No Trespassing
.signs were posted, but Harmony circled around the
property and slipped through a crudely cut opening in
the chainlink fence that caged the almost-extinct
dinosaur. She'd snuck in numerous times as a teenager,
day and night, but nobody had ever bothered her. She'd
roamed the vacant halls in wonder of bygone days. She
felt compelled to visit this place tonight, even though she
was an adult and too old to be breaking and entering.
She entered her usual way and once inside the venerable
building snapped on her flashlight.

Harmony strolled along the familiar corridors.
Everything was gone. At the four-day auction held in
1982, hundreds had swarmed to claim a piece of the
Wentworth's history. The investment company had sold
off all the furniture, linens, kitchen equipment, and
silverware—everything, down to the last muffin tin.
Later, they salvaged the architectural details, the doors,
and the light fixtures. This shadow was all that was left
of a handful of surviving Gilded Age grand hotels along
New England's coast. Harmony thought with grief,
*There is so much history here — even my personal family
history — and it may all be lost if they demolish her.*

4

Entering a room on the second floor, she stood by the window, looking out at the seemingly tranquil waters of the Atlantic Ocean. *She* was out there somewhere, her grandmother, Margaret Parker. Lost at sea, her body never found. Harmony remembered the day last fall when she had been informed about the drowning like it was yesterday...

She'd sat in a lecture hall, listening to her college professor drone on about details of Mesopotamian architecture, when she was tapped on the shoulder. She looked up from her notebook at a lady wearing a dusty-rose suit with boxy shoulder pads. The tiny woman waved for Harmony to follow her. Recognizing the woman as one of the counselors on campus, she grabbed her stuff and left the auditorium. Harmony wondered what could possibly be urgent enough to pull her from class.

The counselor introduced herself in the deserted corridor and said gravely, "We've just received a call from the Portsmouth Coast Guard in New Hampshire. Apparently there's been a boating accident involving your grandmother, Margaret Parker. I'm very sorry to inform you that the boat she was on has sunk, and all three passengers are presumed drowned."

Harmony's thoughts honed in on the fact that her grandmother had *drowned*! Of all the ways to lose someone... Another family member drowning couldn't be a coincidence.

She blinked and focused on the spider web that stretched across the windowpane. With a shake to ward off eerie thoughts of drowning, she inhaled the unpleasant scent of mildew and rotting wood. She lifted her flashlight and circled the perimeter of the dark guestroom. The plaster walls were crumbling, and the slatted boards behind them rose like an old picket fence. Something metallic reflected between them as the beam of light swung by. That caught her attention, and she slowly refocused her torch on the area. There it was again. *What is that?* The dirt shuffled under her feet as she stepped closer.

Harmony slid her fingers between the two-inch-wide boards and yanked. Immediately she withdrew her hand, rubbing the grime between her fingers. Still curious, she tried again, and the board cracked—a little. Putting her shoulder into the next tug, she broke a long section of brittle board away with a snap. Dust billowed, and plaster jingled like loose coins down the wall to the floor. She placed the rough panel at her feet and angled her flashlight inside to get better look. *Hmm, it looks like a bag of some kind. Maybe a purse?* She snapped several more boards away, enough to fit her hand inside the wall. The jagged wood scratched the tender skin of her forearm, and she bit her bottom lip to stifle an oath. Grasping the bag and ignoring the grimy feel of the fabric, she let out the breath she'd been holding. She lifted the bag gingerly toward the opening she'd made, but it was slightly too small, and her arm remained trapped. Wedging the flashlight between her knees, she used her free hand to pop another board, releasing the contents held tightly in her grasp.

Ha! I got it!

She examined the pouch with her flashlight. Its long strap could be worn across the body, and a front flap secured its contents with a buckle. The buckle's metallic reflection had given away its location. The bag looked like leather, but it was so dirty it was hard for Harmony to tell for sure. *Wow, how did the scavengers miss this?* She laughed gleefully at her good fortune. Before she could open it, she heard the *whoop, whoop* of a police siren. Her luck had changed. She heard the cruiser pull up in front of the building, on the ocean side.

The police frequently patrolled this abandoned hotel

to scare away squatters, salvagers, and teenagers. They offered a warning with their siren and gave the fence a onceover, but mostly they just used this quiet spot to stretch their legs.

Oh no...time to go. Harmony clicked off her flashlight and slipped it into her back pocket. In the dark, she maneuvered her way to a room at the back of the hotel. Peering out the open window, she checked to see if the coast was clear and then slipped out onto the fire escape. Her sneakers clanked against the metal steps, and she prayed the patrol officer couldn't hear her. She trekked down the remaining stories. Reaching the ladder, she managed the rungs hand over foot, the satchel awkwardly clamped under her arm, until her foot hit a sturdy pile of long-forgotten boards. She swung as if on a trapeze from the last rung onto the overgrown grass and crouched, listening. A long inhale of salty air replaced the dank smell of the Wentworth's interior, calming her erratic heartbeat.

Harmony picked her way through the dead grass and sticks littering the ground until she reached the chainlink fence. She guessed scavengers, or teenagers wanting a place to party, had made the opening years back. Barehanded, she rolled the cold bouncy metal links, bunching them in her hands as best she could, so the pointed edges wouldn't catch her clothing. She ducked down and slipped through, out of the cage.

Harmony retrieved her bike from the bushes and placed her new-found treasure into the basket that hung off the handle bars. She melted away undetected down the dark, narrow ribbon of road in the mild March night.

2

Harmony, giddy with excitement that she'd found a relic in the Wentworth-by-the-Sea, resisted the tempting urge to stop on the side of the road and open the bag. Luckily, the rest of the road was relatively flat, making it a short, easy ride back to her house. There she could look at her findings in better lighting. On the front lawn, she slipped off the seat and walked her bike around to the back where she usually left it parked by the porch. She was deep in thought, so when she heard "*Psst*," she squeaked in surprise.

At the sound of familiar laughter, Harmony cried, "Samantha! You scared me half to death. What are you doing here so late?"

Samantha emerged from the screen porch, holding her stomach with one hand, laughing over giving her good friend a fright. When her giggles died down she held up a small bottle of Pepsi. "I just got this from your fridge. I saw your bike was gone, so I was going to sit on the porch and wait for you for a few minutes," Samantha said. She commented casually, "It's such a warm night." Indeed, rarely in early March did the evening temperature reach sixty degrees.

Samantha Finch, Harmony's longtime neighbor and best friend since grade school, often made herself at home in the Parker's house. Samantha was home on vacation for a couple of weeks after a year of travel. The production company she worked for produced a weather series that aired on PBS, the Public Broadcast System. Samantha hosted the series.

In high school both girls had joined Drama Club. Harmony had a better singing voice but only felt comfortable singing in the chorus, while Samantha, who had taken voice lessons for years and loved all things theatrical, tried out for every lead. Samantha's perky disposition made her popular, and as a result she managed to star in every production. She'd headed off to college to study meteorology, her sights on becoming the weather girl on a major broadcast news station.

"Yeah, it's unusually warm…balmy even," Harmony agreed, engaging the kickstand.

"Where were you?" Samantha watched Harmony lift something from the basket of her bike. "What's that?"

"I'm not sure. Come on, let's go inside so we can get a better look." Samantha followed Harmony back to the screened porch and waited while she retrieved the hidden key Samantha had used to get in and grab a Pepsi from the fridge. Harmony explained she was inside the Wentworth looking around when she'd spotted this bag hidden in the wall. She replaced the key under the vase filled with silk flowers and opened the door to the kitchen.

"Oh." Samantha didn't sound enthusiastic.

Harmony knew her obsession with the old hotel was puzzling to Samantha. Her friend understood the Wentworth's architecture appealed to Harmony, who majored in architectural history. She even acknowledged that their families had spent a lot of time there years before it closed. But the girls were only sixteen when "The Grand Lady" closed her doors, and those memories were filled with a hotel that was going downhill. At sixteen, Harmony knew Samantha had more important things on her mind, like getting her license, dating, and performing on the stage at the local performing arts center. In the last several years, Harmony had practically begged her to join the preservation group that stormed town meetings on behalf of their town's historic treasure, but Samantha didn't have the emotional connection or the time, so Harmony wasn't surprised by her lackluster reaction.

Inside the kitchen, Harmony flicked the wall switch, and the brass fixture came to light over the oak table. She tore away a paper towel from the roll suspended under a cabinet and wrapped it under the dirty bag before setting it on the table.

"I can't wait to find out what's inside!" She drew her shoulders to her ears and squeezed her fists in excitement before unfastening the clasp. She eased the old leather flap open. *Yes, definitely leather.*

She lifted out a tin not much bigger than the palm of her hand. It was so light she wondered if there was anything inside. She gave it a slight shake and felt something shift. She carefully lifted off the unmarked lid. A thin paper nested within, and she fingered it aside. Peering inside, the only sound she made was "Hmm."

"What is it?" Samantha's face came close to Harmony's, cheek to cheek, to see what was so interesting. "Is that tea?" Samantha slumped into a chair and twisted the lid off her soda. "I wouldn't brew that if I were you. From the looks of that dirty old bag, it's probably been in the wall for fifty years." She took a swig of her Pepsi and commented, "You should get Diet Pepsi. Everyone is switching because it has no calories."

Harmony rooted around inside the bag, but the tin was its only contents, and she felt a little disappointed as she tucked the tin back into its longtime resting place. However, she'd been lucky enough to find something left at the Wentworth, no matter how insignificant.

Harmony eyed her friend critically. Samantha was already thin. She shouldn't worry about drinking a no-calorie soda. But she was, after all, a television celebrity who had to keep her figure. Beautiful, charismatic Samantha kept her dirty-blond hair long enough to fall just past her shoulders. Harmony knew she worked with a curling iron to get it as wavy as Harmony's. Of course, with Samantha being a theater junkie, her only wish to be famous, she had mad hair envy. When strangers asked if they were sisters, Samantha argued it was because they had the same wavy blond hair. Harmony was pleased her best friend had achieved the career she desired, but she'd missed her constantly.

Harmony confessed, "I'm glad you're here. It's been tough coming home without my grandmother here."

"It is strange without her here." Samantha stared off, thinking a moment. "But...she's with Stan now." They exchanged a meaningful look. Margaret and Stanley Parker had been a one-of-a-kind couple. "Well, I'm here for a few more days, so don't worry. I'll help you get things settled." Samantha was no stranger to this family. Stan and Margaret's house had been like a second home to her during her teenage years.

"Thanks," Harmony sighed. She had returned to the university in South Carolina after her grandmother's funeral last fall, going through the motions until finals. Once she'd come home for the Christmas break, she hadn't returned for her final semester. The lonely holiday had taken its toll.

"I'd like to get some of my grandparents' things cleared out. It will help me move on...before I go back to school. Even though I've lived in this house almost my whole life, it's hard to believe this place is mine." She'd had big plans after graduation to move to Boston and get an apartment and a great job at an architectural firm. Leaving her grandmother alone had loomed in the back of her mind...but now there was no one here to hold her back. As much as Harmony was looking forward to her future metropolitan life, leaving this house, and the Wentworth, still left her with a heaviness she couldn't dislodge.

At age six, her grandparents became her guardians, raising her in their typical New Englander home. Her grandparents had purchased the house back in 1945 after the war. They'd left it to her in their will. Not only had her grandparents paid off the house but they'd left her a large trust fund. Every asset went to her, the only surviving relative, her parents deceased. Harmony couldn't even think about selling it. Once she made her move to Boston in the future, she was going to close it up and use it as a summer place. Harmony loved this island, this town, this area, but after the deaths of her grandparents she felt it was time to move on.

Harmony's grandfather, Stanley, had been a sailor during the war. When he returned home he'd met her grandmother Margaret at a soiree at Wentworth-by-the-Sea, the prestigious seaside hotel. That was merely one family connection to the grand hotel.

"This break from filming has been revitalizing." Samantha planted her elbows on the table and looked around the kitchen. "I've spent a lot of time hanging out in this kitchen. There is no place like home. So," Samantha muttered, "how are things going with your committee?"

"Have you read the headlines lately?" Harmony railed, not giving her a chance to answer, but Samantha had got the reaction she wanted. "Henley Properties wants to tear down eight-five percent of the 'newer' section of the Wentworth and build condos. They promise to restore the original building, but we've heard this argument before."

"I'm sorry. I know that place means a lot to you. And I remember it meant so much to your grandparents. They met there at a dance, right?" Samantha suddenly smiled. "Stan and Margaret were always dancing around in this kitchen."

Harmony chuckled at the memory of Stan coaxing his wife away from washing dishes. She'd be clad in her favorite apron, her hands encased in soapy yellow gloves. Unfazed, Stan would waltz her around the table. Harmony would roll her eyes as she sat doing her homework.

"Yeah, they met at a soiree. I wish I could meet someone there at a soiree. Maybe someday it will be saved." Harmony sipped her soda, looking thoughtful.

"I'm sure some company will renovate it." Samantha's voice was high.

Harmony easily detected the white lie. Perhaps Samantha thought it was doubtful anyone would attempt to invest in a lost cause, but Harmony wouldn't give up hope.

The girls chatted late into the night. Samantha told adventurous stories from her travels, and Harmony gave Samantha the rundown of what she planned to do in the house over the next couple of months. Eventually Samantha hugged her dear friend goodnight and walked two houses down to her own childhood home.

By the sink, Harmony took a few minutes to wipe the grime away from the grubby satchel. Once it was as clean as she could get it, she looped the strap around her torso. It rested comfortably across her body, like a messenger bag. She snapped off the kitchen light and strode down the hallway wearing the satchel. Wondering who it could have belonged to, she guessed perhaps a hotel guest or an employee. She entered Papa Stan's study and placed the satchel on the bookshelf for safekeeping. Pulling the door closed on her way out, she rubbed her weary eyes before heading up to bed.

She snuggled under her bedspread even though it was a warm night, and tears filled her eyes as she thought about her grandparents and how they'd be missing out on all the events in her future. She was on the cusp of moving on with her new grown-up life, but that invisible leap felt empty without them to share in her success. She felt alone in this world.

The box fan hummed in the window frame. She watched the blades blur as she considered her love life. She'd broken up with her boyfriend five months ago and had only gone on two very boring dates since then. She counted on her prospects increasing once she moved to Boston.

As for her friends—well, her best friend Samantha was usually off traveling the world, making her dreams come true. Harmony had made some friends at college down south, none of them from the New England area. Despite her thoughts of finishing school and job hunting, she wanted to use this time off to go through the house, and she was still active on the Fight for the Preservation of Wentworth project. A local fellow preservationist had chatted weekly with Harmony about every newspaper article and town meeting while she was away at college, keeping her in the know.

Her grandparents were gone. Her parents were gone. Her life was in limbo, and she desperately needed a fresh start. *Don't feel sorry for yourself!* she scolded. But her loneliness spiked, and she cried herself to sleep.

Harmony was a child, outside on a cold day. Before her stood an outline of a woman in a blue parka, the fur-lined hood secured around her head. The woman was bent forward with her arms outstretched. Her gloves wrapped around Harmony's small mitten-clad hands. She wiggled her fingers inside the thickness of her mittens. Harmony couldn't make out the woman's face, but she knew it was her mother. The overcast gray sky seemed to create the same illusion inside the hood. Her mother's face blurred. She heard her mother's high young voice instruct her how to move her skates over the ice. The metal blades scratched across the frozen surface, and Harmony swayed as her mother skated backward, guiding her along.

Suddenly there was a sound. A horrible, cracking sound! And Harmony heard the panic in her mother's voice as she tried to move them closer to the river's edge. More popping and cracking, followed by a bloodcurdling scream that rang through the air.

The solid ice beneath their skates gave way, and the two of them plunged down, breaking contact with each other in the current. The icy water engulfed Harmony, and her jacket became saturated, pulling her down like an anchor. She pawed through the air bubbles surrounding her, searching for her mother – for anyone to save her!

When the air bubbles vanished she saw a man swim up to her – every detail on his face was vivid, unlike the emptiness inside her mother's hood. He looked far from scary. His large black eyes slanted in his narrow face as they watched her, and his streaming black hair floated outward like long tentacles. His firm lips turned up in a smile and then he flashed his white teeth. Strangely, no effervesce escaped his mouth or nose. Harmony thought he should be cold; he was bare-chested and only a circle of cloth hung from his hips. As he reached for her, Harmony noticed the flash of silvery scales that ran under his arms, from shoulders to elbows. A line of scales also shimmered along his outer thighs down to his ankles.

Was he a man or a fish?

Harmony held out her hands, and he merely yanked at her mittens, which floated just out of reach. Why was he not helping her? Her lungs were starting to feel tight. She was sinking and he was letting her. He was going to let her drown!

Her freezing fingers began to tingle and feel warm. When she held them out to ward off the man who now reached for her, heat surged down her arms. The man *jerked back in shock, as if he'd been struck.*

She wanted to get away from him. Kicking her legs and propelling herself upward, she floated just below the river's surface, the light from above filtering through. The man made several attempts to grab her, but his expression turned angry when her penetrating energy kept him away. He bared his teeth in frustration and swam away. That was when she noticed the blue parka, with her mother trapped inside, being dragged down deeper into the darkness by the man-fish creature.

The back of her jacket was yanked from above, and all went black.

Harmony cried out as she sat up in her bed. *Dry and safe. Another bad dream.* All she could recall was being in deep, icy-cold water. She slid back down to the pillow and glanced at the time. It was morning. Samantha would be over soon.

3

Morning at the Finch house hadn't changed much during Samantha's absence. Mr. Finch made his daughter scrambled eggs, just how she liked them, before she dashed out the door. With a deep inhale of salty air, Samantha sighed, understanding this snug little town gave her a sense of belonging, but she had to admit she was anxious to return to her fast-paced life and her boyfriend. She'd had a great time these past couple weeks with Harmony. New England's weather was unpredictable, and the mild sunny days had melted all the snow. This gave the girls an opportunity to bike the loop around the scenic little island, also New Hampshire's smallest town. Social evenings at their favorite watering hole with the locals in the next town over brought back old memories.

She would be jetting away in two days, so she made sure to put aside some time this morning to help Harmony sort through her grandparents' stuff. She couldn't imagine how hard it would be for Harmony, because she was fighting the sadness too—the Parkers were her second family.

Samantha walked passed the one house that separated their homes and spied Harmony crossing the yard, heading for the garage.

"Morning! Hey, aren't we cleaning out your grandparents' bedroom?" Samantha bounded over at a jog, her arms pumping. "I'm ready for some heavy lifting." Samantha flexed her muscles, and tugged her sweater sleeves tight.

"Hiya, Sam. Yeah, I'm just getting some empty boxes from the garage." Harmony chuckled at her goofball friend and rolled the garage door open, and the girls stepped inside.

Samantha wrinkled her nose at the smell of dust and mildew. Even though Stan kept his garage in top-notch condition, it had gathered a fair share of leaves and cobwebs in the three years since he'd been gone. He was a military man with orderly habits, but his wife, Margaret, sentimentally kept everything. While Harmony contemplated what size boxes she'd need, Samantha snooped around.

"What are you going to do with all this stuff? Like this?" Samantha held up a tennis racquet she'd lifted from its designated bracket on the garage wall. She rummaged in a nearby tote for a ball.

"I used to watch my grandmother play at the Wentworth."

"You haven't started playing, have you?"

Harmony furrowed her brow at Samantha's question. Samantha raised her eyebrows in challenge, and then she launched a tennis ball at Harmony.

Harmony's hand went up in defense, deflecting the yellow torpedo. "Ouch."

The tennis ball rolled under the tool bench.

"Aww, come on. Toss it back." Samantha posed with the racquet, knees bent like a tennis pro. She was athletic and would challenge anyone at any sport—whether she was good at it or not. She laughed off any inabilities; this endearing quality had earned her recognition.

Harmony ignored her and the tennis ball. "Let's go in and get started." Abandoning her animated friend, who was pretending she'd scored the winning point in a tournament, Harmony grabbed a couple boxes and walked away.

"...and the crowd roars!" Samantha bowed to her imaginary fans before tossing the racquet onto a shelf.

The girls entered Stan and Margaret's bedroom, both silent, absorbed in their thoughts. To Samantha, things looked like they had since they were kids, as though Harmony's grandparents would come through the door at any moment. Apparently Margaret had held onto Stan's things after he'd passed on. His pipe still sat atop his chest of drawers, and Samantha watched Harmony instinctively lift it to her nose.

"I can still smell the pipe tobacco."

Harmony set the nest of empty boxes down on the floor and placed a carton of trash bags on the dresser. "I've contacted that consignment place over in Portsmouth. They are willing to sell some of Margaret's clothes and shoes, and the rest goes into these bags to be donated."

Harmony opened the lid of the large jewelry case that historically occupied the dresser. With wide eyes, she looked up and said to Samantha, "Remember these earrings?"

The girls lost track of time as they went through the pieces. They reminisced about brooches worn on special occasions and bracelets and earrings popular throughout the decades, and they admired rings, sparkling with gemstones.

"What are you going to do with Margaret's jewelry? There are some valuable items in here." Samantha lifted a bracelet studded with emeralds. It looked expensive, and she personally adored emeralds.

"Keep it for now." Harmony shrugged.

Samantha watched Harmony. With an exhale, Harmony looked down at the ring hugging her finger. Both girls knew it had been Margaret's favorite piece of jewelry. It was not the diamond that Stan gave her when he proposed—Samantha had noticed that resting between velvety rolls in the jewelry case. The one on Harmony's finger was Margaret's lavender pearl ring. Samantha remembered the emotional moment the day Margaret had gifted it to Harmony after her high school graduation. She had said, "You are like this rare pearl, Harmony, beautiful and one of a kind."

"This was always my grandmother's favorite possession. Papa Stan told me that my grandmother had seen a guest at the Wentworth wearing one. 'Naturally your grandmother wanted one.'" She mimicked her grandfather's voice.

Samantha laughed and said, "Yeah. Lavender was her favorite color, right?"

"Yes. Did you know *Margaret* means *pearl*? Her grandmother was named Pearl. So unsurprisingly, with all those coincidences, lavender pearls happened to be her favorite jewelry. It made good sense."

"That's wicked cool!"

Samantha returned the bracelet and was poking at an emerald earring when she heard Harmony clear her throat. Samantha looked up expectantly.

"Sam, I've been thinking." Harmony hesitated, her eyes looking far off for a second. "Isn't it strange that both my parents drowned...and my grandparents too? Obviously not all at once, but..." Her brows drew together in contemplation. "Papa Stan...a car accident, they said, but his car skidded off a bridge and he was trapped in the river. And now my grandmother drowns just offshore in her friend's boat. Seriously, what are the odds?"

Samantha shook her head, unable to come up with a reasonable explanation. "It is weird that both your grandparents drowned. And even though I never met your parents, their drowning stories are crazy. I guess that validates your fear of deep water." It was all Samantha could come up with. Her expressive eyes washed over her friend, that old protectiveness coiling in Samantha's gut. Kids had talked behind Harmony's back in school. A fellow student being raised by grandparents because her parents had drowned gave the student body

20

something scandalous to talk about. Harmony Parker had been an easy target.

Harmony shrugged her shoulders and slouched on the bed. Her eyes filled with tears as she scanned the possessions that embodied her loved ones. "This is harder than I thought." She sniffed. She wiped way the tears that gathered at the corners of her eyes on the cap sleeves of her tee-shirt.

At her side in an instant, Samantha gave her a hug. "I know. It sucks!" After a few moments, Samantha leaned back. "You'll be fine, you know. You have so much to look forward to. You are so strong...whether you believe it or not." Samantha had watched Harmony overcome adversity in school. And the way she fought for the Wentworth-by-the-Sea was admirable. Plus, she not only had the inner strength to do what she felt was right, but she was tough on the outside.

Samantha would never forget when some punks were tormenting a stray dog years ago, before their friendship, and Harmony had come to its rescue. In a nearby playground after school, three bad-news boys were poking sticks at the whining animal. The delinquents were in the girls' fifth grade class. Samantha had been standing across the field with her friends. She had only known about Harmony then. Samantha and her friends were glued to the unfolding scene, staring in shock.

"Get away from that dog!" Harmony yelled, approaching the trio.

The tallest of the three boys told her to mind her own business, but that just made Harmony seethe with rage. She marched right up to the group of larger boys, stepping between them and the dog, giving them a piece of her mind. Samantha remembered gawking, scared for Harmony's safety. Those boys were bigger and meaner than the girl whose stance was like Wonder Woman's, fists on hips, upholding justice. She was ready to take them on.

"What are you going to do about it?" Each of them taunted her, snickering.

When the tall boy reached forward to shove her, Harmony caught his hand in her fist and swiftly twisted his arm around his back.

"Ahhh, get her off me!" His voice cracked in agony. He bent forward in pain, and she forced his face close to the growling dog. The animal must have sensed his ally.

"Would you like a little payback, dog?" she ground out through clenched teeth at the mutt, who growled and barked in the kid's face.

The other boys raised their sticks to free their whining buddy from the girl who manhandled him.

"Get 'em!" She shouted the command, and the dog leaped to attack the pair of boys, who dropped the sticks and sprinted away, screaming, their friend forgotten. When she shoved the big bully down with unnatural force, his face landed in the dirt. He scrambled away and then sat up, rubbing his shoulder, his bottom lip quivering.

"Cruelty to others will come back to you tenfold. I'll be watching you!"

That kid was scared of her throughout the rest of fifth grade, until his family moved out of state. The other two boys were always polite to her. As for the dog, Samantha had never seen it again.

She had been perplexed by the strange surges of physical strength the quiet and friendly Harmony had displayed. *Thank goodness she's slow to anger and she's never been angry at me,* Samantha thought. Yeah, her gal was strong. She would take care of herself.

Once her emotions settled, Samantha rallied. "I'm here to help, so this is what we are going to do…" She stood and gave instructions and then pulled two trash bags out of the box before handing one to Harmony. She uttered encouragement while they worked diligently over the next couple hours to fill the bags. Of course she couldn't resist trying on an outrageous outfit or two to make Harmony laugh.

Harmony wore chinos and a pale pink shirt with a little green alligator stitched above her breast. Her wavy blond hair hung over her shoulder as she set her lunch plate with the green crazy daisy pattern in the sink. She drank the last swallow from her glass of Pepsi and gazed out the window framed by airy curtains, at a spot somewhere amid the fast-moving water of the river. This over-the-sink window was an ideal lookout. She could see the land across the water in Maine. Boats came and went daily down the Piscataqua River, nautical traffic carrying goods and a fair share of tourists. Fishing and lobstering were booming businesses in this seaside area.

On the days without Samantha's ready smile and upbeat personality, Harmony moped around, continuing her decluttering efforts. She'd sent off a good bit of her grandparents' clothing to a consignment shop and donated books to the library. Open boxes remained stacked all around the house in various states of fullness.

In the living room, she picked up a photo album from the pile that surrounded her on the floor. It was old and there weren't many pages, but it was a favorite of hers. Margaret said it belonged to her grandmother and contained pictures during the time of the famous Russo-Japanese Peace Treaty signed at the Wentworth-by-the-Sea in 1905. Margaret's grandmother, Pearl, had worked at the hotel in those days. There was a picture of her, dressed in her uniform, on the sweeping veranda. Included was a photo of the Russian and Japanese delegates, all wearing suits and fashionable mustaches as they posed for a picture at the Wentworth's front door.

A pensive smile lingered on Harmony's lips. She remembered her grandmother telling one funny story after another about her earlier days carousing with her gals and their gang of friends all around the Wentworth grounds; it occurred to Harmony that in the last couple of years before her death, her grandmother had only laughed so hard when she reminisced about the old days—the prime of her life. Harmony felt envious of their camaraderie. For Margaret, it was a time when the love of her life was still alive, long before the death of her daughter, Harmony's mother.

That was the first of the drownings.

Her smile gone, Harmony nibbled on her lower lip. She wished she could remember her parents. Placing the album back on the pile, she stood and then padded barefoot down the hallway, stopping at the closed door of her grandfather's study. After he passed on, her grandmother kept the door closed to enshrine its scent. Margaret had said it smelled like him in there. The leather chairs, the pipe tobacco, his aftershave—it was combination scent that was Stanley Parker. He had passed away the spring of Harmony's first year away at college. She'd offered to take a break from school, but her grandmother wouldn't hear of it.

She turned the handle and slipped into the room, carefully closing the door behind her. It was another warm day and the room felt stuffy. She should open the windows to let the fresh air in, but the last time she had, Stan's scent dissipated. She told herself she could still smell him, but it was probably only her memories by now.

Returning from school, she'd brought a few things of her own into this study, but they felt out of place. She walked to the bookshelves and glanced at the books, photographs, and memorabilia from World War II. Stanley and Margaret had bought this house and hoped to fill it with children, but they had only one child, her mother, Brook. Harmony gazed at the framed picture of her grandparents with her mother, around age five, on the beach having a picnic. The boxy shape of Margaret's bathing suit dated the photo to the 1950s.

Shifting to the next picture, she picked up the only photograph her grandparents had displayed of her father. Gripping either side of the small frame, she studied it in detail. In the picture, her dad, Eric, stood in front of a fishing vessel with his arm slung around her mother's shoulder, his other hand spread across her large, pregnant belly. His shaggy blond hair was ruffled by the passing breeze. He wore shorts made from jeans, the legs cut away at the knees. Her mom, Brook, wore a halter-style dress and sandals. The picture was faded, but Harmony could see how much she resembled her mom—with the exception of the wavy blond hair she had clearly inherited from her dad.

Stan and Margaret hadn't approved of the fisherman who worked from the docks down in Gloucester. They blamed Harmony's father for luring their daughter away and getting her pregnant. It was the mid-1960s, and Brook had only completed one year of college when she quit school and moved in with Eric. Brook gave birth to a baby girl and settled into a tiny apartment near the wharf despite their protests. Stan and Margret felt like they'd lost her.

Margaret had explained the whole situation to Harmony years later when pubescent curiosity drove her to ask a lot of questions. She'd explained Brook was a free spirit who lived fully and loved deeply. Brook loved to sing and so had named her daughter Harmony. Harmony was more cautious than her mother, but she did have her mother's gift—an amazing singing voice.

Brook's drowning was devastating for all of them. After the heartbreaking loss of his wife, Eric, having no other family, was forced to let his daughter stay with Brook's parents. His commercial fishing job kept him away at sea for long periods. It was the best he could do for his little daughter.

Not even a year had passed since Brook's death when Eric was lost at sea. The authorities informed the Parkers that the fishing company's boat sank during a storm, and all souls were lost—presumed drowned. Six-year-old Harmony became a permanent resident in her grandparent's house. "Little Harmony Parker," she would sing to her grandparents to make them smile.

Harmony thought it was ironic what she remembered from childhood. What was awful was that she could recall the actions of strangers but not much of her own mother. She had an early memory of people stopping her grandmother and shaking their heads at the tragedy. "It was so senseless," they'd say. She scarcely remembered her father either.

She set the gilt-framed photograph back on the shiny line that marked its place on the dusty shelf. On the lower ledge was a decorative cardboard box. She lifted the lid and drew out a newspaper clipping.

TRAGIC DROWNING ON SATURDAY. A young woman fell through the ice into north river while ice-skating. She was swiftly pulled under and found a day later downstream.

Harmony slipped the newspaper back into the box, choosing not to read the article again. Instead she grabbed the satchel she'd found while snooping inside her favorite building, the Wentworth-by-the-Sea. Sitting in the comfortable chair at Stan's desk, she flipped open the flap and rooted around inside. Disappointed the only content was the tin filled with dried leaves, she put the tin on the desk and turned the bag in her hands, examining it closely. The stitching looked hand sewn.

She dropped the bag onto the desk and turned her attention to the tin.

As Harmony opened the baseball-size container it made a *thook* sound. She lifted out the old paper, brittle and yellowed. Inside its folds she examined the crushed leaves. *Maybe tea leaves?* Harmony bent forward to smell them. Beyond the stale, dusty aroma was something faint…something she didn't recognize. She set the paper on a letter tray.

She lifted the now-empty tin, turning it in her hands, looking for a word or a mark. When she flipped it upside down, she noticed a symbol on the bottom, a simple circle with three wavy lines inside. *What does this stand for?*

She leaned back and wondered how the satchel had gotten into the wall. Mindlessly, she picked up her grandfather's lighter and began flicking it. It wasn't near the leaves, but suddenly the parched paper ignited and started to smolder before flames licked upwards. In a panic, she smacked her hand against the small flames, but it only stirred up the herbs. A pungent odor wafted up as smoke infiltrated the surrounding air.

Harmony choked on the burning fumes. *Why is this smoking so much?* The wee flames only kissed the paper's edges, but the smoke from the smoldering herbs continued to burn her eyes; she was starting to feel dizzy. Surely it would die out on the metal letter tray. Maybe she should open the window after all, or at least the door. She abandoned her efforts to try and put the fire out and stood, thinking she'd head to the window to release the smell. After only one step, she was coughing uncontrollably, gripped by some kind of fit. Her eyes blurred with tears as she observed the tray. There were no more flames, just the smoking herbs. *What is that stuff…maybe a drug?* Harmony wasn't getting any air. Tears rolled down her cheeks. Her lungs were burning.

She staggered around the desk, trying to get to the door, which was closer than the window. She needed to escape! *What is happening?* She was almost there, and she put her hand out to grasp the knob, but she fell flat on the floor. Her perception had been off; she was still several feet away. She felt a wave of nausea before everything went black.

5

The Other Realm 1989

Harmony had the sensation she was a leaf tossed on a blustery New England day. She was completely engulfed, a pulling sensation reaching every part of her body, her clothing, her hair, her skin. When she opened her mouth to take a breath it was immediately filled with ice-cold, salty seawater. Her eyes flew open and the sleepiness she'd felt immediately dissolved.

She was underwater.

She was terrified of deep water.

Harmony flailed, coughing and sputtering as she broke the surface, her eyes stinging from the saltwater. It was dark, but her other senses confirmed she was in the ocean. She knew how to swim, and she instinctively treaded water. Her teeth chattered nonstop. Pure adrenaline forced her to swim toward shore, toward the lights. All the while the question begged over and over …

How did I get here?

She struggled not to panic. Her pent-up screams of terror escaped as moans as she pushed on. Thoughts of drowning in the deep abyss beneath her were forced behind a closed door in her mind. Drowning, the fate of her family—she wouldn't allow it to happen to her.

It was a long swim, and her arms were heavy and tired by the time she reached the rocky beach. Her lungs burned, and there was a cramp in her side. The sand was filled with slimy, slippery rocks of all sizes, and the seaweed trapped within the clusters tangled around her legs. Once her feet were on solid ground, away from the tidal pools, she stood, huffing catching her breath. Her burning eyes scanned her surroundings. *Where am I?*

Her eyes scaled the steep hill she'd have to climb to get a better view. It was grassy, with dense brush. She looked over her shoulder at the resounding waves as they pounded over the rocks and rushed toward her, grasping at her heels. She staggered a few steps, not allowing the water to touch her again. An involuntary convulsion gripped her, and the air in her lungs pulsed out. The moon wasn't full but provided her with enough light to see the inky ocean. She cried with relief that she'd just survived the torturous swim.

A movement, something large breaking the surface, scared her, and she rushed toward the hill. She climbed on all fours, clawing at the ground and grasping at branches of shrubbery. A strangled cry escaped her lips, and she blinked back tears.

Harmony clambered through the rough brush, finally reaching an area where the landscape changed to a tended lawn. She looked back with anguish at the hill she'd just climbed, then down at her stinging limbs, covered with angry scratches. Her hands were dirty, her clothes drenched. Mud and grass stuck to her pale shirt and pants, and her hair, hanging around her shoulders, was tangled in waves.

"Where am I? Where the hell am I!" she whined aloud as she looked back over the moonlit sea. This time she recognized a familiar curve of land. She was looking out over Little Harbor. She'd spent hours at the Wentworth looking out at this view. She knew it like the back of her hand.

How did I get here…at night…in the ocean? Last she remembered she was in the study—with those smoking herbs. When no answer to her questions came to mind, she turned and continued toward what should be the Wentworth, at the top of the crest.

Once I get to the road I'll follow it to the next house

and get some help. She didn't think she could make the trek to her house on the other side of the island in her condition. When Harmony reached the top of the hill she stared wide-eyed in disbelief. Before her was a structure resembling the Wentworth, but not as it had last appeared to her, dilapidated and abandoned. It seemed fully restored but with altered architecture. In the moonlight her eyes detected the three iconic mansard towers, but the mansard part flared out as in Japanese design. Past them, the coned turrets remained the same. Harmony rubbed her eyes and looked again, not believing what she saw. Not only did it still appear altered, warm lights glowed from within. Wentworth-by-the-Sea, the hotel she was trying to save, stood before her eyes, restored.

How can this be? This must be a dream.

"Wake up!" She hissed the words out loud. She shook with chill, and her teeth continued to chatter. *This is crazy!* She moved toward the building and glanced at the sign in an arch over on the portico: Wentworth-by-the-Sea.

No, wait. That's not what it says.

She focused on the letters. *Wellness-by-the-Sea. Why does "Wellness" replace "Wentworth"?*

She passed through the open doors into the front lobby. There was no carved paneling, no gilded mirrors, patterned carpet, wallpaper, not even the News Nook, the Wentworth's in-house post office; nothing familiar could be found. This was...plain. The floor she dripped on was slate tiles, the walls painted an airy blue like a summer sky. Just off to the side was a counter. Behind the counter, a doorframe opened to an alcove housing books in floor-to-ceiling bookshelves. A pair of dark-haired girls chatted just inside, placing volumes back into slots. They looked over at the wild-eyed, drenched stranger who'd appeared late in the evening.

One of the girls walked up to greet her, bewilderment evident in her unusually bright eyes. "Welcome to Wellness-by-the-Sea. How can I help you?"

"W-w-w...Where am I?" Harmony vibrated. "W-w-w...what is this place?"

"Wellness-by-the-Sea," the girl repeated. She swept her pale eyes down Harmony's torso, past her muddy clothing to the pool of water she'd left on the floor. Harmony followed her eyes downward and gave an apologetic half-smile for the puddle. The girl reached beyond the counter for a towel, one of many rolled and stacked neatly on shelves, and offered it to Harmony, who quickly rubbed down her hair and face and then wrapped it around her shoulders.

"You are welcome here in our sanctuary. I will give you a room so you can clean up and change out of your wet clothes. This way," she gently coaxed. "It is okay. We are here at the Wellness to help."

Harmony agreed to follow her. At this point she felt frozen, and her brain was about to shut down. Harmony thought, *This slip of a girl seems harmless enough, and I'm probably in a dream anyway.*

They mounted the steps and trudged upward, circling each floor, Harmony's hand trailing the smooth surface of the uniquely carved railing. They stopped on the second floor and advanced to the end of the hall. The girl stopped at a door. Harmony knew the room within was ocean facing; she knew every room by heart after her illegal explorations. Once inside, the girl waved her hand over a symbol of a sun on the wall. The lights overhead softly illuminated the space. The room was sparsely furnished with two pairs of fabric chairs, each set with a small wooden table between them.

The girl motioned Harmony to follow her down a hallway, away from the main room. "This way. You can change into something dry. All the rooms are stocked with tunics for our guests." Harmony noticed the girl wore a free flowing tunic herself.

"Thank you." Harmony still gripped the towel around her shoulders. Her teeth had ceased chattering, and she was starting to feel warmth seep back into her skin. "What's your name?"

"Oh, forgive me. My name is Lynn," she avowed. They passed a small washroom before entering a bedroom. It was minimal, just a bed on a platform and a nightstand. Lynn waved on more lights as they passed through the space.

"Lynn, my name is Harmony Parker."

"Harmony," Lynn whispered. "How unusual to have a name with no meaning related to water! Harmony is... musical." Lynn's curious eyes widened as she asked, "You don't sing, do you? Singing is prohibited." Lynn slid open a shoji screen and collected folded clothes from the shelf behind it. She added a pair of soft slippers to her pile, all the while casting nervous glances over her shoulder at Harmony.

"I sing a little." Harmony was trying to figure out what Lynn meant by "singing is prohibited." *Maybe it is a silent kind of sanctuary, like for meditation?* She watched the girl, whose hospitable gracefulness became shadowed with nervousness. She'd been surprised by Harmony's name. "My name means unity. What's the deal with water? What does your name mean?"

"As everyone knows, we are given aquatic names to honor our god...although some have abandoned that practice. *Lynn* means cascade." She set the items on the bed and pointed to the washroom. "You should find everything you need in there. I will return shortly with food and hot tea." Lynn gave her a small nod and slipped away.

Harmony wanted to stop her from leaving and demand she answer more questions, but at this point she just needed to get out of her wet, filthy clothes so she wouldn't catch a chill. Once the girl was gone, Harmony dropped the towel and stripped off her wet pants, shirt, and undergarments. In the washroom she looked around at the various jars of soap, lotion, and tooth polish. In the shower, she opened the faucet, hoping for hot water. She exhaled with relief when she felt the warm temperature and stepped inside. She scrubbed away the salt and grime. Wearily, she worked the shampoo through her snarled hair until it rinsed clean and smooth, flowing down to her waist. She gently soaped the scratches caked with blood and dirt. Reaching for a clean towel, she dried her limbs with a brisk rubdown, promoting blood flow, careful though to avoid the scratches.

On the bed lay fresh clothes. She slipped the tunic over her head and sighed at its remarkably soft fabric. It fit relatively well. The moccasin-style slippers also provided a good fit. And there she stood, in a strange place wearing strange clothes.

Harmony pinched herself for the fifth time—she wasn't dreaming. *If this isn't a dream, then what? Did I go back in time?* Harmony noted the automatic lights and running hot water. *Maybe I'm in the future...or maybe the stress of cleaning out my home, my grandparents' home of forty-four years, has finally gotten to me. I've gone crazy.*

She roamed the room searching for a phone but didn't see one. She strode back to the washroom and unraveled the towel from her hair. She had seen a comb earlier and used it now to detangle her long blond tresses. As she worked the knots free she looked around. All the walls in this room were paneled in a pale wood sparingly inlayed with Japanese designs. The floor was tile, the porcelain fixtures minimal in design. They looked futuristic to Harmony. *Yes, possibly the future.* She returned the comb to its resting place.

6

Harmony heard Lynn's greeting, and she shuffled her slipper-clad feet into the main room. She was thankful the girl was setting down a tray of food; her stomach rumbled at the delicious smells. Lynn immediately handed her a steaming mug from the tray. Restored by the hot shower and dry clothes, Harmony felt awareness easing back into her cranium after a few sips of the strong black tea. She'd been terrified in the ocean, and her nerves were still frazzled.

Lynn stared openly at Harmony.

Obviously I don't belong here, and obviously Lynn can tell.

Suddenly, a knock sounded at the door, and both girls jumped.

"I've called for the elders of the council to come speak with you. I hope you don't mind." Lynn crossed to the door, opened it, and ushered in two noble figures.

Harmony took a few hesitant steps toward the door as Lynn opened it. A tall, white-haired couple smiled at her as they entered. They both appeared to be in their seventies, with only a few wrinkles between them. The willowy and graceful woman held her body like a ballerina. The man's round face sported bushy, old-man eyebrows, his white hair combed back to rest at his collar. Their bizarre eyes made Harmony's gears turn. She'd thought Lynn's irises were unusual, and the couple's eyes carried a similar luminescent glow.

"Hello, I am Morie, the caretaker of the Wellness-by-the-Sea, and this is our Linker, Calder." She gestured to the man beside her. "We are both members of the council. May we speak with you?"

"Yes. My name is Harmony Parker, and I have a lot

of questions to ask you." Harmony considered their titles as she offered them a seat.

Morie dismissed Lynn, who gave Harmony a lingering gaze before leaving.

"Thank you for giving me a room and everything. I'm afraid I can't pay until I can retrieve some money from home—that is, once I figure out exactly where I am." Harmony lowered herself into a chair, amazed she still had manners when all she wanted to do was shout out her question: *Elders of the council, what is happening to me?*

The woman waved her slender hand in response to Harmony's concern. "Payment is not necessary. We are not a hotel. This is a temple, built to honor the water god Suijin. In this sanctuary, we house those who seek knowledge, worship, and healing. Our top-floor galleries contain our vast library. The lower floors contain birthing pools. We also assist in sending off our loved ones in death. Calder assists in all these matters through spiritual guidance and uses healing energy and herbal medicine as needed."

"Wellness-by-the-Sea is a temple." Harmony repeated the words aloud. Trying to formulate their meaning, she concluded, "Okay. This place is a religious hospital whose guests worship a water deity, and it's also a library." She blinked as visions of *The Twilight Zone* rerun episodes flashed before her.

She held the mug of scalding black tea, and now she swallowed another sip, feeling it scorch her tongue and throat before she set the mug on the table at her elbow.

Morie exchanged a glance with Calder, who nodded for her to continue. "Harmony, there are two realms of Earth. You have left the human realm and crossed in to our realm. You are in the world of the Aquapopulo, the water people."

"Realm! World!" Harmony's voice broke and she

swallowed hard. *I'm not in my own world?* "I don't understand."

"In this world we worship our one god, Suijin, the god of water, the creator of our kind. I believe your Japanese culture recognizes Suijin among others, and the rest of your cultures worship many gods. Water is everything to us." Morie, apparently focused on the Devine, held her hands together in prayer style, like a nun.

Harmony had not heard of the water god Suijin. Japan was on the other side of the world, a world it didn't sound like she was even in anymore. *Things are getting stranger by the minute.* She glanced again at Calder; there was something familiar about him.

Calder pressed his fingers together like a steeple, and Harmony noted the delicate webbing between his fingers as he began to explain.

"The realms are the same in space and time, but you've crossed into another dimension."

Harmony tried to absorb what the man had said. He'd answered her question about where she was, but she couldn't fathom how she'd arrived in another world. Why would *she* be in another dimension?

After several moments of silence, Morie spoke. "Lynn has told us you wandered into our temple, wet and confused. Can you tell us what you remember before you were in the sea?"

Harmony's gnashing assault on her bottom lip subsided, and she blinked several times, resurfacing from her deep thoughts. She focused on a space somewhere between the two people who sat across from her. Her tone was slightly high and hollow. "I was at my house, sitting at my grandfather's desk. I had found a satchel hidden in the walls of the building that sits here—like yours, but different. In the satchel was a tin containing what I thought were tea leaves. The leaves were loose within some paper. I pulled out the paper containing the leaves and laid it on the letter tray on the desk. I was looking for a name on the tin, maybe a manufacturer of the tea. Anyway, after a while, I was playing with my grandfather's lighter, and suddenly the paper and dried leaves caught fire." Her voice sped up. "I tried to squelch the fire, but it smoked and smoldered. And the smell! There was an awful smell, and I was choking." Her hand moved up to encompass her throat as she remembered the terrifying experience. "I was so dizzy, and I couldn't stop coughing. There was too much smoke for just a tiny fire. It should have gone out, but it didn't. It was as if the smoke were swirling around me. And then...I blacked out." Her eyes flicked from one elder to the other, her heart pounding a little faster. "I woke up out there," Harmony pointed toward the window, "under the water."

"It is okay. You are safe now." Morie's gentle voice was soothing. "Those were not tea leaves that you found, but they were responsible for bringing you here. Calder can help explain better. He is our expert in these matters."

Calder's kind eyes caressed the girl sitting on the edge of her seat before him. He nodded his head respectfully and stated sincerely, "Please allow me to back up a moment and say it is an honor to meet you, Harmony Parker." He scrutinized her features as she smiled grimly, returning his nod less enthusiastically.

Harmony returned his open stare and surveyed the man who'd listened politely to her story. *He must remind me of someone. Obviously I've never met him before – he lives in an alternate world. What exactly is this old man an expert of?*

His expression became serious, and he continued. "The herbs that you spoke of are effective. They are specially blended for one purpose. They allow a select few of us, called Linkers, like myself, to pass through to your world and return back to ours. The portal lies just off the coast of this island, in a slice of broken water."

"The Linkers, for thousands of generations, have gone into your realm to gain knowledge—linking your realm to ours," Morie explained. "They travel there and live anonymously among your people. Our libraries are filled with the life and times of the human race. We have studied your kind quite extensively."

"So the leaves I found brought me to this realm? Why me? Why here? Do other humans know about you?" After her rapid-fire questions, Harmony's mind continued working the puzzle.

That stupid old building! A sudden rush of regret and frustration flushed through her. *I shouldn't have been in there. If I'd just obeyed the law and not trespassed, I never would have found that cursed satchel.*

"Harmony!" Calder recaptured her attention. "Humans are unaware of our existence. You have a powerful connection to this place, this sacred ground."

Despite the eruption of panic she experienced a few moments ago, she digested what he said. Calder seemed to understand where she was coming from, both literally and emotionally, so she spoke to Morie. "Wentworth-by-the-Sea, this building's name in my world, is very important to me. It's abandoned, and I've been fighting to have it preserved because some want to tear it down. I have to admit this place has always haunted me. I don't know why."

"This island is where the birth of our people took place." Morie looked fixedly at her.

Harmony, whose drying hair had begun to curl around her temple, was intrigued by the possibility of another race.

Morie's hands retained their prayer pose. "Our ancestors, the people of the sea, came upon the shore, making us primarily land dwellers once again and transformed us into the Aquapopulo race we are today. We owe so much to Suijin." Morie's eyelids fluttered closed for a brief moment while she devoutly whispered, "Hear my praise." Opening her eyes, she smiled at Harmony.

As nice as the lady seemed, Harmony pegged her for a religious fanatic, although she certainly didn't get that impression from Calder.

"Harmony." When Calder called her name she snapped her gaze away from Morie, who was now giving her the creeps. Calder eyed her critically, and she felt weary, and scared. No longer interested in talking, she just wanted to go home.

He asked, "Do you know the theory of human evolution?"

Harmony wondered where this was going. "You mean, like, at some point in the past, our ape-like ancestors descended from the trees and moved into the African savannah to undergo the evolutionary changes that separate us from the apes? And the rest is history." She had been an A student, and anything to do with history was her strong suit.

Calder grinned. "Yes, very good. Now, what do you know of aquatic ape theory?"

Harmony shrugged. "I've never heard of it."

Calder pressed his lips together seeming to expect as much. "Our dimensions started out the same. As you said, the ancestors of Homo sapiens, the early apes, descended from the trees. However, some of your anthropologists believe there was a time when the early apes lived along the water's edge, spending the majority of time wading and living off what was available from the sea. These scientists theorize that is how evolution changed you from apes to humans. This is known as the aquatic ape theory in your realm."

Harmony studied their expressions and mannerisms, which seemed slightly foreign, while she pondered the idea of an alternative evolution theory. Since she'd been transported to another realm, she guessed anything could be possible.

Calder explained further. "The aquatic ape theorists agree with the balance of evolution theory, that your early ancestors moved into the African savannah four million years ago, but only after undergoing a great deal of evolution during the aquatic phase."

"What about bones and fossils? Don't scientists have proof of evolution?" Harmony recalled the controversy between evolution versus creation.

"There is a time period between four and eight million years when scientists have found no fossils. Why?" Calder's thick eyebrows lifted. "Because the skeletons are under the water, and anthologists dig on dry land." He pursed his lips before adding, "Your modern-day Africa was covered by much more water then, and the temperatures were much cooler."

Harmony was intrigued by the story but failed to see the connection. "Humans evolved in water instead of out on the savannah. Okay, but why are you telling me this?"

"Ah. Well, first off," Calder leaned forward in his seat, "it is not a hypothesis—it is indeed a fact. This is where our races split—yours became humans and ours the Aquapopulo. Our race, after being in a similar environment as yours four million years ago, stayed in the sea for several more million years. As Earth's atmosphere changed over time, our ancestors migrated away from the current African coast where your race began and voyaged by sea to North America. Our ancestors came ashore here on this very island of New Castle on your New England coast." Harmony's eyes widened. "We have only one race, but a second group

42

that migrated inland has evolved differently than us. And we do not inhabit this entire planet. The sea and waterways are still the core of our existence today. We thrive where there is abundant water."

Morie gushed, "Our connection to the sea and all waterways is strong. It nourishes us with its food, cleanses our bodies from the Earth's dust, and receives our dead to be transformed again into the circle of life. We are born in water. We are spiritual people who worship our aquatic lord."

"Sea people?" Harmony skeptically asked. "Your ancestors came from the sea, like mermaids and mermen?"

The man frowned. He knew of the tales of such creatures in Harmony's world. "Our ancestors did not have fish tails. Remember, the early ape entered the water for survival. Wading in water for long periods of time adapted them with features now known in modern humans. There are the differences in our races. Aquapopulo have a thicker layer of fat to adapt to the colder waters. We are not affected by the cooler air temperatures as you humans are. We don't get extremely cold, but tropical, humid temperatures bother us, so we remain in the agreeable temperatures of the northern climates."

Calder held up his hands to display his webbed fingers, and Morie did the same. "You may have noticed we have webbed fingers and toes. You may notice our eyes are paler than human eyes and refract light differently. Our ancestors have always needed oxygen to breathe. But we have the ability to hold our breath for long periods of time. Some special people, known as Divers, can hold their breath for up to twenty minutes underwater—quite a feat. I can only hold mine for eight minutes." His face crinkled, and his smile reached his eyes.

But his smiled faded as he continued. "Since history concludes that this is the home of the great transformation from sea people to land dwellers, we have deemed it sacred."

Harmony nodded, processing all that he said.

"Our clan has always had a temple in honor of Suijin on this island. This newer building was built from drawings brought back from your realm not so long ago." Calder gave a heavy sigh. "If people in your world are going to tear down the building upon this land and use if for anything less than a tranquil place, it will interrupt our spiritual energy. Such a negative shift could threaten our sanctuary. It must maintain positive energy. I am afraid, because what has been done so far in your realm has already started to make shifts in ours."

Morie's melodic voice was wrought with emotion. "The balance is shifting. In the last ten years the things our people have asked from Suijin are no longer received. The harvests have been poor, babies are not conceived, and violent storms have destroyed many homes along our coast. Some of our people have stopped worshipping him. We fear the disruptions caused in your world have angered our god. As a result, Suijin is sending out his Kami, the water spirits, to steal our people and return their souls to the depths of the oceans."

It seemed to Harmony that Morie's faith in Suijin would never falter, and it seemed to baffle the devout woman that others would cease to worship. Learning more about these people's current struggle nudged Harmony toward wanting to help, especially if the cause was coming from her side of the dimension. "You need to send me back. I will try to stop the demolition of the Wentworth if I can," Harmony responded passionately. She watched them exchange a look, which prompted her question: "Can you send me back?" She felt a sinking sensation in the pit of her stomach.

Calder's mouth was grim, but he nodded optimistically. "Our Linkers have used the herbs to pass into your world and back for thousands of years. I know the herbs that will send you back, but the hour grows late. Let us get some rest. We will talk about this tomorrow."

They stood, and Harmony, burdened by her apparent fate, followed them to the door.

Morie paused and stated calmly, "You should find everything you need here for your comfort. I'll send Lynn to you in the morning."

"Rest well, Harmony," Calder said before they closed the door, leaving Harmony alone to wrestle with her thoughts. She was extremely fatigued. With a wistful glance over her shoulder at her cold tea and the tray of untouched food, she sighed and headed to the bedroom. Her last thought as her head hit the pillow was that no one was going to miss her. Samantha had left to return to her job overseas. No one was going to look for her. She had no one.

7

The next morning Lynn entered Elder Morie's private chamber, meekly murmuring, "Good morning."

Morie spoke calmly, but her words were filled with insinuation. "Good morning, Lynn, I trust you were discreet after your encounter with our guest last night."

Lynn had been curious about why Harmony had come to Wellness alone, apparently traumatized. There was definitely something strange about her besides her name. Lynn couldn't help wondering if maybe this girl had been sent by their god—a siren, able to leave the water and walk on land! Everyone feared the sirens— they were killers. She looked sheepishly at Morie, knowing the staff was buzzing with excitement this morning after her loose tongue. Fear prompted her to ask, "Is…is that girl…is she a siren?"

Morie looked taken aback by Lynn's assessment. "A siren! Where ever did you get that idea? Never mind." Morie studied the young employee. "No, Harmony is not a siren. She is human."

With a sharp intake of breath, Lynn stared at the mistress of Wellness with astonishment. She had met a real human! "Oh, thank goodness she is not a siren!" She breathed out, holding a slim hand over her pounding heart. "But human! Wow, I can't believe it!"

"Yes, and it's probably best if we keep this quiet," Morie affirmed.

Lynn knew there was no hiding the fact that a human girl walked among them. Anyone who saw her would know she wasn't of the Aquapopulean race. *I knew she looked different – beautiful, but definitely different.* This was even more interesting than her being a siren!

"Lynn, I'd like you to look after Harmony this

morning. Get her breakfast, clothing, whatever she requires until Calder can take charge of her. He is performing a transition of death ceremony this morning."

Lynn beamed at Morie's request. It wasn't every day one got to look after a human. She walked as calmly as she could to Harmony's room, feeling exalted by her huge responsibility.

Harmony answered her door. Lynn gasped. Never before had she seen hair the color of honey. Last night Harmony's hair was wet, camouflaging its light color. Besides, Lynn had thought she was a siren, and all she could concentrate on was getting out of the room safely. After hearing local reports of sirens luring people to their deaths, she was on alert, even if she couldn't explain why this siren was out of the water. But what if humans were dangerous? The thought hadn't occurred to her before. *She doesn't seem dangerous. And her hair!* "Wow, it's beautiful!" Lynn paused with her hand in midair. "May I touch your hair?"

Harmony allowed the girl in and presented her back so Lynn could lift the wavy locks. "I could use a haircut I guess, but thanks."

Harmony turned to face Lynn and inquired, "Is it possible to have my clothes washed?"

"I can ask." Lynn didn't think Harmony's clothes would stand out as much as her veil of blond hair did. The tunic appeared to fit her curvy body well.

"I'd like to talk to Calder. I've been up since sunrise waiting for the opportunity to continue our conversation."

"He will meet with you later. He's performing a transition of death ceremony this morning. Shall I fetch you something to eat? Tea?"

Harmony shook her head, pacing the floor. "Do we have to stay in this room? Maybe you could show me around?"

Morie hadn't said the human couldn't leave her room. *And,* Lynn thought, *wait until the others see that I am in charge of a human!*

Lynn obliged. "Would you like to see the library?"

8

Harmony noticed that the top floor contained room after room of a vast library. Globes stood in several areas, some marked with the geography of her human world. She studied one particular sphere that represented the world she was in. She studied each continent, the same shapes as in her own world, but no countries appeared, only elements: copper, gold, aluminum, and others. Several salt mines were noted.

One book featuring architectural drawings lay open. Harmony looked with interest. When her fingertips turned the page she noted the paper felt strange, almost like canvas but not quite.

Scholarly appearing men and women gathered around tables speaking quietly, each group eyeing her with curiosity as she passed by. In another section of the library rolls of paper, containing geometry, hung like maps in a classroom. Young students copied what their instructor had marked on a roll. Once one student caught a glimpse of Harmony, shoulder tapping and head turning had the group of kids staring at her. When the instructor cleared his throat gruffly, Harmony sent him an apologetic smile for the interruption. Harmony suggested they head downstairs.

There were four main floors to this building with extended spaces in the tower rooms. As they descended past the two middle corridors containing similar guestrooms to hers, Harmony heard the hubbub of a busy staff and flurry of activities. The main floor offered treatment rooms for the elderly. Lynn explained that the seniors staying there were awaiting their transition ceremonies. "Families are summoned at the end." Harmony glimpsed inside the open door of one of the rooms, where an old woman rested in a chair by the window. A caregiver was setting up a standing tray containing a bowl of pureed food. The woman's sunken eyes focused on Harmony, and she gave her a toothless smile. Harmony smiled back, sending her a little wave.

Harmony and Lynn continued on until they reached a large dining room. It was emptying out, and the staff of young girls cleared away the dishes. It reminded Harmony of the staff at the Wentworth when she was a child and she ate there with her grandparents.

"One second!" Lynn chirped to Harmony before rushing over to a friend and whispering into her ear. The friend rounded her wide eyes and found Harmony. She looked back at Lynn with a nod and then disappeared for a brief moment. Lynn waved Harmony over. When the girl returned, playing nervously with the braid that hung over her breast, she thrust a basket forward, offering Harmony some type of bread.

"Thank you." Harmony lifted the small roll and sank her teeth into it, surprised when jelly squirted from its center. "Mmm, it's like a donut!" she said, her mouth full. She realized she hadn't eaten the food brought to her last night, and she'd passed on Lynn's offer of breakfast earlier. She practically inhaled the roll. Lynn's friend lifted the basket again, and Harmony took another. "Mmm, really good. Thank you." Just then the friend was called, and she waved good-bye before dashing away.

Lynn ushered Harmony back into the hallway and down the corridor toward the birthing rooms. "I heard this morning there's a mother in labor. She already has a son, so maybe we will watch her daughter being born! Let's have a look. The birthing rooms are this way."

"How do you know it will be a girl?" *Maybe in this realm there is some cool scientific way to know what sex a baby will be.*

"Females can only produce two offspring. We are born with two eggs, one male and one female. As I said, she's already birthed her son."

That is certainly thought-provoking. Harmony, an only child like her mother and grandmother, wondered how many children her mother might have had if she had lived longer.

She trailed alongside Lynn, peering into the rooms they passed. Through the open doors, Harmony noticed that each room was equipped with a waist-deep pool. According to what Morie had explained yesterday and her tour guide now reiterated, all women gave birth in water in this realm.

"Is it safe to have a baby under the water? What if the baby drowns?" Harmony reasoned that surely the hospital was the safest place to have a baby.

Lynn laughed out loud. "Babies don't drown. Everyone knows even human newborns can hold their breath for upward of forty-five seconds. Plus we have white fat for water insulation and buoyancy. Also, the white creamy stuff babies are born covered with protects their new skin in water, just like infant harbor seals."

A closed door swung open, and a girl carrying clothing stepped out. Lynn pointed past the girl's shoulder. "There's the birthing mother. Do you want to watch?"

Before Harmony could protest, Lynn clasped her hand and stepped into the room. Lynn offered a greeting to the woman laboring in the pool. Several other women in the room conversed, waiting for the baby's arrival. The chattering died down as one by one all eyes rested on Harmony.

Lynn introduced Harmony as coming from the other realm, and gasps echoed in the sparsely furnished chamber.

Harmony smiled politely and asked Lynn out of the

corner of her mouth, "Should you be telling people where I'm from?" From the shocked expressions on the faces around her, she gathered this wasn't common. She understood from Calder that Linkers were known to pass into the human realm, but no one had mentioned humans coming into their world.

"I already told a least a dozen people before I came to your room this morning." Lynn shrugged, apparently unfazed by any consequences.

Harmony thought that by now the entire Wellness complex knew she was here.

Lynn explained to the ladies that Harmony had never seen a water birth. They sucked in air at the shocking statement. They glanced among themselves, seeming confused. No one appeared to want to talk to Harmony, but they politely tolerated her presence.

The pregnant mother bared her teeth and moaned, "She's coming!"

The other women moved to the pool's edge for a better view, forgetting about Harmony for a moment. An older woman, the only one with white hair in the group of brunettes, wearing what looked like a two-piece bathing suit, entered the water. Harmony sat along the edge beside Lynn watching as the nude pregnant woman closed her eyes and concentrated on breathing. The white-haired woman chanted a prayer and then guided the group in a meditation ritual. She called upon the water god to send healing waters. She called upon the energy in the room, drawing from the women around her to give strength to the mother and baby. The laboring mother's breathing intensified. She blew out several long, loud puffs of air. After one great, strangled cry, the water below her turned murky. The women cheered as the white-haired woman in the water guided the newborn girl to its mother's small, full breast. The mother stood, clutching her newborn, and the baby gave several lusty cries. The mother snuggled the infant while the matrons wished the new mother well. The elder released a plug in the pool and the murky water drained away and was replaced with fresh water. Mother and daughter reclined in the warm water, relaxing.

Lynn and Harmony congratulated the new mother before they quietly slipped from the room.

Hours later, Harmony stood on the veranda at the Wellness, her hands wrapped around a mug of tea. It was overcast, and there was a slight chill to the breeze. Lynn stood beside her as they respectfully watched the procession of people in flowing white robes snake down the hill toward the dock. If only she had noticed that dock last night before she swam ashore to climb the overgrown hill with some difficulty. She watched two men carry a stretcher that held a body wrapped in linens. At the dock, a small unadorned boat waited, and the men placed the stretcher into it. A single passenger climbed in and began rowing with the outgoing tide.

"Lynn, does everyone come to this spot to bury their dead in the sea?"

"People will travel a great distance to bury their family members off the coast here, as this is our most sacred place, but some bury them closer to where they live, always returning the bodies to the water." Lynn moved to the railing. "There are other towns with Wellness Centers along the coast, none as grand as this. I've never been much farther than this island. My parents live just over the bridge."

Harmony continued to watch the rower as he propelled the craft out a good distance. Then he stood in the tiny boat and lifted out a stick that he tossed into the sea. "What is he doing?" She stepped up to the rail next to Lynn and shielded her eyes from the glare.

"That stick plugs the hole in the bottom of the boat. They are made to sink easily once the vessel is out to sea. He will swim back." The young man was bare-chested and wore pants that tapered above the knee. In one swift move he dove off the side of the boat. Harmony squinted, watching for him to resurface.

The small group on the dock turned and made their way up the steps toward the Wellness Temple. Harmony recognized Calder's white hair. He lingered, apparently saying a prayer. Harmony again searched for the man who dove from the boat. No one seemed concerned that he hadn't yet appeared. About ten minutes later, when the last of the people were reaching the building, was when the man's head finally broke the surface—much to Harmony's relief. Being told that someone could hold his breath for fifteen minutes or more was totally different from actually seeing it.

Harmony scooted behind a large potted palm, hidden from the view of the arrivers. She only stepped forward when Calder said final quiet words to someone nearby, who then walked away. Lynn said good-bye to Harmony and slipped back inside, leaving her in his care.

Calder turned and smiled at her. "Good morning, Harmony. Are you well today?"

Harmony just shrugged. "Can we talk now?" The words rushed out. She felt a pang of guilt for being rude, but her anxiety was overtaking her manners.

"Of course." Calder's voice was soothing. "Let me put away my robe and get my satchel, and we will be on our way." He left the porch and entered the building, Harmony on his heels.

"On our way? Where are we going?" She followed him through a set of doors into a corridor she hadn't been down before. She noticed this layout was slightly different than the Wentworth's.

"Do not fear. We are going to my family's dwelling. It's not far." He opened a door, and they entered a comfortable room, similar to the one on the upper floor she occupied. Calder slipped out of his robe and hung it on a peg next to several others. He removed his satchel from another peg. Harmony noticed it was almost identical to the one she'd found in the wall at the Wentworth-by-the-Sea.

"Okay, I'm ready."

They exited the back of the building and followed a path through thick brush and spruce trees. "It's on the other side of the island, so we'll drive." The path jogged, then opened up to what looked like a gravel parking lot. Instead of cars and trucks, there were covered four-wheel bikes with double bench seats that sat up to four passengers, like a golf cart with pedals. They resembled the bikes in seaside vacation towns you could rent for an hour of family fun. Harmony counted by twos in her head. The twenty-four bikes were all very similar.

"Wow, does everyone have one of these? Do you have cars?"

"This is our only mode of overland transportation in the coastal regions. Many of us travel in canoes on the waterways. We will just use the roads today." Calder smiled at her bewildered reaction. "There are many differences between our worlds, Harmony. We live a much simpler life here. We are spiritual people and choose to live this way."

She climbed onto the bench seat next to him and placed her feet on the pedals, as he did. "We know of your technologies and how they are affecting your race. We choose only things that benefit us without harming nature or our people."

Harmony thought back to a newscast last week and knew all too well what Calder was getting at. But how exactly did his race know of her kind? She hadn't noticed any televisions so they could watch otherworldly broadcasts. They were spiritual; perhaps they could see subconsciously? She was lost in thought for some time.

The breeze tugged at her hair, and she felt the sun warm her skin as the overcast skies cleared. She awakened from her thoughts, inhaling the clean ocean air. *The same smell as home.* One deep breath was all she needed before a sense of calm washed over her. Harmony asked, "How do you know about us? You said Linkers have crossed over? You're a Linker, and you knew about the peace treaty. Have you been in my world?"

"Yes, I traveled to your world long ago." He held out a hand, signaling for her to stop pedaling as he applied the brake. The bike slowed as it rolled downhill. "Linkers have brought back information in journals for centuries filled with notes and drawings. It is a difficult crossing, as you've experienced, and gathering herbs can be just as perilous. When we enter your realm it is an enormous responsibility to be discreet and keep our presence a secret."

"Wow, so you know what it's like where I'm from. This is...surreal." She studied his profile. Again, something about him seemed familiar. "Have we ever met?"

"No, Harmony, you've never met me. I know who you are though. I know quite a bit about your island town and the older folks there," he answered evasively. Before she could ask when the last time he'd visited her town had been, he added something just as intriguing.

"I am approaching my hundred and twenty-seventh birthday. I'm an old man." He chuckled when she gasped in surprise. "Our lifespans are slightly longer here. The oldest person on record is one hundred forty-two." After a short pause, he changed the subject. "You may find it interesting that many of our animal species are different. In your world, for instance, the bird species have flourished, but here we have no flying birds."

Harmony's eyes flicked upward and her ears perked. She hadn't seen any birds. No crying seagulls, no sandpipers, nothing.

Calder continued. "Our seafaring ancestors brought flightless birds over by boat from the east. In your world that area is known as Great Britain. They are domesticated, so we can eat their eggs—very tasty." The lines around his eyes crinkled when he smiled. "You will spot them in the village. There!" He pointed into the brush along the roadside, houses just feet away. "There is a pair." The birds walked along, pecking at the ground like chickens, but they were darker with more slender necks. Harmony studied them curiously and then turned her attention to the houses.

They had rolled over roads made of packed gravel and ground shells into a complex of dwellings. On the inland side of the road, the houses were built on the ground, each containing a turret attached to a box-shaped building. The tiled rooflines sloped upward at the corners in the ancient Asian fashion. Behind them, up the sloping hills, were large gardens, being tended by numerous villagers and their children. The dwellings on the shore side were constructed on stilts, like boxes stacked upon boxes. Each of the two- or three-level homes were wrapped by decks and docks, with canoes and longboats tied up at most.

"These houses are unusual," she commented. "Like the Wentworth, they are a blend of architectures. I went to college to study architectural history." She glanced at him, wondering if she'd have to explain college, but he nodded as though he knew what she was talking about.

"Yes, our Linkers spent a considerable amount of time in the Orient throughout the centuries. Later others visited extensively during the Victorian era. The builders cleverly blended the styles from the journal drawings the Linkers brought back. You'll see this style in our coastal regions."

"Why is the Wentworth strangely similar in name

and structure to Wellness?"

"The builders recreated it from a drawing brought back, and the altered name seemed a natural fit. It is a fairly new structure, less than one hundred years old— like yours. Before that, the original structure was primitive. The community gathered after seeing the drawings and decided we wanted to make it more comfortable for our visitors."

Harmony had many questions. "So how long have your people been traveling to our world? How did they even figure it out?"

Calder chuckled. "Accidentally! A Linker was making herbal blends for tooth pain. When he lit the herbs, he found himself in ancient Mesopotamia."

While she considered his words, Calder announced, "We have arrived." Between the roadways was a grassy median where several bikes were parked. Calder pulled into an empty space and stepped out.

"Come," he instructed Harmony, walking toward a water dwelling. As they approached, a young man rested his tool on the deck and waved.

"Hello, Rio," Calder bellowed. "I'm glad you are home."

"Yes, Grandfather. I didn't go out fishing because I had some repairs to tend to." He pointed to the broken railing on the deck that he'd abandoned to greet his guests. His handsome face was friendly, and he approached them in an easy manner. Harmony noticed his reflective eyes, like everyone else's here, as he regarded her with sudden curiosity.

"Rio, this is Harmony. Harmony, this is my grandson, Rio."

Rio politely gave her a slight head bow, and she returned his gesture.

"Rio, are your mother and sister at home?" Calder inquired. "I need to speak to all of you. Time is of the essence."

9

Rio wasted no time escorting Calder and Harmony inside the family's home. His dark, shoulder-length hair was pin straight and worn parted to the side. Everyone Harmony saw wore similar undyed, light-weight fabrics in the tunic fashion—the people at the Wellness and in the fields and Rio, who walked in front of her.

Inside the dwelling, cluttered and lived in, Rio offered them comfortable seats. Harmony felt the atmosphere of this home lift her mood—it was a true family home—she envied them.

"Hello, Father. I didn't expect you back until next week," said the brunette woman who abandoned her beadwork and joined them. She hugged her father and settled into the chair next to her son. Her attention was captured as a similar-looking younger version came down the stairs carrying several books.

"Grandfather!" The girl sounded delighted and rushed down the last few steps. When she reached the group her expression became guarded.

"Hello. Yes, I came early because something of great importance has come to light. I must speak with you all, as I will need your help." His family gathered around him on the edges of their seats. Calder introduced his daughter, Nami, and his granddaughter, Binda. "This is Harmony Parker."

"Welcome to our home, Harmony." Nami's tight smile stretched across her concerned face. She shifted her gaze back to her father, alarm raising her voice. "What has happened?"

Harmony watched Calder's daughter shift uncomfortably. "She is obviously a stranger to this land, Father. Everyone knows only humans have hair the colors of sunshine, coal, or fire."

The siblings exchanged glances but said nothing.

"Yes, Harmony has come from the other realm. She has warned us that the sacred land where our temple sits is in danger of being destroyed in her world. This may have grave implications for us."

Harmony, like Calder's family, waited to hear what help he needed.

"Can't Suijin do something about the destruction in her realm?" Rio asked.

Binda spoke up. "No, he can do nothing! You should know most humans do not recognize Suijin as the water god. His power is weak in their realm."

All eyes landed on Harmony, who tried not to squirm under their scrutiny. Calder defended her. "She came here quite by accident...and all because of me."

Now all attention was directed back on him.

"Because of you?" Harmony asked. "Why? How could my being here be your fault?"

"It was I who put the satchel in the wall at the Wentworth-by-the-Sea back in 1905." He looked at the shocked faces of his grandchildren, but Nami averted her eyes, as if she were aware of this information. Everyone talked over each other at him, but Calder held up a hand to silence them. "I'm afraid I must start at the beginning." His audience obediently settled back to listen.

"When I was a boy, on the cusp of becoming a man, I trained with the Linker of my generation. I was born with the mark." He pulled aside the collar of his shirt for Harmony's benefit. Just below his collarbone was a tattoo, a circle with three waves.

"I've seen that!" Harmony injected. "On the tin I found."

"It is the symbol of our race—earth and water," Binda explained, solving the mystery.

Calder nodded, releasing the fabric, which slipped back into place. "We traveled for years, collecting plant leaves, berries, flowers, and many other samplings. My master taught me how to dry and preserve them. We meditated and harnessed the healing energies of our Earth. We traveled with some people from the Forest Tribe as we made our journey through the forests and mountains of that region. The coastal clans assisted us when we needed Divers to go into the sea and collect underwater plant specimens.

"One morning my master woke me and said I would be going on a solo journey. I was to prepare." He pressed his fingertips together like a steeple and drew in a long inhale. "That was the day he sent me into your world." He exhaled.

Harmony saw confusion in the youthful faces of Calder's grandchildren. She understood. Surely they all felt the gravity of what was happening as Calder's story unfolded—that is—except Nami, who slipped from her seat and quietly announced she'd get them tea.

"I emerged from the sea, just as you did, Harmony. It is like that every time. A difficult passage, not always survivable." Calder spoke those words directly to Harmony, and she shuddered at the horrific memory. The thought of having to go through that experience again to return home made bile rise in her throat. She forced a swallow as Calder continued.

"The year was 1900. I went aboard a merchant ship and traveled around the world for five years. I was on a mission to gather and learn about healing herbs from your realm. When I was in the Orient I discovered many. After five years, I was ready to return to my home. So I made my way back to our sacred place, by way of a Japanese political group on their way to that very spot for peace negotiations. When I returned to the island of New Castle, which was once only a small fishing village, I discovered the transformation of the hotel, Wentworth-by-the-Sea. A man by the name of Frank Jones had bought it and spared no expense to reshape the Colonial Revival hotel. It now had steam-powered elevators, electric lights, and flushing toilets."

"They have had the conveniences of electricity and flushing toilets for less than one hundred years, Grandfather?" Rio questioned with disbelief. "And what is an elevator?"

Calder's mouth curved into a smile. "I'm afraid so. I will tell you of elevators and otherworldly inventions at another time, Rio," he promised. "Harmony, that was the summer I met your great-great-grandmother, Pearl."

Harmony gasped. "Wow, my grandmother Margaret told me stories of her grandmother Pearl working for the hotel during the signing of the peace treaty in 1905. That's incredible—I can't believe you met her. What are the chances..." The words failed on her lips as a thought occurred to her. "How did you meet her? How well did you know her?"

She recalled what her grandmother had told her. Pearl had worked at the hotel for a few summer seasons, one of the most famous being the summer of 1905, her final year there. At the end of the season a wealthy local had asked her to marry him. Pearl was very beautiful and very young. She had married a man twenty-two years her senior. Pearl moved into his comfortable house and soon gave birth to a daughter. It was the only child they had. They rose in society, and her daughter became a sought-after socialite. However, there had been rumors that the child didn't belong to her husband.

Harmony had discussed the timeline of Pearl's marriage with her grandmother many times; they agreed the conception of the child didn't add up. They had always figured Pearl had become pregnant out of wedlock that summer, and they never believed the man she married was the father.

"Maybe you also met my great-great-grandfather?" She waited for his reply.

Calder noted the accusation in her tone. He disregarded her questions. "Pearl was very beautiful. Every man, woman, and child stopped to glance her way when she walked into a room." His expression softened, and he had a faraway look in his eyes. "She would set the tables in the dining hall in the afternoons before dinner service or stroll the long verandas, making sure linens were clean and everything was as it should be. The manager made sure only the prettiest of the girls were visible to guests.

"One day when the delegates traveled to the shipyard where the negotiations were taking place I stayed behind. I told the gentlemen I was not feeling well, but in reality I was planning to leave their world. I was sitting alone on the veranda reflecting on my five years of travel when Pearl walked up to me. She asked if I was all right and if she could get me anything. The manager was on her heels, and when I replied I'd like her company, the manager insisted she sit and entertain me until I tired of her."

Calder chucked at the memory. "The manager had another girl bring us tea, and the two of us talked all morning and over lunch. She was fascinated by where I had traveled. I could have looked at her sweet smile all day. We became friends that day, and I couldn't bring myself to leave just then. We met again and again before I told her I was leaving. She asked me to take her with me, but I couldn't." He looked at Harmony, Binda, and Rio, hoping they'd understand his struggle. "I wanted to. I considered trying it. I knew we were in love, but I couldn't stay. Linkers are forbidden to have romances with humans." The apologetic twist of his lips convinced Harmony that her suspicions were correct.

"Did you know she was pregnant when you left?" Harmony felt her anger rising. She'd put together the puzzle easy enough. She glared into familiar eyes— Calder's eyes. She'd inherited those pale, amber eyes, as had the generations of Pearl's descendants before her.

Nami returned then with the tea tray and set it before them on the low table. No one reached for a cup except her father. Harmony flicked her gaze at Nami figuring she'd been listening from the nearby kitchen. There was no shock on Nami's face, only compassion.

"We knew, and we had a plan. Someone else was already interested in her, someone who could give her everything she could want in your world."

"What about *my* grandmother? She was of *this* world." Binda reacted with jealous rage. Her chin thrust upward and she barked at her mother. "You knew of this!"

"It was long ago, before he met my mother, Binda. Be silent and let him finish," Nami scolded her daughter.

"I came back. Your grandmother and I were married many years later," Calder clarified for his grandchildren before he lifted the steaming cup to his lips.

"Oh my…That means…we are related!" Harmony said with mixed emotions, suddenly realizing she wasn't the only one left in her family line. She was related to Calder, Nami, Rio, and Binda. Harmony dared not say anything more to Binda, whose mouth was grimly set.

"Distantly related," Calder confirmed. "I met your great-great-grandmother when I was very young. I mentioned my advanced age to you earlier. Well, you see, my grandchildren are the same age as you are, but you are my great-great-grandchild."

Harmony lifted her fingers to her lips and slipped her thumbnail between her teeth. She had felt a connection with Calder that she couldn't explain. He'd looked familiar to her. Growing up, she'd always had a weird sense that she was different. She'd just convinced herself she was different from other kids because her parents had died.

"Wow, this is so unbelievable. You are my great-great-grandfather. My grandmother Margaret and I were the last, and now she is gone." Her eyes met Calder's as an idea occurred to her. "She was your granddaughter...and she drowned last fall."

Calder nodded, looking grief-stricken.

A thought echoed in Harmony's mind: was it a strange coincidence that her parents and grandparents had drowned? *And here I am, in a world with an angry water god.* "Can your water god actually cross into my world?" she asked. She returned to chewing on her fingernail, remembering that Morie had said something about this aquatic god in Japanese culture.

Calder pressed his lips together, nodding. His answer was grim. "Yes. He may be a minor, overlooked god in your world, but we can only assume he has used his power to take human souls as he's been doing in this realm."

"My father's commercial fishing vessel sank and all were lost. And my mother drowned when she fell through the ice." Harmony looked at the faces before her. They were her family now. Rio gave her a sympathetic smile, as did his mother. Binda's face was impassive as she stared into the teacup her mother handed her.

Calder apologized. "I am sorry, Harmony, but I don't think your family's drownings were accidents."

"I knew it wasn't just a coincidence," she rasped painfully.

"My mentor had sent me through not only to gather knowledge from the humans but to look into things Suijin might be responsible for—sunken ships for example. Several of the council members of that time wondered if the disturbance of our sacred ground had caused him to become vengeful. We felt the earthquakes when ground was broken for the great building the Wentworth-by-the-Sea and any other time the land there was majorly altered."

Nami sat next to her son, Rio. "The reason we built our temple was to appease Suijin's anger."

Rio chewed on some nuts from the tea tray. After he swallowed he said, "He's been luring our people into the water with his sea sirens and drowning them. He is even sending them up rivers to reach the inland people of the Forest Tribe."

Nami fretted. "The Forest Tribe is not innocent in this. I've heard many of them no longer worship!"

Binda rolled her eyes at her mother's comment. "Mother, you get this information from gossiping friends. I have frequented the traders' village, and I have found the same could be said about the coastal dwellers. The truth is, worshipping is fading out with the younger generations. Though the tribe is barbaric by my standards, they are still my best customers."

Calder halted their chatter, looking to each of them. "We need to send Harmony back to her world. She is our only hope for stopping these disturbances. If Suijin is behind this, I don't know what any of us can do."

"How can we help her, Grandfather?" Rio asked.

"The herbs that got her here will get her back, but I do not have them." Calder's bushy brows drew together. "There are three ingredients. And they must be gathered from three locations. Each one is extremely difficult to get to and located in very dangerous areas. Everyone knows of the first location, but not many know the plants that grow there are special."

He focused on Harmony. "The first is a plant from deep under the sea, inside a cave. Once you obtain the first plants and bring them back to me, I will sun-dry and crush them. To get there you will follow the coast north. Binda and Rio will take you. This place is not far, and they know the way."

Rio murmured, "The sea serpent's cave." His eyes widened. "You've told us never to swim there because of the danger lurking in the water."

"Wait... You expect me to go in deep water? I...I can't!" Harmony stuttered as her uncontrollable fear of deep water flooded her.

Calder shook his head. "Not you. Collection will require the skill and endurance of an Aquapopulean Diver. As I mentioned to you last night, the Divers are our strongest swimmers. They can hold their breath underwater for around twenty minutes. You will need such a person for the gathering of this plant."

"Right." Harmony's shoulders eased away from her ears.

Turning to his grandchildren, he said, "I trust you know where to find your friend Kodiak Night?" Binda and Rio nodded. "Bring him back here."

Binda argued that Harmony need not accompany them, but Rio sided with Calder. "Having Harmony with us might help convince Kodi to help us." Rio stretched his hand in Harmony's direction. "Just look at her."

After giving Harmony a once-over, Binda narrowed her eyes at Rio, remaining silent.

"What is that supposed to mean?"

"Sorry, Harmony. I only meant that after seeing what you look like...I mean, your luxurious golden hair... Well, I just mean you could help persuade our accomplished Diver friend."

Harmony waved away his attempt to explain, knowing he wasn't trying to be disrespectful. "I'll do what I can to convince him," she added helpfully.

Rio exhaled with relief. Harmony was unaware that they were a race of brunettes, with no exceptions. And they all knew Kodiak had a weakness for rare finds.

Later Nami stood at her father's shoulder, watching her children paddle away with the stranger. She was the daughter of a Linker, though not one herself.

"I fear for my children," she admitted.

"I fear for our future existence," Calder countered. He wrapped his arm around his daughter's shoulders and gave her a fatherly squeeze.

10

Harmony stepped gingerly into the canoe tied at the dock attached to Rio and Binda's family dwelling. She loathed boats—especially as the water got deeper beneath them. The thought of her father's fishing vessel sinking and, worse, the thought of him drowning in cold, abysmal water plagued her.

The canoe set out for deeper water. Binda paddled at one end, avoiding Harmony, while Rio paddled at the other. Rio conversed with Harmony as he maneuvered the small canoe out to sea. He soon lifted a small sail that whisked their vessel over the white crests.

Rio wanted to know the details about exactly how she'd arrived in their world. Harmony explained how she'd found the herbs and said that burning them yesterday had sent her into the ocean in their dimension.

"I've read in school and heard tales from my grandfather about the human realm, but Grandfather never explained how perilous crossing over was," Rio said to Harmony. He remarked to Binda, "Wow, can you believe that?"

"I already knew about that, Rio. Every Linker learns that in training," Binda said smugly.

Harmony could tell Binda was irked that Calder had kept the story of his personal time in the human realm with her great-great-grandmother a secret. She hoped her cousin would come around so they could get to know one another better. Finding out she had family had been almost as shocking as waking up in another realm.

"Where did you say we are going?" Harmony asked. A drop of sweat beaded on her brow, not from the heat but fear. She gripped the seat, her knuckles white, her heart pounding.

"Out there." Rio pointed beyond the speckles of other boats to an island visible on the horizon. His smile was genuine. He was much more outgoing than his sister, who sat tight-lipped during the majority of the trip.

"Oh, the Isles of Shoals." It was odd to recognize landmarks in this other world.

Harmony regarded Binda over her shoulder and attempted to cut the tension between them. "What do you do, Binda? Do you go to school?"

"School is for little children," she snapped.

"Oh." Harmony shrugged her shoulders at Rio, not sure why Binda seemed annoyed.

Rio chuckled at his sister's expense. "We attend school from toddler age to age fourteen for basic education, and then we work in our trade. The common trades along the coast are fishing, building, farming, and teaching. There are shop owners, like in your culture, I expect. There are other skills, such as scholars, artists, and crafters. The inland Forest Tribe is known for their weavers who produce skillfully crafted cloth. We trade goods or use gold coins."

"What about Linkers?" Harmony again wondered about Calder's title.

Rio tapped just under his collarbone, where she had seen Calder's mark of the circle symbol with three waves. "Linkers are born with their mark. They have a huge responsibility in our race. There are only six alive that we know of. Binda also bears the mark. It is extremely rare to have two in one family."

Harmony couldn't picture Binda handling all the differences in the human realm if she crossed over. Binda gave her a pointed look, and Harmony turned back to Rio, feeling guilty that she'd been staring at her cousin.

"Only Linkers have markings. Our elders, who started off as young leaders, are chosen and educated to

71

lead the communities, tribes, and temples. Binda has been working closely with Grandfather. That is why she is so angry he didn't tell her about meeting your relative in your world. I think she feels entitled to know all things."

This last comment provoked a glare from Binda. The siblings had the same pale-blue eye color as their mother, their brightness like a pool's reflection. "I'm sure he was planning on telling me, Rio. And besides, being a Linker is not the only thing I will do with my life. I have other gifts," Binda retorted.

Rio took pity on his elder sister and said, "Yes, she is a very talented artist, and the tribal tattooists find her drawings very valuable. We've gone several times to the large trade gatherings during the year. Binda is highly sought after."

Her chin tilted up a notch at her brother's praise.

Harmony swiped a handful of her windblown hair out of her face and tried to secure it by tucking it into the crook of her neck. "I like to draw too, mostly buildings. I go to school to study about historic buildings. I'm hoping to get a job restoring the local architecture—when I get home, that is." She attempted again to recapture her hair, and explained, "We go to regular school until age eighteen and then continue if we want to specialize in a trade. Anyway, I should have finished when I was twenty-two years old. I only have one semester left. I'm twenty-three now."

Rio steered toward the islands. Though his long hair was tied at the nape, strands whipped loose around his face. He swung his head, allowing the wind to direct the hair away from his lips. He responded, "I am twenty-two. Binda is a couple years older." The girls regarded one another when Rio stated what they were most likely thinking. "You are similar in age, and you both like to draw—two things in common already."

"We are approaching," Binda said, ignoring his observation. "Pull up to the third dock." Rio dropped the small sail and paddled among the other boats that crowded the lively harbor area.

Harmony scrambled from the boat as soon as it bumped the dock and blew out a long, thankful breath that she was again on dry land. The churning in her stomach returned when she remember this was a tiny island and they'd soon be making a return trip across cold, abysmal water.

Boats of all sizes floated nearby, but none resembled the modern motor boats she knew. The larger vessels were reminiscent of Viking long boats. The miniscule island seemed to be full with people. Harmony smiled at the children fishing from the pier as she walked past. They jumped to their feet, poles forgotten, as they watched her walk away. Several young men unloading barrels rested their loads at their feet to give her their full attention. Beyond the docks was a makeshift town of basic buildings—no fancy architecture. Fish vendors were trading, and open-air cooking and eating were ongoing. The maritime people wore sleeveless, weather-worn tunics. Many covered their clothing with large aprons to protect them from the messy seafood.

"Who are we here to see?" Harmony stayed close to Rio, feeling apprehensive.

"My good friend Kodiak Night. He's a renowned Diver. Just who we need to help us. All we have to do is convince him." Rio ignored the stares his cousin was getting and led her past the buildings to an opening where the rocky, grassy ground rolled toward the open sea. "When Kodi isn't diving he's digging for oysters. He loves to hunt for pearls. He's quite lucky and finds the best ones."

The tide was out and several men were digging in the mud around rocks, some pulling up trapped oyster shells.

"Wait here," Rio directed the girls. He trudged down toward one man who was crouched alongside a large bolder.

The man stood when Rio approached and called to him. The first thing Harmony noticed about him was his short hair. So far all the men she'd seen wore their hair either straight to their collar or to their shoulders. It varied more with the women. But everyone had very straight hair, in various shades of brunette. The only other hair color Harmony had seen was white on the older generation.

She watched Rio and his friend Kodiak talk for a bit. Rio used emphatic hand gestures, and his companion shook his head several times. When Rio finally gestured in the direction of the girls, Kodiak looked over and paused, focusing on them.

Binda waved to Kodiak, mumbling to Harmony, "He doesn't look happy."

Kodiak nodded to acknowledge her wave but continued his debate with Rio.

11

Kodiak considered the gravity of what Rio had confided. It was madness that a human was in their realm, but even crazier that Calder wanted him to help. Diving into the sea serpent's cave was dangerous, and would require sufficient payment to go along with the risk. "So a stray human has found her way into our realm. Why would we risk our lives for her?" Kodiak raised his brows, waiting for a justifiable answer.

"Calder is hoping by sending her back we can avoid unknown destruction to our island." Rio suddenly gave a nervous laugh. He revealed, "The funny thing is…she's not just any stray human. Turns out she's our cousin."

Kodiak shook his head. Amusement twinkled in his eyes. "Who knew Calder was such a rule breaker?" He knew it was strictly forbidden for Linkers to have relations with humans during their journeys. Kodiak never pictured the old Linker as a ladies man.

"Calder doesn't want the girls to know, but he is willing to pay you—a large sum. He said the monetary offering would seal the deal," Rio enticed.

Kodiak tugged off his gloves, tossed them into the net bag filled with shells, and hoisted the bag over his shoulder. The men left the shore side by side, engaged in rapid conversation. The closer Kodiak got, the more he was impressed by the dazzling beauty before him.

Rio's smile was overly enthusiastic, and he spoke in an "I'm trying to stay positive" tone. "Kodi, this is Harmony Parker from…" He lowered his voice and looked around. "From the human realm."

Kodiak nodded politely, distracted by her untamed blond hair.

"Kodi wanted to meet you before he decided if he

will join us on our journey." Rio gave him a pleading look.

On cue the flaxen-haired human turned on her charm. "Kodi, it is an honor to meet you. I hear you are an amazing diver."

His eyes flitted away briefly at her praise, but they shifted back to rest on her lips as she spoke. Plump and pouty: he wondered how they would feel against his own.

"We need your help. I..." She placed her slim hand under the hollow of her throat. "I need your help."

Kodiak tore his eyes away from her mouth and noticed the gold ring with a lavender pearl on her finger. His eyes widened in surprise. In all his finds he had never seen a pearl of this color. "Your ring," he said. "What kind of pearl is that?"

"Oh!" Harmony looked down at her heirloom ring, smiling fondly at it. "This was my grandmother's lavender pearl ring. Lavender pearls are rare."

"I will accept it as payment for helping you." He leveled his gaze at her.

"What—*no!*" Her other hand covered the ring, protecting it from view. She looked at Rio. "This was my grandmother's!" she said in anguish. She turned to Binda, who responded with a shrug.

"Kodi, must you *insist* on payment?" Rio tried to intervene. Rio said Calder was offering to pay him, but a rare pearl was much more enticing then gold coins.

Kodi turned to his friend. "I will only help you—for that. I will dive into the serpent's cave and retrieve what you need for that." He pointed to Harmony's hand, now tucked safely under her armpit.

Kodiak watched Harmony read the distress on Rio's face. There was no changing his mind. What could she do? They needed him.

"I just want to go home. Calder said each place was

difficult." She frowned. "Okay, I'll give it to you as payment, but only if you help us collect *all* the leaves we need from the three different locations. We start at the serpent's cave."

"But we don't need a Diver for the other two," Binda piped in.

"If you are going to take this ring, then you are going to earn it." Harmony's declaration intrigued him.

"Deal." Kodiak smirked at her tenacity. She had both beauty and brains. He knew what she asked was risky at best, but he lived for adventure and thrived on challenges. Besides, the ring wasn't the only thrill he was planning on getting out of this deal. Once more his eyes swept over her waving hair, and he anticipated the day when he could lock his hands in it.

12

Harmony was relieved she'd convinced Kodiak to help, but her heart squeezed in anguish at the thought of turning over her grandmother's ring. Of course, all the jewelry her grandmother had ever owned had passed down to her, but she'd trade every piece, some more valuable than the pearl, to keep this one ring.

"Let me collect my things. Then I'm all yours," he said, looking into Harmony's eyes. Kodi's smirk and comment left her with a keen awareness of the need to be careful with this guy.

He strode away, and the others kept his pace.

Side by side, Kodiak was almost a foot taller than Rio and more slender. The sleeveless tunic exposed his arms, which Harmony noticed rippled with muscles. From his physique she imagined he was a powerful diver and swimmer. And his face was quite handsome, the most handsome face Harmony had seen so far in this world. After the rocky start, she wondered about her conflicting feelings.

The block buildings on the island were similar to human apartments, sandwiched together. They waited outside in a narrow alley for Kodiak to return from his room.

Harmony thumbed the pearl on her ring. *Why is this all happening to me? Because of Calder's indiscretions with my kind, his blood runs through my veins, connecting me to this world. The herbs he hid ultimately brought me here! Is he to blame? Or is this water god responsible for my family drowning? Why would he drown my family? And what of Kodi? He wants the only thing I hold dear.*

"Cousin."

Harmony's heart pulsed at Rio's endearment. He accepted her no matter what, and she was grateful to him.

"I'm sorry you have to trade your ring for Kodi's help. He has a crazy obsession with pearls. But honestly, no one is a better diver. You were smart to commit him to collecting all the herbs. He is smart and strong, and he can be persuasive when he wants to be."

"You speak highly of him—why?" Harmony considered Kodiak kind of a jerk. He seemed overly confident, and his commanding presence annoyed her.

"I have known Kodi all my life. He lived with his father in my village when he was a boy, and we grew up together. Once we had our trades, his father moved south, and he moved to this island. He keeps to himself now, when he's not diving for customers. Kodi is someone you can trust. Just give him a chance."

Rio's reassurance did little to comfort Harmony. After all, Rio's enthusiastic outlook on life might be biased. He was sweet but somewhat inexperienced.

Kodiak returned with fresh clothes, a satchel he carried across his body, and another bag slung over his broad shoulder. Before they could walk away, a door across the alleyway swung open. A pretty girl rushed out, calling his name, her voice wistful. "Kodi, are you going somewhere? You agreed to dine with us. My mother thought perhaps tonight..."

The obvious infatuation in her eyes made Binda and Rio smile. Binda said under her breath, "Kodi is not only sought after by many girls, but their mamas too."

Harmony looked on with curiosity, thinking this naive slip of a girl was fishing way out of her league.

"Sorry. I'll be away for a while," Kodiak said kindly.

"Oh." She sounded disappointed. "Okay, but be sure to come by when you return."

Kodiak gave her a wink, turned, and strutted down

the narrow lane. The group followed his lead.

Harmony glimpsed the girl leaning against the door, dreamy-eyed, watching Kodiak walk away. *Oh brother!* Harmony thought. *So this is how it's going to be!*

On the long row back to the mainland, Kodiak took Binda's seat and helped Rio paddle until they were beyond the cluster of boats into the open water. Harmony tried not to look at his arms as they moved against the water in long, controlling stokes. He was impressive, but she wasn't going to like him—not if he was going to take her grandmother's ring. She couldn't like him. In fact, she decided she disliked him.

Harmony shared the center seat with Binda, uncomfortably close to the edge of the canoe. When the vessel rocked Harmony squeezed her eyes shut. She desperately tried to control her shaking knees.

Binda's voice sounded in her ear. "Are you all right?"

Harmony gave Binda a pathetic look and shook her head. "No. I have an immense fear of deep water."

"What! You are afraid of water? Did you hear that?" Binda laughed. "She's afraid of water." Kodiak smiled at Binda's amusement. Rio had a puzzled look on his face.

"Not *water — deep* water!" Harmony corrected. Her anger diluted some of her distress. Then Harmony realized these were Aquapopulo, water people. Of course what she confessed sounded ridiculous.

Kodiak, who hadn't spoken to Harmony since they'd made their deal over her grandmother's ring, now seemed interested. He said, "When Rio told me that you are from the human realm, I didn't believe him until I got up close and saw your hair. Do all the people on your world have hair your color? And are all of them afraid of deep water?"

Binda laughed, which startled Harmony. "Ha! Kodi, you should have spent a little more time reading when you were a kid instead of daydreaming."

"Binda, you know I hated being cooped up in a library. Besides, there are plenty of interesting things in our own world. It just takes a little exploration," Kodi justified.

Harmony sighed at his stupid questions. "Of course not. People fear all kinds of things," she said. "Some are afraid of deep water or high places or bugs, or whatever…" She ran her hand through her hair to drag it back from her face. "And people have blond hair, or red hair, or black or brown hair. Older folk have gray or white hair."

She observed that Kodiak was openly admiring her, and Harmony chided herself for noticing his attractive smile. Her strong feelings toward him were definitely feelings of dislike.

"Haven't you ever seen blond hair before?" Harmony flicked away the locks breezing over her shoulders.

"No, no one in this realm has your hair color. You are quite unique," Kodiak remarked.

"Oh." Harmony felt a flutter of pleasure at the way he said she was unique. Then she looked at Binda, who was eyeing the strands that touched Harmony's arm. "So that is why everyone has been staring at me?" She recalled Lynn admiring her hair at the Wellness.

Binda wore the hair above her forehead braided to keep strands from blowing around. The loose hair in the back touched her cheeks. "Not everyone has seen the color drawings of your people in the library. In the thousands of journals are descriptions of your world, the many kinds of people and their cultures, and lots and lots of stories." Binda admitted she had studied a large portion of them. "As a Linker, I'm expected to cross into your realm, but I have no desire to go. I've read about great wars, famine, plagues, and other horrible things."

The boys listened intently. Harmony wanted to

defend her species from Binda's verbal attack, but she couldn't deny the facts.

Binda glanced sideways at Harmony. "I'm thankful I was born in this realm, where there is peace and balance. The Aquapopulean race is one of concord. In fact, I don't think it's Suijin who is causing us strife. I think it's the destruction humankind is wreaking on their planet that's causing a rift in this realm. And to make matters worse, it turns out we are distantly related to a human!"

"Binda!" Rio admonished.

"It's not that bad!" Harmony argued, ignoring her barb. "Well, the stuff you said is bad, but there are good things—great things even."

Kodiak jumped into the conflict. "I don't know what to believe. Some say Suijin is a vengeful god and sends his sirens to reclaim souls. Why? What does that really get him? And Binda, you imply the ramifications have more to do with quantum mechanics."

"Well, genius," Binda clucked sarcastically, "tell us more about quantum mechanics."

"Forget quantum mechanics," Rio interjected. "What happens on her island seems to effect ours. Harmony told us the structure that sits where our temple does is going to be torn down. The land will be disturbed. We need to gather the ingredients to send Harmony back. She is our only hope to avoid possible destruction."

Harmony watched Kodiak who seemed to mull over Rio's words while adjusting the sail. "Maybe they won't tear down the structure in her world. Even if they do, do we know *how* it will affect us exactly? How does Calder know for certain?" He received blank stares. "I'm just saying, we are possibly risking our lives by going into the sea serpent's cave...and for what?" He looked pointedly at Harmony. "What is it you are planning to do when you get back? How are you planning on stopping this destruction?"

Harmony considered his tough questions. She had accepted Calder's word that something devastating would happen here, but he'd never said what exactly. And true, she was asking these strangers to do something dangerous for her, but she couldn't stay here. She looked at Kodiak and said with determination, "Calder is a respected man, and if he says there will be danger to your kind, then I think it's worth heeding his warning. I will do whatever I can to stop the destruction of your hallowed land, but I certainly can't do anything about it here."

Rio nodded. Harmony figured Binda would never doubt her grandfather's warning and probably wanted to be rid of their human guest. Clearly there was no perfect answer.

Calder was wise, but was he right?

Kodiak looked at a far-off spot on the horizon and drew in a long breath. Exhaling, he smiled at the faces yawning and dipping with the waves. He shrugged and said. "I will take the risk for the promised reimbursement."

Harmony couldn't look at him again after that.

They rode in silence until they reached the deck at Rio and Binda's dwelling. Harmony swayed up the dock, without sea legs, as if still rocking in the canoe. Calder met them at the door and greeted them. "Just in time for dinner." Harmony's stomach was still in knots, and food was the last thing on her mind.

After their meal, Calder unfolded a map and spread it across the table. They gathered around him curiously. Harmony recognized the island of New Castle and the surrounding area. "Binda, Rio—you know this land," he touched the map with his finger. "We are here. You will follow the river to here and cross over the land on foot until you reach the cliff. At the cliff there is a path to the beach below, where you can enter the water."

Kodiak nodded. "I know of the sea serpent's cave. Another diver told me he attempted to go in but was nearly killed by the serpent."

"Wait!" Harmony held up her hands. "Are you telling me there's a real sea serpent—a monster in the ocean?" She scanned each of their faces, but Kodi's eyes held her captive. She hadn't even glanced in his direction since they'd returned to the dwelling. Outside, with the glaring sun shining off the sea, she hadn't noticed the color of his eyes. Now she observed they were incredible. The light flared though them; they glowed like brushed copper. The outermost circle of the iris was a ring of black that outlined their brilliance. For a moment she totally forgot what she was concerned about.

Kodiak replied, "Yes a real sea serpent—and a big, mean one at that."

"If you can avoid him it would be best. Binda, be sure to carry salve with you," Calder advised. "Kodiak, you will need to go into the cave and collect this plant." He opened a leather-bound journal he'd laid on the table earlier. He stopped at a page, indicating a drawing. "Rio and Binda, you must draw the serpent away from the cave."

"How will we do that, Grandfather?" Rio sounded anxious.

"I've heard the serpent has a liking for dolphins. Luckily he stays close to the cave. Only a stray dolphin that finds itself in those waters becomes his meal." Calder's furry eyebrows rose. "I was able to obtain dolphin blood today from an old friend." He pulled a bottle out of his satchel. "A little goes a long way."

All together, they agreed to concentrate solely on this mission before talking about what was to come next. Calder wished them luck and left to go back to the Wellness Temple. They retired early, anticipating they'd leave at dawn.

13

At dawn Kodiak, along with Binda, Rio, and Nami, dove off the dock into the bay for the habitual Aquapopulo morning swim. It helped ground him and awaken him for a new day. The salty water caressed his skin while he flexed and stretched his muscles, connecting with the living sea. The underwater sounds cleared his mind and allowed his creative thoughts to generate. He contemplated Harmony. She was unusual and incomparable, which intrigued him. A human in their realm was unprecedented, and the rules probably still applied: no mixing of Aquapopulo and human blood. Kodi broke the surface to head back to the dwelling. He knew she would be on the deck watching her extended family. He wondered again about Calder breaking the rules. Rio said he'd fallen in love with Harmony's great-great-grandmother. Could it be true? Could one fall in love with a human?

A quarter of an hour later he swam closer, watching her golden mane hang around her shoulders as she leaned over the railing, her forearms resting on the banister. In her hands she held a mug, which she lifted to her alluring lips. He could feel his rising desire, a desire he told himself to cool. Although there were rules, he battled the thought of breaking them. Rules could be bent.

Kodiak caught up to the others. They swam up to the dock, refreshed and smiling, and climbed the steps. Each of them sprawled in the morning sun to dry. Kodiak felt eyes bearing down on him, and when he squinted up at the railing above, he saw Harmony move to go inside. At her movement, Nami rose to her feet. "I'll prepare breakfast."

Now dry, Kodiak sat with his longtime friends, pensive as they ate, knowing the difficult task ahead. They packed food in their satchels for later, and Nami hugged her children good-bye. They paddled away.

The boys rowed effortlessly upriver for some time before finally pulling off on a grassy area. Kodiak leaped out and pulled the canoe onto the shore. Binda handed him his satchel and grabbed her own before stepping out. Kodiak offered his hand to Harmony and held her still once she stood on firm ground. He exhaled in surprise.

"What is it?" Harmony asked, alarmed.

"Your hand!" He couldn't help himself and reached out his other hand to touch her cheek. "Your skin is so...warm." It was not that he hadn't read about the unusual body temperature of humans, but he hadn't given it much thought until he held her warm-blooded body in his grasp.

"Try sleeping next to her. I felt like I was sleeping in the hearth with a fire blazing." At her mother's request Binda had shared her bed with her new cousin last night.

The thought of sleeping with Harmony caused Kodiak to drop his hold on her and clear his throat.

"What do you mean?" Harmony chased after Binda, who was already heading up a path.

"You humans are warm-blooded—not that we are cold-blooded, but our internal temperature runs way lower than yours. That's one of the reasons we can stay under the water so long and dive to deeper depths. We are mostly unaffected by our mild climate. The fat under our skin layer is more efficient than yours."

Harmony was fascinated. "Are your lungs different?"

"Yeah, our lung capacity is...expandable." Binda glanced back at Kodiak and tipped her head. "His is supersized."

"That is so amazing. If I could hold my breath underwater as long as you all can, I probably wouldn't be so scared of deep water."

Kodiak took her words as a compliment, that *he* was amazing, and flashed a charming smile at her. Harmony dropped her lashes and stayed on Binda's heels. The boys trailed close behind.

"Shh." Binda stopped and looked around.

"Which way?" Kodiak regarded the path that split in two directions.

Binda took a moment to remember. "This way." Her brother nodded, and then he turned to Harmony. He held out his hand, winking at Kodiak.

Kodiak watched her laugh at Rio's curiosity as she slipped her hand in his.

Rio's face lit up. "That is remarkable." He nodded at Kodiak, now understanding his amazement.

Kodiak stared jealously at his friend's hand, tucked where he wanted his to be. That kind of warmth needed more exploration. Yes, in the future he looked forward to bending the rules!

"Rio, have you studied much about humans? I took a tour of the library yesterday morning. It's huge!" Harmony picked up her pace.

Still holding her hand as they continued to walk, Rio nodded. "I've read the basics that we are required to learn in school. Kodiak and I spent a lot more time outdoors, so we don't know as much as Binda." Rio's easy smile reached his friend, who fell in beside Harmony when the path widened.

"I wish we humans knew about this world as you do ours. But I guess I can see why your race has wanted to keep us separate. Binda is right; it is more peaceful here. I find your world somewhat enchanting." Harmony lifted her face, looking into the tree branches overhead. "It's so quiet."

The woods were silent except for the leaves rustling in the breeze. Kodiak noted the sun was high overhead, its light filtering through the trees. "It's noon. We should be getting close."

Rio bobbed his head at Kodiak's estimate. "Harmony, Binda just needs some time to adjust to you. Being marked as a Linker comes with a lot of pressure, and she has been a dedicated student for many years now." The three of them watched his sister trudge ahead. "Someday she may pass over to your world. She could benefit from your experiences. You should talk to her. Don't give up."

Kodiak listened to his friend advocate on his sister's behalf and wondered if Harmony would continue with her efforts to make peace. Binda had been rude to her. Kodiak figured Binda must feel jealous—she didn't normally act this way. Binda had always been looked upon as Calder's special and gifted granddaughter, but now she had competition. According to Rio, she'd felt slighted by being kept in the dark about Harmony's existence, and she was taking her frustration out on Harmony. Rio told him that he just wished his sister would give Harmony a chance.

Harmony shrugged and sighed. "I'm trying, Rio." After a pause she let go of his hand and caught up to Binda.

"Binda, I have a question," she shouted, making Binda stop and turn. "Why do only Linkers cross over? Can others cross if they want to?"

As the boys caught up, Kodiak could read the annoyance on her face over Harmony's inquiry. At first he wasn't sure if she'd bother to answer, but she did.

"Linkers have special training. They are mentally prepared for the conditions they will need to adjust for. They learn about languages and cultures in depth and study herbal remedies to protect themselves against the diseases we don't have here. Linkers have a strong spiritual connection through meditation that takes them to a level beyond our realms." Binda looked at her brother. "Grandfather was young, too young, when he first went over. If I go, I will be better prepared."

Kodiak assumed Binda referred to not repeating the mistake Calder made by falling in love with a human. *Wow, she just isn't letting that go.*

They arrived at the edge of the cliff. "This is it. This is the place Calder brought us to before." Binda indicated herself and Rio. "But not in the ocean, of course. This cove includes Suijin's consecrated waters."

Kodiak was eyeing the drop to see if he could safely jump from the cliff top. He observed the rocks waiting beneath the waves and understood it wasn't a viable jump.

Binda raised her voice over the wind and pounding waves. "The beach is this way."

Kodiak and the others followed Binda to an obscure, overgrown path, and they descended. When they reached the beach Binda opened her satchel and took out her sketchbook. She opened it to the page where she had drawn a picture of the plant Kodiak needed to retrieve.

Kodiak studied it again, committing it to memory. He recalled every detail he could from a friend who had narrowly escaped the serpent's cave and lived to tell about it.

At the base of the path, all three dropped their satchels, slipped out of their sandals, and pulled off their shirts. The boys were bare-chested; Binda wore what looked like a fitted cropped tank top, which covered the chest of her boyishly slender body. All of them wore loose-fitting knee-length pants. They secured their belts and checked the variety of knives held by belts at their waists.

Kodiak surveyed the inlet, stretching his shoulder muscles. Before any dive, he calmed his enthusiasm and focused on the task at hand. He faced the group, ready.

Binda collected the bottle of dolphin's blood from her bag and repeated the plan. "We will swim out there and dump the blood," she instructed Rio, and then she told Kodiak, "The cave is that way. Once the serpent detects the smell of blood and exits the cave, swim inside and collect the leaves as quickly as you can."

"We will circle around and check on your progress," Rio assured his old friend.

As they moved toward the water's edge, Kodi stopped. He eyed Harmony before he spoke to her. "Stay back, out of sight, there in the brush." He pointed to where they had left their shirts and satchels. "If we are detected by the serpent and it comes here to the shore, it might be able to reach you if you are too close to the water's edge."

"It can't come on shore though," Rio assured Harmony.

"Hopefully I can sneak in and out without discovery," Kodiak commented, his eyes lingering on her. *Stay focused!*

"Okay. Good luck!" Harmony headed to safety while the others entered the water. Kodiak dragged his hand through this mussed hair, trying to remove her from his thoughts.

14

Harmony watched them dive down and then break the surface several times. Only Rio turned and waved before they disappeared from sight. Keeping vigil for ten solid minutes, her eyes never leaving the surface, she wondered what it would be like to stay underwater for so long. Her eyes drifted skyward, thinking how strange it was not to hear seagulls cry. The sun was warm on her face, but the glare was intense. She dropped her eyes to scan the satchels at her feet, wondering what kinds of things the Aquapopuleans carried around. Everyone seemed to have one. She allowing her thoughts to wander, instead of worrying, but she jumped when she heard something break the surface.

Thank goodness! Instead of her friends, she saw a bulky snake-like body adorned with fins briefly skim the water's surface before disappearing back under the water. *Oh no, the serpent!* She wanted to scream a warning, but it would be futile. They were deep underwater by now.

The serpent was heading toward where Binda said the cave was—and right for Kodiak! Minutes passed. Harmony was beside herself with worry.

Finally two figures appeared at the shore and stood up in the breaking waves—Rio's arm was slung around Kodiak's neck, his body slack. Kodiak lifted Rio into his arms as he marched among the waves that crashed onto the beach, and Harmony rushed forward. "Get back!" Kodiak yelled.

"Where's Binda?" Harmony froze, her eyes wildly searching for her.

"Get back!" Kodiak yelled louder as he heaved his burden to a more secure hold. He continued up the beach as fast as he could. "It's coming."

Harmony was reluctant to follow him. She couldn't leave Binda. Where was she? Then she saw the sea begin to bubble and foam about one hundred yards out. There was that sound again, the one she'd heard that night when she passed over to this world. It sounded like a tree knocking, cracking, and splintering before falling, followed by a clanging noise. Her heart was pounding, and tears started to well in her eyes. *Oh, Binda, where are you? You can't be lost because of me!*

As if answering her silent plea, Binda surfaced, the waves pushing her to her knees and dumping her into the surf. She dragged herself back to her knees, pausing in the waves as they battered her. Harmony knew something was wrong. Binda stood and staggered forward, stumbling, limping, pain evident on her face. Harmony leaped forward to help her, but Binda screamed for her to stay back. A large wave knocked Binda underwater again.

Binda lifted her head above the breaking waves; sand plastered her cheek. Harmony refocused on a spot behind Binda to try to see what was making that sound. The water in the middle of the cove became choppy. Water bubbled and foamed and then erupted as the sea serpent reared its massive head, towering above them. Sea spray misted the air. Harmony felt the seawater slosh at her sandaled feet and stared in horror at the monster. The sound it now made was between a barking seal and a jackhammer, as loud as a horn blast from an eighteen wheeler. It swung its head sideways, one coal black eye visible. It narrowed that eye on Binda.

The beast rose out of the water in a giant *S* shape. It was entirely covered by maroon scales, as shimmery as an oil spill. Its face looked like a dragon out of ancient folklore, with several sets of wickedly pointed horns above its eyes, under its chin, and from its jaw. The fins under its eyes opened like an accordion, making its head appear larger. A dorsal fin extended from the top if its head, running down to disappear into the foaming sea. As it snaked its way forward, it opened its mouth, exposing razor sharp teeth and a forked tongue. It lifted its head, ready to strike at Binda. Without thinking, Harmony ran in front of her friend, her kin, to block her from the blow. Harmony held up her arms, screaming. The sea serpent recoiled with an indignant cry as loud as a police siren. It swung its head from side to side, like a bird, to give each of its eyes a better look at what was blocking its advance. The girl stalked across the sand with her palms out stretched. She emitted an energy pulse that threated the indomitable beast.

Kodiak ran down the beach and helped Binda up, dashing away from the danger with her. The sea serpent made a second attempt to strike but was unable to penetrate the energy coming from Harmony.

"Harmony!" Binda cried as Kodiak dragged her up the beach.

"She is blocking him somehow," Kodiak huffed. "It won't go near her."

It was true! Harmony walked along the shoreline with her arms up as the sea serpent followed, agitated. It would not come closer. Finally, the sea serpent rose up snorting and bellowing, only to dive with a violent downward thrust into the water, leaving a loud splash in its wake. Its snake-like body rounded over the water until the point of its tail made the final plunge, leaving the ocean fizzing.

Harmony dropped her suddenly heavy arms to her sides. The tingling was going away. Her ears rang from the deafening blasts the monster had terrorized them with. She shook with adrenaline.

Harmony watched the waves become calm as her heart rate returned to normal. *What was that? How did I do that?* It was strange, but she wasn't afraid—not of the energy she emitted or the sea serpent after she'd engaged it. It was as if she knew what she was doing, like she'd done this before. She numbly walked back toward the path, a safe distance from the sea.

Rio lay barely conscious in the grass. Binda sat next to him, examining the severe burn on her leg. Harmony was roused at the sight of them. "What happened down there!" she asked frantically.

Kodiak pulled a tin from Binda's bag. "I claimed the leaves and was on my way out of the cave when Binda and Rio swam up. I thought we were clear, but the serpent came out of nowhere and wrapped his body around Rio. I was able to cut him free and secure him between some rocks. Binda lured the monster away. Then I hauled Rio out." Kodiak popped the lid off, stuck two fingers into the greenish-brown goop, and smeared it across Rio's chest. The skin was blistering and red, like a bad sunburn. Rio moaned. His eyes rolled before his body went limp.

"What is that? I thought he was squeezed by the sea serpent?"

Binda sucked air through her teeth when she touched the infected skin on her calf, the same blistered red as Rio's. Through clinched teeth Binda said, "The serpent can secrete poison through its dorsal fin. It looks like a burn, but it can be deadly. We need to get Rio back as fast as we can."

"How can I help?" Harmony kneeled at Rio's side, smoothing a strand of hair from his forehead.

After applying three more smears to Rio's bare chest, Kodiak handed the tin to Binda, who applied the salve to her leg. Kodiak grabbed Rio's shirt and tossed it to Harmony. "Help me get this on him. The sun will make it worse." Kodiak lifted Rio to a sitting position, and Harmony carefully pulled his shirt into place.

No one spoke again.

Kodiak and Binda slipped their shirts on and slung their satchels across their bodies. Harmony secured Rio's bag around her chest and collected the net filled with a seaweed-type plant Kodiak had removed from his belt. Kodiak squatted and eased Rio into his arms. He lifted him and adjusted his weight, nodding at the girls when he was ready. Harmony offered her arm to Binda, who gladly accepted it; she hobbled along on her damaged leg as best she could. They climbed up the path to the top of the cliff and circled inland through the trees until they reached their canoe, stashed at the river's edge. Harmony and Binda pulled the wooden canoe into the water. Kodiak stepped in carrying Rio. He sat and placed his friend on the bottom, resting Rio's head against his knee. The girls hopped in and settled just as Kodiak started paddling downstream.

Harmony felt Binda's eyes on her and avoided her intense gaze, instead scrutinizing the contents of the net bag.

"How did you do that? How did you hold off the serpent?"

Kodiak responded to Binda's breathy question. "She saved you. She saved us," he said. "This isn't a land of magic, but harnessing one's energy to heal is proven. Maybe Harmony's energy force is unique because of her mixed race."

Binda ignored Kodiak. "How were you able to shield us? How did you do it?"

"I don't know." Harmony sighed. "I just felt something, a tingling sensation that started in my shoulders when I raised my arms. Then waves of heat washed down them, rushing through my limbs, and I felt a buzzing sensation in the palms of my hands." Harmony's gaze shifted from Binda to Kodiak. "I don't know how I did it. I just knew I could." Anger, fear, and desperation had sparked that flame. Harmony shook with trepidation, realizing that power felt…good.

***

It was just getting dark when Nami watched her injured children return to her. She stood on the dock wringing her hands.

"What happened? Did you get it?" she fretted, hoping they'd succeed and wouldn't have to try another attempt.

"We were successful, but they've both been poisoned," Kodiak told her urgently.

Nami immediately sent Kodiak to fetch Calder, and she saw to her children's comfort.

Once Kodiak returned with Calder, Nami sagged with relief. Moving with efficiency, he applied fresh salves and bandages to his grandchildren's burned skin. Then he sat with his hands stretched over Rio's body, eyes closed. Like a shaman, Calder used his spiritual energy to heal Rio. After an hour, which seemed to sail by, Rio opened his eyes, and drank thirstily. Calder reassured Nami her son would be fine. He turned his talent to Binda next. She sat with her leg elevated. They bowed their heads and closed their eyes in concentration while Calder made waving motions over her calf.

Afterwards Binda quietly told her mother and grandfather about the day's events. Most notable was the talent Harmony seemed to possess. Nami's children were well enough to join them at the dinner table for a light supper of fish and vegetables.

"Are you feeling better, Rio?" Harmony inquired, lifting the pitcher of water and filling the empty glass he'd just set down.

"Thanks!" He took a long swallow. "Yes, much better, but my skin feels itchy where the burn was." He demonstrated by scratching at his chest.

"Leave it," his mother scolded, but she rested loving eyes on him.

He gave her a grin before turning back to Harmony. "Hey, cousin."

Nami watched the exchange between her son and Harmony and smiled inwardly over the kinship name he used to refer to her.

"I wanted to thank you. Kodi told me about how you blocked the sea serpent with your magic energy."

"I didn't say *magic*," Kodiak corrected.

Nami noticed Harmony's cheeks turn red when she saw that all their eyes were on her.

Harmony said to Calder, "I don't know how I did that—I just felt something. Do you know anything about that kind of ability?"

Calder understood that times were changing; this group needed to be in the know. Their very lives depended on it. "I don't have an answer for you. But remember, you are not only human. Perhaps your unique blend of our two races has afforded you this gift. Never underestimate your abilities, Harmony. Holding Suijin's serpent at bay was no small feat, and I can't even imagine how Suijin would react if he knew."

"Perhaps Suijin is unhappy that you are here? Maybe he is threatened by you?" Nami's faith was strong, but even she believed this god could be angered. She allowed the group a moment to ponder her words.

Instead of answers the discussion brought only more questions. Why would Suijin, a god, be threatened by a girl? What else might Harmony be capable of? Would her power help them get through the dangerous missions they faced in the future? Could she harness her power?

15

Kodiak wandered out to the deck that surrounded the sea dwelling. The ocean lapped around its stilted legs. Cloaked in stars, the air had cooled considerably, and Kodiak welcomed the evening breeze. The moon was making an appearance through the clouds, and its light reflected off the water, beckoning him to go for a swim. He contemplated the idea.

"Kodi?" When he heard the sound of a feminine voice he recognized who called to him. Harmony's vocal sound was pleasant, her slight accent barely audible.

"Good evening, Harmony." He watched her approach and wrap her arms around her slender shoulders as the breeze lifted her hair.

"Wow, the temperature really drops here at night," she observed, "but I guess you don't get cold."

"Not really." He flashed back to when he'd touched her warm skin and wondered again what it would be like to engulf her in his arms. She stopped near him and leaned against the rail. The moon cast her face in glowing light. Kodiak didn't waste the opportunity to study the heart shape of her face, the delicate eyebrows that gave her unique expressions, and her mouth—so full and pouty and pink. He had to blink several times to focus on what she was saying.

"...and risked so much helping us. So I wanted to say thank you." Harmony started to tug her lavender pearl ring from her finger, but Kodiak placed his hand over hers.

Immediately he felt the heat from her skin. He knew he should have pulled his hand away, but instead he clasped her fingers. He looked down at her rare lavender pearl. "You keep it until we have completed *all* of our missions. You can give it to me before returning to your world." As the corners of her mouth lifted he added, "I will do what I can to help you get home." He wasn't sure why he'd told her to hang onto her ring for now, but it felt like the right thing to do.

"Thank you!" she gushed and flung her arms around him. Kodiak was caught off guard by her emotion, until he remembered she was not here of her own choosing. He was suddenly overwhelmed by the sensations of her body against his body. She stood on her toes with her torso flattened against his, her arms wrapped around his tense shoulders. *This is what her heat feels like ...all-pervading* ... and he didn't want it to stop. His hands, in brief confusion, had paused in midair, but now they dropped to the small of her back. Harmony's hug lingered. In their intimate nearness he felt her body relax, secure in his arms. When he slid his arms tighter, encircling her, she sighed. His body was responding rapidly. As her nose brushed the taut column of his neck, he bit his lip to control his sharp intake of breath. Her breathing quickened, and he turned his head so his lips brushed her hair. She tilted her head back and they regarded one another. What was this energy between them? They were like two magnets locking together with a force difficult to dislodge.

They heard someone inside summon them, and Harmony swallowed. Feeling her stir, Kodiak reluctantly allowed her to peel away from him. He turned toward the rail, gripping it for support, allowing a blast of fresh air to cool the skin Harmony had left uncomfortably warm.

She cleared her throat and barely whispered, "I also came out to tell you that Calder is getting ready to leave. He said he will be back tomorrow to go over the details for our next two quests."

He nodded at her and proceeded inside. Out of sight,

he raised his brows and blew out a long breath. That intensity left him tingling all over. Forget bending the rules, or breaking the rules… He was playing with fire!

***

Something about Kodiak's intimate closeness set her at ease. Harmony felt secure for the first time since she'd crossed over. When Kodiak's arms encircled her, she'd sighed, longing to remain there, wondering what could be. She recalled when her nose brushed his neck and she'd inhaled his earthy smell of sand and surf. For the second time that day she'd felt an awakening within her.

Lying in bed, listening to Binda's soft breathing, Harmony wondered how she was going to make it through or if she'd ever get home. In the human realm, everything was familiar, but here she had family…and an ability, or gift—she didn't know what to call it. All she knew was that it made her feel powerful—and she wondered if she would get to feel that again.

Harmony looked up at the face in the fur-lined parka. She sensed her mother smiling at her, but the sun, trying to burn through the overcast sky, was blinding her. It was quiet. No one was around, and all she could hear was the scraping of the ice-skate blades. Then she heard the cracking, her mother's cries, and her own screams as she plunged into the frigid water.

He swam up to her and smiled, his milky skin and teeth bright white in the murky water. Although he reached for her, she sensed it wasn't to rescue her. It was more like he wanted to keep her, like capturing a prize. She watched her mittens wave bye as they disappeared into the darkness. Heat was building. She grew more wary of the man approaching and reaching for her. Suddenly a flash reflected against his scales, like onyx and silver, that traveled from his elbows up to his broad shoulders. He crossed his arms in front of his face.

He then swam around her, attempting to reach her, but somehow she deflected his energy. His dark, slanted eyes darted around, trying to figure out where her weak spot was. He paused like a ghost before her, studying her face, and then he swam away. Before she was pulled from the water she caught sight of him dragging away a body in a blue parka. Mother!

Harmony woke with a start. She was shaken, as she always was when she dreamed of being in deep water. The man's face was a clear image in her mind. This man...he'd been in her dreams before, she was sure of it.

16

After a long morning swim, a remarkably healed Rio sat at breakfast with his sister, Kodiak, and Harmony. Calder arrived and was happy to see his grandchildren restored. The fruit plates and tea cups were pushed aside, and he unfolded a map and spread it across the table. Calder prepared to give them an overview of what to expect.

"To start, you will travel by canoe to the closest trading village, which is not far, and acquire elk to take you overland for the remainder of your journey."

"Elk—as in reindeer?" Harmony was trying to picture how they would manage that.

Each of her companions grimaced at the thought. "We avoid traveling overland. We prefer bikes to animals," Binda groaned.

"The elk are useful and fast, easily covering fifty miles a day while carrying people and goods. Thousands of years of breeding has perfected this animal's performance. They are underutilized here, in my opinion. Only the coastal traders use them to move goods to the outposts. I think our aquatic ways have given us little tolerance for the large terrestrial animals." Calder pinned his eyes on Binda, who shrugged a shoulder in response.

Calder informed Harmony there were no horses in this world. That was profound news. *Where would humans be without horses,* she thought. Empires were built because the horse could travel great distances. The horse revolutionized warfare, transportation of people and goods, and communication. But here apparently the elk replaced the horse, and, according to the praise Calder afforded them, seemed to be superior in every way. *This is something to think about another time.* She focused on the map.

"This journey will be long and dangerous." Calder surveyed the group. "You need to travel near the Great Falls, four hundred miles away, and back, a total of eight hundred miles."

"So far!" Harmony was alarmed. "There must be another way…or maybe there's another way to send me back."

"This is the only way," Calder assured her. "It will take approximately eight to ten day to reach your farthest destination, if all goes well. And then the return journey."

Harmony fell silent, numb at the thought of being trapped in this world for so long.

"But before you go as far as the Great Falls you will stop to collect the next component we need from a swamp. The swamp lies in a small, dense valley just before you intercept the Muhheakantuck River." He pointed to a place on the map so everyone could follow along.

Harmony leaned in, recognizing each point of interest. In her world the Great Falls were Niagara Falls, and the Muhheakantuck River was the Hudson River, both located in New York. Muhheakantuck was the original Native American name for the river, meaning the river that flows both ways. She narrowed her eyes at where Calder's webbed finger indicated a swamp. Frowning, she thought, *There definitely aren't any swamps in New York.*

"Take great caution. Dangerous creatures lurk in that swamp." Calder seemed to ponder a thought but didn't say more. This worried Harmony, and she exchanged knowing looks with the rest of the group. He moved on and explained that the item they sought hung from the indigenous trees that only grew in this particular swamp.

He flipped open a journal to a hand-drawn picture. Harmony thought the long gray tails resembled Spanish moss.

"Well, at least it's in the trees and not in the swamp water. I'm sure that swamp smell is hard to get out of your hair." Rio bared his teeth in disgust.

Kodiak jumped into the conversation for the first time. "Okay, if we leave at first light and pick up the elk here," he said, pointing to the map, "we can be on our way by midmorning." Calder agreed. "It looks like the south road will take us closer to the swamp than the north road."

"Yes, and the southern route will keep you in the foothills of the mountains, where the roads are well maintained and flatter, which makes them easier to travel." Calder's finger snaked along the route on the map. "Every fifty miles is an outpost where you can get fresh mounts. Lodging is available if you choose to stay the night."

Binda offered more information. "The tribes have two large trading ports on the Muhheakantuck, one crossing the river here in the north and the other here in the south, near the swamp." Binda bragged that she'd been over each of the bridges with her grandfather several years ago. Harmony ignored her lofty tone when Binda added, "The natural trails made by the animals over hundreds of thousands of years on their journeys to the salt licks near the Great Lakes have become the roadways of the traders."

"Yes, but you should avoid the trading ports." Binda's eyes widened at Calder's remark. "You can follow the roads for a while, but I advise you to veer off and cross the river here instead. We don't want the tribe to see you cross into their territory, for once you cross Muhheakantuck River you are on their land. If at all possible avoid the tribespeople out there. You will see them at the trading village on our side of the river to be sure, but do not tell them where you are going. The plant we need is on their land, just east of the falls, and they will want to trade for something valuable. If you stay on this side of the falls, well within the surrounding forest, you should be able to pass undetected." He looked pointedly at each of them and held up a hand to emphasize the importance of his statements. "I do not know what they might ask for, but if you find yourselves in their city, before their chieftain, you will need to decide the right thing to do. Take warning—tread lightly. It will be best to obtain the leaves undetected," Calder stressed again.

The Forest Tribe was untraditional. They'd been adapting to river life for more than twenty thousand years and had had built a primitive city on the falls. Forest Linkers journeyed to the human realm and emerged during the height of the Roman Empire. After that visit, the Forest people labored to build a grand city to rival the city of Rome itself. They used their precious salt resource near the Great Lakes to raise funds, similar to Rome's tax on salt. They brought back knowledge for crops that could be spun into fine cloth. Soon they were producing the finest cloth in their realm and establishing trade with other coastal villages. Gold coins began to be used as currency, as was still true.

Calder's finger touched where the place Harmony knew as Niagara Falls was located. Then he slid his finger just east of it, along Lake Ontario. "There is a grove in a clearing here. You will know it by its yellow flowers." Calder flipped to another page in his worn journal. "This flower blooms most of year and it looks like this—very distinct." Binda sketched it in her own journal. She also sketched the map before her. "And these are the leaves." He tapped the drawing, and Binda scratched out a duplicate in ink.

"The trails there are more natural and hard to follow. There are dangerous animals in the forests and the mountains. Make your camps alongside the water and burn a fire. I urge you to stay close to the waterways when you can as they will offer your best escape routes. The tribespeople can only hold their breath for a few minutes—they've lost the ability after being on land for thousands of years."

"They're not Aquapopulo?" Harmony's mind went wild with thoughts of alien beings roaming the realm.

Calder sat back in his chair considering her question. "It is true our race evolved through the sacred island, but as in your world, people diversified over time as they migrated. Africans have darker skin, Asians have distinctly shaped eyes. You follow? Adaptations change us all."

Harmony nodded, and he went on. "Here in this world we have mainly the coastal dwellers, who occupy this coastline from your world's Chesapeake Bay up to the Bay of Fundy. The secondary group, known to us as the Forest Tribe, has occupied what you know as Niagara Falls for twenty thousand years. Our population is small, and we live by meager means. Through meditation and prayer we ask Suijin for peace and positive spiritual energy.

"Peace," Harmony sighed. "True peace seems to be unachievable in my world."

"Unfortunately, in recent generations the Forest Tribe has made changes that are not like the ways of the rest of us. It is causing strife between us." Calder's disappointment rang clear.

"Are they aggressive?" Harmony certainly didn't get the sense the coastal people were.

"They can be. The Forest people are fierce hunters. They utilize every part of the animals they hunt. They eat them, wear the hides, and use the bones and teeth for various things. Anything left they feed to the big cats, which are extinct in your world. Known as the American lion, the biggest cats in the Americas became extinct during your last Ice Age. Our world did not experience that ice age. Anyway, the tribal people, the women especially, have a spiritual connection to the big cats, and they have become their guardians."

Binda sniffed, clearly repulsed. "They keep the cats at their sides always. Years ago Calder took me to their city for the negotiations on the price of salt. Those cats looked at me like I'd make a good lunch."

Calder snorted. "The cats certainly weren't the only fierce-looking members of that tribe. The females resemble pictures I've seen of the famed Amazon warriors. The men, though more passive than the females, are thickly muscled and can run for miles without tiring. When you see them you'll know them by their tattoos, adorned animal skins, feathers, beads… They love trinkets, like shell jewelry of any kind, which is fortunate for us when it comes to trading with them. They are exceptional weavers. The cloth is extraordinary. We make very little cloth of our own. We either buy cloth and salt or trade with our shell jewelry, soaps, and such."

"Our mother makes some of the bracelets we take for trade," Rio said to Harmony. He then turned in his chair and called to his mother. "Mother, show Harmony your jewelry."

Nami stood in the nearby kitchen, polishing fruit and pretending to look occupied as she listened intently to her father's plan. At her son's request she crossed the room toward a freestanding cupboard. She reached in and retrieved a box. The box made a clinking sound when she put it on the counter. Harmony stood and left the men to discuss details about the terrain. Binda was still actively sketching away. Reaching her aunt's side, she marveled at the variety of lovely shell bracelets resting in the box.

"I made these bracelets with local shells I found. Please take one, a gift from me."

Harmony lifted one that caught her eye right away. "Wow, I've never seen these shells before. These are lovely. They must have taken you a while to make." She rotated the bracelet this way and that, admiring the perfectly knotted threads holding the shells in place. Harmony was touched and reached to hug her aunt. "Thank you, Aunt Nami," she said gratefully.

When she drew back her aunt held her still and stroked her hair. "Your great-grandmother was my sister. I wish I could have met her. I was very excited about the idea of having a sister when Calder had told me of her existence years ago." Nami's genuine smile was very much like her son's.

"I wish you could have known my family."

"Even though the circumstances are strained, I want you to know I'm glad I've met you, Harmony."

"Knowing I have family, even if far away...well, it means more to me than you know. There is no relative left in my realm, I'm afraid." Harmony spoke with the only aunt she'd ever had, feeling the bond strengthen. Nami tipped her head toward the door, suggesting a private moment outside.

They settled in chairs to bask in the sunshine. Then Nami confided in her niece. "Being the daughter of a Linker has its challenges, especially when the honor passes you over." Harmony remembered when Rio told her it was rare to have two Linkers in one family. Nami seemed to wish it was her instead of her daughter. "I've seen a lot of things most don't. My father has confided in me my whole life. And Harmony, I understand what it's like to lose a mother."

During the discussion of Calder falling in love with

Harmony's human great-great-grandmother, Harmony learned Calder returned to this realm and later married Nami's mother.

"How did she die? I was told your race doesn't get sick like mine."

Nami nodded. "We do have sickness, but not like in your world. The herbs my father kept can be poisonous if taken in large doses. While my father was away on one of his inconspicuous trips to the other realm my mother took a powerful mixture to ensure she'd not waken. My father came home to find her lifeless."

"I'm sorry," she whispered, shocked. *Why would she do that?* It hit her. "Wait—what do you mean by 'inconspicuous trips' to the human realm? He went back to visit her! Does Binda know?" Harmony recalled her cousin's mistrust when he'd told them of falling in love with Pearl. *No, she couldn't possibly suspect.*

Nami glanced at the door and shook her head. "Binda is still young and has much to learn of the ways of love and sacrifice. Yes, my father returned many times to your realm, and his health suffered for it. My mother suffered, too, from heartache. The man she loved, who stayed with her, fathered her children, loved someone else. Actually, he loved both women, and he couldn't choose. She prayed he'd forget the human. He promised that his past was over and my mother was the one he needed to be with, but she sensed his words were hollow." She sighed. "I watched my father grieve the loss of his wife. It took him many years of meditation and prayer to ease his guilty soul. I forgave him. I couldn't lose him too. He told me many things about his family on the other side, my half-human relatives. His openness brought us closer." They smiled knowingly at one another. Suffering from heartache was something they had in common.

"Wow, I thought my life was complicated, but

compared to his..." Her words trailed away, and Harmony became lost in thought. "Nami, you forgave him. You have incredible compassion."

"I meditated and prayed to achieve forgiveness. Anger has its purpose in the moment, but it's how you resolve the issues afterward that counts."

Sage advice, Harmony thought.

17

Kodiak paddled the canoe toward a network of docks at the river's bend. A carved wooden gateway simply read Trader's Village, like a supermarket brand, Harmony thought. They followed the plan they'd formulated on their way there. The canoe had to be emptied and stored until their return. Once the canoe was maneuvered into an empty slip on a dock, the group slung their satchels across their bodies and stepped onto the dock. Binda reminded them to be discreet.

Harmony had gathered up her golden hair during the approach and hid it under the hood of her cape. Calder had suggested she take one of his ceremonial robes for this purpose, since they did not wear hats. The hood seemed the only logical thing to wear on her head without drawing suspicion. Plus, the cape doubled as a coat during the cooler evenings in this realm.

The town around them teemed with activity. "I pictured this place as a small village, but it looks like a thriving town." Harmony strained to get a better look as the boys shouldered their packs, filled with supplies from home.

When an attendant approached them about storing the canoe, Binda grabbed Harmony's arm and drew her off the docks onto the dirt pathway. The ground was hard-packed enough for vendors to move local goods up and down the roadways on large tricycles, with deep barrels attached to the backs, different than those used in the coastal village. Goods were transported from the boats to the bike-barrels that crisscrossed the marketplace. Elk carrying men and goods mingled among them.

Harmony got her first look at the infamous Forest Tribe people she'd heard about. Several men, scarcely clothed, carried large packs brimming with animal skins on their backs. They stood out not only from their abundant tattoos but their barrel-chested physiques differed from the slender men of the coastal villages. Their skin was darker, but their smooth faces and chests were hairless like the coastal men.

Kodiak spoke to the girls as he shifted his load. "Okay, the canoe is taken care of. Now we need to acquire the elk. Let's head over there, by that hitching post." He pointed across the square to a vacant spot. They crossed and dropped their goods in a pile. "You girls stay here. We'll get the animals." Kodiak hesitated glancing around.

"Go on, we'll be fine." Binda said, shooing him off. "I've been to this village many times. I can handle it."

"I know you can handle yourself, but you've never had a human along." He looked again at Harmony's disguise. "Yeah, okay, it's just odd she's wearing a cloak without a ceremony." Kodiak glowered at some men that were already beginning to stare at Harmony. "We'll be right back." He hurried Rio along, looking apprehensive.

Despite having so much to look at, Harmony found her eyes following Kodiak as he waltzed through a crowd of other boys. He was taller than most. She had to admit she wasn't sure how she felt about him. She was furious that he'd bargained for her ring, but he'd told her to keep it until she returned home. She was pleased to feel it snug on her finger now. He'd seemed sincere when he told her he'd do what he could to help her return to her home.

"Binda, what do you think of Kodi?"

Binda had removed her long-sleeved tunic and was tucking it into the bag at her feet. She looked down the lane at Kodiak and Rio, who'd reached an establishment featuring a large elk carved on its sign. She said, "If I could have two brothers, Kodi would be one of them.

Aside from being a know-it-all and flirt, he's a good guy. I trust him with my life."

When Binda sent her a scowl, Harmony nervously changed topic. "Mmm, what's that delicious smell?" Harmony rose on her tiptoes to see further down the market square. In that direction, a concentration of cooks labored over grills laden with smoking meats. Her mouth watered, but there was no way to get to the grills without encountering dozens of tribesmen. For several minutes she tried to convince Binda to go buy some, but Binda was horrified to learn Harmony ate meat. Finally, Harmony gave up. Apparently, she would be on a seafood and vegetation diet while she was here. *When I get home, I'm going straight out to get a hamburger!*

Harmony asked, "Where are the tribal women?"

"Probably in the vegetable market or by the jewelry vendors. Mostly men come to trade. They carry their loads of skins or fabrics on the elk; the big cats carry only women and are useless otherwise." Harmony glanced around apprehensively, looking for the big cats, relieved none were in sight.

Binda eyed a young man who was restocking vegetables under the canvas where the market area began. He glanced back at her, smiling. Harmony observed the exchange.

It wasn't the only detail Harmony had noticed concerning her cousin. Binda had changed from her modest tunic into a fitted vest-style tunic that was cropped at her waist, displaying six tattoos around her shoulders and on her arms, not including the Linker's mark. Of course she'd seen the tattoos when Binda was swimming near the sea serpent's cave, but it seemed she was now making her style known once she was free of her peers. She wore more tattoos than Harmony had seen on any other coastal person. She hoped Binda was feeling more comfortable; maybe she'd be more receptive now.

"He's cute," Harmony commented. Binda sliced a glance at Harmony's grin. "What is he selling?"

Binda returned her gaze to the interesting target. "Pears. Maybe we should buy some." A grin spread across her face. Harmony thought she was quite cute with her smile and sparkling azure eyes.

Kodiak and Rio returned just then with two elk in tow. This was another of those times when Harmony's reality felt surreal. They should be horses! As Kodiak and Rio secured them to the post Harmony stepped back, not eager to get too close yet.

"Hey, Kodi. Binda, and I are going over there to buy some fruit while you get the gear loaded. We'll only be a few minutes."

Kodiak studied the market and the nearby grill mobbed with tribesmen, seeming concerned. "Binda can go. I want you to stay nearby."

Harmony sent Binda a pleading look, hoping she'd tell Kodiak that she could go with her, but instead her insufferable cousin gave a half-shrug and walked away. Harmony crossed her arms over her chest and sullenly watched Rio, who was double checking the straps on the saddle before he started to load the supply bundles. He straightened, his brow furrowed.

"I just realized we need an additional bedroll. I'll go purchase one."

***

Kodiak instructed Harmony to stay close by him, and he watched her out of the corner of his eye. He could tell she was irritated that she wasn't allowed to explore, but under the circumstances he knew he'd made the right choice.

She inched closer and closer to the animals before

asking him, "Are these things friendly? Can I pat them or will they bite me?"

"They are completely docile and will only bite if you stick a finger in their mouth."

Tentatively she reached her hand out to touch the elk's velvety, plush antlers. A smile stretched across her face. Her earlier annoyance seemed forgotten. She lowered her hand to rub his nose and looked into his dark eyes, which looked back with interest. The animal sniffed around for food, causing giggles to bubble within her. "You are a handsome fellow. I'm sorry I don't have anything for you," she cooed.

Kodiak couldn't help but grin as he watched her talk to the dumb animal. "He doesn't know what you're saying. He only takes commands."

Harmony pressed her lips together, but before she could retort, the animal dropped its head to the grass. Harmony let out a cry and jumped back to avoid being knocked down by its wide antlers. "Those things are a hazard!" She burst out laughing but immediately remembered she was supposed to be discrete. She pressed her fist to her lips, stifling further noise. She scanned the square. Many dark heads were turned in her direction.

"Can they see my hair?" She drew the hood closer to her eyebrows.

Kodiak suppressed a laugh. "No, it's not your hair." He'd been captivated by her giggles and attempts to befriend the beast. He bent to pick up a bed roll and caught the eyes of two males elbowing each other and looking at Harmony.

"My laugh?" She stepped over to him, and he shook his head, avoiding her. "What is it then?" she whispered, stepping closer still, placing her slim hand on his arm, her eyes wide with concern.

At first he kept his gaze lowered, looking down at the

wool fabric in his hands, but then his coppery eyes blazed over her face. He said, "It's not only your hair that is striking. You are beautifully exotic."

His statement left her swallowing her embarrassment. She backed away, dropping her hand. "That's absurd."

Rio walked up with his load then and swung the bundles onto the back of the saddle. Binda appeared behind him, adjusting her full satchel. Binda nodded when everything was loaded. "Looks like we are ready. We'd better get moving."

"I'll ride with you, Rio, if that's all right?" Harmony asked. "I'll tell you stories from the human realm."

Kodiak watched Rio climbed on and pull her up behind him, her arms wrapped around his waist. With Binda mounted behind him, who leaned back easily against the supplies, he couldn't help but think Harmony was too close to Rio's shoulder. When she whispered in his ear, Rio laughed. Kodiak was slightly irked. As the trader's village disappeared behind them, he watched Harmony slid her hood back. The golden hues in her hair reflect the morning sunlight, his fingers itching to touch it.

18

They rode for hours, stopping once at an outpost to feed the animals and themselves. After they dismounted, Harmony chuckled at her stretching companions, glad she wasn't the only one suffering after the long ride in the saddle. The outpost reminded her of a giant general store with barns and yards for elk and not much more around it. Harmony did notice rooms were available for rent on the upper floor, but it seemed like most people were just passing through, like at a rest stop along an interstate.

During the ride after their hurried meal, Harmony forgot about how she felt when Kodiak was near her and how his words of praise made her belly feel all fluttery. *You are beautifully exotic — flatterer!* She enjoyed her constant conversation with her cousin.

Eventually the group slowed to a stop beside one another.

"It's getting dark. We should make camp soon," Binda suggested. "We're too far from the next outpost to make it there tonight." Just ahead was a stream, precisely what they needed to water the animals and wash off after the dusty ride.

"Good. We'll make camp here for the night," Kodi replied.

Binda hopped down and offered to gather firewood. Harmony flexed her back once her feet were firmly planted on the grass, and then she helped Rio unload the goods from the animals.

They made quick work of settling the elk, starting a fire, and warming a meal. Riding the elk had been bizarre but fun, Harmony thought. She considered what Calder said about the cats. Was it so unusual to have big cats as pets? She had not seen any pets around, not a stray dog or cat. She'd had a cat when she was a kid, and she often fed strays on the back porch.

"Do any of you have pets? Do people *have* pets here? I'm aware of the big cats, but do you have little cats too?" Harmony inquired, watching their bright eyes blaze in the firelight. Binda and Rio's blues seemed translucent, while the copper in Kodi's seemed to burn like two flames.

Binda clucked and set her dinner bowl aside. "Yes, there are smaller cats, but who would want to touch a dirty animal or have one in their dwelling—yuk!"

"I would! I happen to like cats!"

"Well, I guess humans have more in common with the tribes!" Binda's remark was condescending.

"Just because you don't like what humans like doesn't mean you should look down on us." Harmony had had it. After everything that had happened and many hours of riding, she was tired, sore, and cranky. She'd been denied meat and dined on rice in broth; her stomach still growled. But as soon as she barked at her cousin, she felt remorseful.

She sighed quietly. "I'm sorry. I shouldn't have yelled. I'm just tired…and still feeling a bit lost."

Rio gave her a reassuring smile, and Kodiak looked thoughtfully at her.

Binda's tone eased up. "The pets you are talking about seem to form a similar relationship as we have with dolphins. As we are an aquatic race, it's natural we have a close connection to sea-going mammals. We'll play with pods when we are out for a leisurely swim. South of here people train dolphins, like you would a dog."

"Oh, I remember learning about dogs." Rio tapped at his temple, recalling. "They look like wolves."

The talk died down and they laid their bedrolls just

outside the ring of dying embers. Rio was the first one asleep and began snoring softly. Binda settled quickly too.

Harmony imagined swimming and frolicking with dolphins, but they kept evaporating from her mind. She wiggled around, trying to get comfortable and stay warm. She wasn't used to sleeping on the ground, despite the soft moss and her padded bed roll, and she just couldn't get comfy. The soft breeze was persistent, tugging her robe back regardless of her efforts to tuck it between her knees. She was sore from riding, which added to her miserable mood.

Is this how it's going to be, sleeping on the hard, cold ground for weeks!

"Harmony…"

She lifted her head at the sound of her name. "What?"

"Are you cold?" Kodiak asked, lifting himself up on one elbow.

"Yes. Very."

Kodiak rose and disappeared into the woods for a few minutes. He came back with some more dead branches and put them on the barely warm fire. He poked around, waking several flames, and they popped and crackled. The sound was music to Harmony's ears.

"Thank you, Kodi." Harmony could barely make out his outline in the firelight. She watched him drag his bedroll behind hers.

"I'll block the wind. Although I don't have much body heat to offer you, I'm willing to share my blanket." He sat down and adjusted his wool blanket over their legs. "I know you're exhausted. Try to get some rest. We leave at first light." Kodiak presented his back to her and tossed the remaining covers over their shoulders.

Harmony mumbled another thanks. She may not have drawn heat from him, but his nearness flooded her senses, and her awakened pulse warmed her. When she wiggled her bottom against his lower back she heard him groan.

Hmm, if he's feeling anything like I'm feeling, then he deserves to be uncomfortable.

She didn't like that her body responded strongly when he was near her, or that his handsome face invaded her daydreams. It was unlike her to be mean, but she found herself rolling over and gluing her body to his back. "This is better."

Her arm slid around his ribcage and she sighed against him. Although the thought of him roused her senses, Harmony felt secure with him as well. She soon fell asleep.

***

Her words blew through Kodiak's soft hair into his ear, sending a chill rocketing down his spine. *The imp!* He regretted his decision to assist her. Kind of. Once he relaxed, he enjoyed the sensation of her breasts pressed so snugly against him as he felt the rise and fall of her breath. And that breath! It was like warm kisses against his neck every time she exhaled. Kodiak was confused as to why she'd chosen this intimate position with him. There were times when she was blatantly angry with him, like when he'd bargained for her ring. Even though she'd hugged him when he'd told her to hold onto the ring for now, she hadn't shown a complete turnaround. She'd tried to avoid him at all costs, especially when their eyes met now and again.

Once he heard the even breathing of sleep he reached for her hand, which rested comfortably against his chest. It was too dark to see it, but he felt the smooth pearl with his thumb. *I can't wait until this belongs to me.*

19

The next two nights, the elks proved efficient, covering a sizable amount of ground every day. Calder had promised the elk could easily travel fifty miles a day, and they did so with no complaint. Each day, Harmony, and her cousin Rio rode together, conversing companionably. The days trekking through the mountain roads wore Harmony's nerves thin. Riding was agony. Even her arm muscles were sore from holding on so tightly over the endlessly rolling terrain.

When they settled in for the night, everyone went silently about their duties making camp and ate accompanied by quiet conversation. Her belly full, Binda thumbed through her journal, making notes. Rio played a small flute he pulled from his pocket.

Harmony was enjoying the song Rio played. "That reminds me of an old song from my world," she remarked when he finished. She hummed a few bars of the song.

"Do you play an instrument?" Rio asked, hopeful his cousin was a fellow musician.

"No, but I used to sing at church with my grandmother."

With Rio's encouragement, Harmony sang a ballad, much to Rio and Kodiak's delight.

Binda reprimanded her brother. "Rio, you know singing is not allowed." Responding to Harmony's astonished look, Binda explained, "It's unholy."

"Don't listen to her. You have a beautiful voice. Can you sing another?" Kodiak asked, giving Binda a challenging stare.

"Maybe another time. I'm kind of tired." She was making an effort not to aggravate Binda, but she wasn't sure it was working.

The following night, still in neutral territory, they stayed at an outpost. The girls shared one room and the boys another. This allowed them to acquire fresh mounts. In the morning, while the others loaded gear onto the traded elk, Harmony greeted the animals with vigorous neck rubs. The group laughed at her human need for affection toward their living transportation.

On the fourth day they approached the swamp valley before sunset. Binda and Rio agreed to stay with the elk on high ground, above the smell that permeated up from the valley, while Kodiak and Harmony braved their way far enough into the swamp to find a tree draped with the botanical they sought.

Dry ground was present, but many trees grew straight out of the marsh. Loud squawking followed them, and they glimpsed monkey-like animals leaping from tree limb to tree limb. Several seemed annoyed with their uninvited guests. Harmony held her hand up toward the closest howler, hoping to send the pests running in the other direction. She felt neither a warming sensation nor energy project from her hand. *Maybe what happened with the sea serpent was a one-time occurrence? Or maybe it only works with serpents.* She wasn't pleased these creatures were making so much noise. She allowed Kodiak to take her hand and guide her quickly toward their goal.

"Okay, this one has a low branch. I'll boost you up. You can scoot down the branch until you reach those mossy things." Kodiak clasped her waist.

"Wait," she protested. "You want me to climb? Why not you?"

"I'm better in the water." She noticed the copper flecks in his amber eyes. "I'm not too good with trees." She pressed her lips together, giving him her best pout, but he only raised his eyebrows.

"Okay, but what if I fall in?" She surveyed the floating brush and patches of green scum. "How deep do you think that is?" She tried to shake off her fear of deep water, not wanting it to affect her mission.

"It doesn't matter." He turned her face, forcing her to look at him. "If you fall I will jump in and save you." Her fear left her for a fraction of a second, but as it returned, she inhaled resolve.

With a nod he lifted her, and she clutched the branch. He shoved her up, his large and strong hands on her rump, and she swung her leg over to straddle the tree limb. She found her balance and peered down at him. He watched her intently and she blushed, thinking about where his hands had just touched her. She inched her way along the far-reaching branch and leaned forward to gather a fistful of stringy moss. She carefully tucked several more handfuls into her satchel. She started to scoot backward. A monkey leaped onto the branch in front of her, startling her. She wobbled. She began to tilt to one side and lost her balance. She screamed to Kodiak as she fell, landing with a noisy splash in the marsh.

The moment Harmony hit the water there was a movement in the nearby brush—she saw a gator slip into the murky water.

Kodiak dove in, grasped her arms, and pulled her to the surface. The water wasn't as deep as Harmony had thought. She'd landed feet-first against the mushy bottom before she sprang back up. Immediately the smell and taste of the swamp filled her nose and mouth.

"Blaah!" She spat and stood, but she found she couldn't step forward. "My foot is stuck!" Harmony was tangled in the undergrowth. The bulky alligator swam past, investigating a possible meal. She watched in horror as the gator turned back toward them and disappeared below the surface. She thrashed and struggled to free her foot.

"Hold on!" Kodiak dove down, and she felt her foot come loose in seconds. He resurfaced and commanded, "Swim!"

She did. Suddenly she was in clear water, away from the reeds, and she swam for the minimal land ahead. Dragging her shaking body out of the water, she patted her chest for the satchel, but it was gone. She spun to tell Kodiak, but he wasn't there. He had been right behind her! But now the water was empty, save for a few ripples.

"Kodi! Oh my God, Kodi!" she screamed, hoping Rio and Binda might hear her. Minutes passed. Tears blurred her eyes as she called his name over and over. The monkeys she'd noticed in the trees around her moved to a safer distance away from the wet, shrieking visitor. When one of them ventured in for a closer look Harmony picked up a rock and hurled it, missing the monkey by several inches. "You stupid monkey! It's your fault!" As she crouched to find another missile Kodiak broke the surface of the water and quickly pulled himself onto land. He stood there holding her satchel.

"We can't leave this behind!" Rivers of murky water dripped from his dark hair, and he wiped the nasty water away from his mouth with the back of his hand.

"Oh, Kodi!" She grasped his saturated shirt in her fist, tugging him farther away from the water's edge. Once she'd made sure nothing had followed him from the swamp, she rested her head against his chest briefly. "Kodi, I thought he ate you." She trembled.

"He almost did. It took me a while to untangle the satchel. It was caught in the branches of a fallen tree. Before I became his dinner something bigger swam by, and he became *its* dinner." He looked incredulously over his shoulder. "Let's get out of here."

Harmony quickly checked the contents of the bag before they leaped along the islands of solid ground until they escaped the mysteries of the swamp. Visions of the 1982 *Swamp Thing* movie passed through her imagination. She looked over her shoulder, still expecting to be chased by a swamp creature. *So this is what it feels like to be in a horror movie.* Harmony was giddy with relief when it was finally behind them.

The others jumped to their feet when they saw their friends arrive dripping wet. "What happened? I thought you had to get into the trees." Binda laughed, "What…did you fall in?"

"It's no laughing matter, Binda. We came face to face with a huge alligator." Harmony's words won the surprised reaction she anticipated. She wouldn't say anything else until they were moving forward on the backs of the elks. Harmony mounted behind Kodi this time, since they were both wet and grimy from the swamp. She clung to him more tightly than she had when she rode behind Rio. A flicker of guilt sparked, when she thought of the night she'd snuggle-tortured him. The look on Kodiak's face the next morning had told her volumes. Relief that Kodiak was safe and not being digested in that beast's stomach almost brought her to tears again. Harmony let her eyes drift closed as she clung to Kodiak, and she reproached her weak heart. *I wasn't going to like him.*

20

It was almost dark before cooler air was carried downstream by the Hudson River. They selected a secluded inlet to make camp, alongside a stream that fed the river. Rio offered to tend the animals; Binda declared she'd build a fire. Harmony slid off the warm beast, wondering if she smelled much worse than the animal did. Kodiak suggested they wash in the river and said he'd brought soap along. He grabbed some towels from the saddlebags and revealed the soap, which he handed to Harmony. She put the bar to her nose and inhaled the heavenly scent.

The two of them found a suitable spot to enter the swollen river. Kodiak undressed and trudged in, diving under as soon as he could. Harmony kept her undergarments on after removing the rest of her clothing. She trudged in, sank down, and swam around, trying to warm her body. She floated on her back, watching the stars appear. There wasn't a cloud in the sky. The moon's light was soft. Harmony allowed the water to wash away the day's anxieties.

Kodiak finally broke the surface. She was getting used to the fact he could hold his breath for so long underwater. He swam up, and she offered him the bar of soap. He stood in the waist-deep water and scrubbed his hair, face, neck, and his smooth, muscled chest. Harmony thought she should give him privacy but she was enjoying the view. He slipped under to rinse. She swam to the spot he'd just occupied, careful not to stray too far from the shore. He reappeared by her side and she smiled at him. Her resolution not to like him was dissolving.

She floated on her back, absorbing the blanket of

stars above. "The night sky in this realm, without the light pollution from city lights, is breathtaking. Billions of stars are twinkling!" He was still, and she lifted her head to ask, "Don't you think?" Under the moonlight, she could see the curve of Kodiak's lean face, down to his strong chin. In the quiet moment they regarded one another.

"I'll wash your hair if you stand up," he offered, already lathering the soap bar in his hands. She stood, knowing the white fabric of her bra was completely transparent when wet, but no matter—he'd just gotten an eyeful while she was floating. Kodiak closed the gap between them, the water encircling their waists. He handed her the soap. His eyes appraised her—and she watched him watching her...

He orbited around, lifting the curtain of her hair. His fingers gathered it and worked in the lather.

Today she'd ridden behind him and wondered what he thought when she pressed tightly against his back. It was not the way she'd sat behind Rio the day before. Unlike the relaxed way she held onto Rio, she had wound her arms around Kodiak's waist, resting her cheek on his shoulder.

While Kodiak gently caressed away the grime, Harmony sighed at his skilled touch. She recalled what Binda said about Kodiak being a flirt and wondered if the girl on the island was his girlfriend. "You have a talent. How often do you wash young ladies' hair?"

She heard the deep rumble of his chuckle. "You are the first." His hands rested on the bare skin of her shoulders. He massaged the tension from her neck, and his large hand slid over her collarbone, his fingertips touching the edge of the bra's fabric. Her breath caught before his hands retreated. She felt the bulk of her soapy hair lift and drape against her chest. Kodiak's thumbs circled the blades of her shoulders.

Harmony arched slightly. "Ahh, I'm so sore from riding." She closed her eyes, lost in the sweet sensation. "I've never even been horseback riding. I'm sure it's similar."

"Mmmhmm." The timber of his voice vibrated close to her ear. His hands splayed across the width of her back, a thumb positioned on either side of her spine, his longest fingers reaching her ribs. Kodiak eased his slick, soapy hands around her torso and slightly upward, lifting the heaviness of her breasts, before he pressed his sturdy hands downward over her hipbones. "I have never seen a woman as curvy as you. The women in this world are rail-thin, a good shape for swimmers." His voice was husky. "Your body is fascinating." That's when his hands dipped into the water and squeezed her behind. He dipped his head to kiss the tender skin behind her ear.

At that moment the spell was broken. Knowing he desired her and wanted more from her—well, she couldn't let that happen! She admitted to herself that Kodiak was the kind of guy she needed to safeguard her heart from. He was a flirt as Binda had said. Maybe that was all this was, but Harmony reminded herself the day would come when she would have to say good-bye. She couldn't become attached to him…or to anyone! She slipped away and sank down so only her neck and head were exposed.

She finished rinsing the soap from her hair, wondering what to say to him. He went too far. She reminded herself again that Kodiak was helping them so he could take away her grandmother's ring. *He is helping me only to collect his prize.* The ring was already costing her enough emotion strife. She didn't need him claiming a much more personal prize—her body.

"Wow, sorry, I got caught up…" He swallowed and ran his fingers through his hair. "You are so…so very…"

"Human," she interjected.

"Right," he agreed, looking up at the stars. "You are not from this world, and you want to leave this place. It's best if we don't complicate things." He flicked his gaze to rest on her face. "Even if you are magnetic, exotic, beautiful, and...human."

A sound caught in her throat. "If only we were in another time and another place..."

"If only," he grunted before swimming away.

Wading to shore, her emotions were torn. She collected her clothes to give them a quick wash. Kodiak swam out to gather some fresh fish for dinner. She saw his clothes strew in the grass and decided to wash them as well. She'd dried her hair first and then circled the towel around her body, clamping it under her arms.

Kodiak strode up the grassy cove, a fish held dangling from the two fingers plugged into its gills. The fish flapped its tail against Kodiak's leg, and he tossed it to the grass to finish its final movements.

Harmony glimpsed him in all his naked glory and sank her teeth against her bottom lip. She forced her eyes to stare at her feet. He didn't bother to dry off. He reached for a towel and circled it around his waist. He thanked Harmony when she handed him his clean, wet clothes.

When she got back to camp, she hung her wet clothes on some branches to dry overnight and put on dry ones she fished out of the saddlebag.

Rio and Binda sat by a roaring fire and were pleased to see Kodiak hold up food.

With a full belly and two missions down, Harmony finally slept soundly in the warmth from the fire—alone on her bedroll.

They both felt the attraction. They both knew it. They both denied it.

They sat on the backs of the elks facing the Hudson River. Harmony sat behind Kodiak, who reassured her again. "These animals are excellent swimmers. We are weighted down, but they will easily keep our chest, head, and shoulders above the water. Just hang on to me."

She nodded, her cheek against his shoulder. Through the veil of her lowered lashes she watched Rio and Binda's elk move forward and pick its way down before entering the river. She felt the elk move beneath her when Kodiak urged him on. Her feet dipped in, and then they sank to their waists. Her arms instinctively tightened around Kodiak.

"We're okay."

She thought he was kind to reassure her.

Harmony watched the saddlebags; the lighter ones floated a bit, secured to the saddle. She realized their bedding was soaking up the water, and it suddenly occurred to her that the map and Binda's journals were probably getting wet.

"Binda, your journals!" She called across the open water. They were more than halfway across the river, the elks' powerful legs moving swiftly.

Binda looked over her shoulder. "What about them?"

"They're probably wet! The map and drawings of the plants will be ruined!"

"Oh no! All will be lost!" Binda waved her arm dramatically. "Maybe we should turn back and forget this whole charade."

"What is she talking about!" Harmony's fear was forgotten as anger built. Binda was clearly mocking her.

"Now don't get upset. It's all right, Harmony. Our paper and ink are waterproof. Nothing will be ruined."

Kodiak, frowning at Binda's bad joke, turned and assured Harmony, "She is just jesting."

By the time Kodiak and Harmony reached the shore, minutes behind Rio and Binda, Harmony was fuming. They all dismounted, giving the animals a few minutes to rest. The buckled saddlebags would need to be rechecked.

Harmony marched over to Binda and unleashed her fury. "What is your problem with me?"

Binda, though much shorter then Harmony, stood her ground. "My problem with you is that you exist!" She stepped closer, not intimidated by her human cousin. "You had to go and find my grandfather's herbs in the building. As if he hadn't caused enough trouble with his irresponsible relationship, now, after all this time, you show up."

"It's not like I want to be here, Binda! I didn't ask to be put in this situation. And you can't blame Calder for everything." Harmony knew Binda's pain had been bottled up, but she wasn't a child, even though Binda was acting like one.

"Yeah, well, if it wasn't for your selfish race of humans, these problems wouldn't be happening to our world. Your world is full of wars that kill its own people, diseases spread because of ignorance! Your Earth is overpopulated and polluted, and your race will never know true peace," Binda jeered.

"Binda!" Rio barked. "This isn't Harmony's fault. You are being mean and unfair."

Harmony ignored Rio's intervention and returned words of anger. "Well, at least we have passion. We are creative, multicultural, colorful people! We have singing, technology, and amazing inventions... I can get on an airplane and fly through the sky," she whisked her arm overhead, "and go to any place on the planet. You're just hippies hiding in the water." She immediately felt guilty for saying that. She didn't mean it and was angry that Binda was goading her so.

"Girls!" Kodi barked. All eyes turned to him. "You need to be quiet now. We have crossed the river. Now we're on the lands of the Forest Tribe."

"Fine. Let's just get this last mission over with," Binda snapped.

"Fine by me." Harmony crossed her arms over her chest and marched away.

Rio's eyes were wide. He exclaimed, "They share the same genes for temper!"

21

They rode, practically in silence for the next three days, largely because they were deep in the Forest Tribe's territory and didn't want to be discovered. They were nearly at their final destination to collect the last herb. In the evenings their campfires were meager. Kodiak was pleased that Harmony allowed him to join their bedding together, offering warmth. Also he liked that Harmony had chosen to ride behind him the last three days. After his advances on her in the river, he wasn't' sure she'd ever come near him again. What had possessed him to touch her like that? Now he couldn't get the feel of her soft curves out of his mind. Each night as she slept beside him he laid awake thinking of her.

During the quiet days of riding he couldn't get the song she'd sung out of his mind. When she hummed, softly nestled behind him in the saddle, it relaxed him. Her voice haunted him. She was complex, to be sure. Even her temper surprised him. Binda deserved it after the way she'd been treating Harmony, he thought. Despite Binda's attitude and his advances, Harmony had managed to smooth things over. This morning proved this theory, when she asked to mount his elk and proceeded to ask him friendly questions about diving and what kinds of things he'd found under the sea.

As the afternoon sun bore down on them Harmony sighed wearily behind Kodiak, and he felt her stretching her torso. "Do you need a break?" he asked. "The elk could use a drink—me too."

"Yes, I'm thirsty. I can't feel my legs. How much longer?" She wondered if traveling Aquapopulean children asked, "Are we there yet?"

"We'll start heading north now and should be there

tomorrow, maybe the day after. We've made good time. These beasts are worthy." Kodiak slapped the thick neck in front of him affectionately. "Binda told me we are close to the city, so let's make this stop brief."

They refilled their canteens from the stream under the shade of the surrounding trees and allowed the elk to graze. Kodiak watched Harmony pull her hair aside and rinse her face. Then she stood and swiveled her golden head before she started into the woods.

"Where are you going?" Kodiak ran to catch up to her. "You need to stay close. We are well within the tribe's lands."

"I need a moment of privacy." She raised her eyebrows, a hint.

"Okay, but not alone." He turned to Binda, who sat in the leaves adjusting the buckle on her sandal. He sent a low whistle to get her attention. When she looked up he pointed to Harmony, who stood with her hands on her hips, impatiently tapping her foot. Binda nodded and stood to follow Harmony into the brush.

Kodiak stood ankle deep in the stream and plucked berries off a bush. He popped them into his mouth, intently listening for the girls' return. The water was shallow for several feet before the bend, where deeper water flowed south. Suddenly something whistled past him and thumped into a tree a few feet away. The arrow vibrated within its target. Kodiak was moving before it stopped.

Harmony! He raced toward the direction the girls had taken, but they quickly emerged, crashing through the brush and screaming. On their heels came the fierce looking tribal hunters mounted on their spirit animals. The powerful animal paws pounded the earth chasing prey. Breaking sticks and war cries filled the air. Several more arrows whizzed by. Rio turned to urge the elk into the stream. Then he drew his knife.

"Into the water," Kodiak hissed as the girls passed him. "Swim downstream." Coastal people were powerful swimmers, unlike the Forest Tribe people, who had lost their agility in the water when they adapted to life on the land. The stream would allow them an advantage; they could dive down and swim safely away, he knew. The elk could swim fast. Hopefully they'd be able to retrieve the animals later. They just needed to make it to the deeper water. But as they rushed into the streambed that was covered with slick rocks, warriors jumped from the riverbank downstream, blocking their escape.

The sudden roar of a lion stopped them all in their tracks. The biggest lion Harmony had ever seen leaped from the bushes and drove down one of the lagging elk. The elk bellowed in surprise as it landed in the shallow water, puffing out its last breath when the lion's vice-like jaws circled its neck. The water turned red around them. Harmony screamed and covered her eyes. When she opened them, a second lion appeared. It stopped and sniffed the fresh kill. Rio tried to control the other elk that yanked at its reins.

The warriors, covered in tattoos and animal skins, advanced toward the streambed with knives in hand. Two more lions appeared, with archers on their backs, poised to continue the attack. A woman astride a big cat advanced to the water's edge and demanded, "Halt!"

Kodiak knew they were trapped. He looked to the others, each frozen in place, chests heaving. "Okay. We don't want any trouble." Kodiak held up his empty hands, his knives still tucked into his belt.

The woman slid off her cat and waved Kodiak closer. "Who are you and why are you on our lands?" A fur-covered headband with cat ears held back her chin-length hair.

He said, "We have only come to gather herbs. We didn't mean to disturb you."

"What have you brought to trade?" she demanded, waving Kodiak closer still.

"I am a Linker." Wading back to shore, Binda pulled aside her tunic to reveal her mark.

Kodiak realized they had not discussed what they'd do if they were caught; Binda's quick thinking might have saved them. He'd heard the tribe currently had no Linker in their city.

"We will take you to our city. You can speak with the chieftain. The chieftain will decide on a fair trade." She motioned to the hunters to put down their arms. "Come, we will give you safe passage."

Kodiak nodded, and the bedraggled foursome trudged through the stream and up the bank, Rio leading the remaining elk.

"This is Binda and her brother Rio. That's Harmony, and I'm Kodiak. We are from the coastal village near the sacred island." Kodiak observed the way the group's leader eyed him. To his advantage, he offered her a lopsided grin along with an open stare of admiration for her prowess.

The huntress's lips curled at his meaningful look.

"I am Catori," she announced, her stance displaying her power and beauty. "I am the lead huntress of our city, and these are my fellow hunters. I apologize for your animal." She motioned to two men, who quickly bound the lifeless elk to a pole for easy carrying. The big cat, still licking blood from its mouth, watched every move the men made with his kill.

Rio led the last elk out of the water, patting it and murmuring reassuringly when it balked as the men hauled its dead companion up the bank.

Binda asked, "May I retrieve our saddlebags?" At Catori's command the men removed the saddlebags that contained their maps and her journal and handed them to Binda.

Kodiak glanced over his shoulder at Harmony, who was staring in disbelief at the big cats. When she tore her focus away from the brutal death scene, she caught his eye and moved closer behind him. He felt her hand slip into his, and he squeezed it for reassurance. Then he turned his attention back to Catori.

The lion the huntress had been riding circled them before it stopped at Catori's side. "This is Chaser." She swung her leg over Chaser's back. "Kodiak, you can ride with me." Catori scrutinized Harmony and narrowed her eyes when she observed their linked hands "You, with the hair the color of my lion, can ride with her." A woman astride a massive lion urged the cat forward, looking pointedly at Harmony.

Kodiak turned to Harmony, who looked like she wanted to bolt. "It's okay," he whispered softly. "You like cats, remember." His comment brought her eyes back to his, and they locked. With one last squeeze of her hand, he let go and strode up to Catori's lion. Catori offered her arm, her lips pouty and inviting as her eyes slid up and down his torso. He clasped her wrist and swung up behind her. He rested his large hands on her muscular shoulders. Looking over the huntress's dark head and headband fashioned from lion's ears, Kodiak kept a watchful eye on Harmony.

Rio quickly climbed onto the still-skittish elk, and his sister scrambled up behind him. Kodiak glared at them. Never had he heard of a coastal person riding a big cat. He swallowed his pride. What could he do? Catori chose him as her passenger.

The other rider gestured for Harmony to climb on behind her. Harmony inched her way forward as the cat sniffed the air. When it turned its orange eyes on her she froze in fear. "It is all right, he won't hurt you. I have told him you will ride with me," the woman said softly to Harmony and held out her arm to help her up.

Harmony clasped her elbow and hoisted herself up, swinging her leg over the soft, bare back of the giant lion.

***

Harmony watched the four women riding on the backs of lions. A dozen men, who jogged together as if practicing for track, made up the rest of the party. Even the pair carrying the pole supporting the dead elk on their shoulders didn't lag far behind. She glanced to one side, clinging to the woman in front of her, her arms locked around her ribcage. She couldn't hold the huntress's waist because it was belted with weapons, her dress slit open to the hips, exposing her powerful leg muscles. Harmony's legs could barely grip the beast beneath her.

Rio guided the elk as close as the animal would go to the lion, and he glanced over, giving Harmony reassuring smiles and nods. Binda's mouth was set grimly. She looked away from Harmony, clearly disgusted. Harmony figured Binda blamed her for getting captured. After their privacy break, Harmony had heard something and went to investigate, despite Binda's protests. Harmony had spotted the group of warriors and stepped closer for a better look. But she stepped on a stick that broke with a snap, and their heads had turned toward her. The girls had dashed away, but the tribespeople pursued them straight to the others.

Harmony closed her eyes and turned her head away. It *was* her fault. Binda's look made her feel ashamed. What had she been thinking, sneaking over to look? But all her shame left her when she opened her eyes and saw Kodiak riding snug up against Catori, talking in her ear as if he were enjoying himself. Not long ago, she was the one riding snug up behind *him*. A rush of heat and something else flushed through her when Catori smiled seductively over her shoulder at Kodiak. She slid her free hand along the forearm that was now wrapped around her waist. Neither of them were aware of Harmony's condemning stare.

By the time they reached the city, Harmony was seething with anger at Kodi. She couldn't keep her eyes from straying back to them. *Making friends with the enemy...harrumph!*

Harmony became aware of the roar of the great falls, which she knew as Niagara Falls, a good distance away, getting louder as they traveled. As the group broke through the trees, the city revealed to them, the falls crashing loudly. The dramatic sight and sounds distracted Harmony from Kodiak. She gasped at the vision of the beautiful metropolis. The stonework was classic Greek and Roman design. The walls of the buildings below were stacked with protruding balconies and encased by balustrades, arches, and Romanesque columns. The wall of stonework continued downwards into the falls, cut into the side of the earth. A bridge shaped like a Roman aqueduct spanned the falls, connecting to the city gateway on the other side. Instead of finding herself in a different dimension, Harmony felt like she'd gone back in time to ancient Rome.

The big cats and the men slowed to a walk once their feet touched the stone surface of the bridge. Harmony peeked down, over the low curb of the bridge. The buildings below were shrouded by mist from the falls. A pair of massive, seated stone lions towered over them at the city's gateway. Then the cats came to a stop. She slipped to the ground as the rest of them did.

Several of the men carried the dead elk through an archway and disappeared. A man came forward to lead its companion away, and Rio removed the saddlebags.

Kodiak sent a handsome smile to Catori, who looked

up into his eyes. He murmured something to her before joining Rio and Binda. Catori strutted to meet the women who entered the open courtyard to greet them. After exchanging quiet words, Catori turned to her guests and said, "It appears the chieftain is in the forest but will be back soon. We will wait in the great hall. This way."

22

The guests moved along with the flow of residents into the great hall, which, with its flying buttresses and vaulted ceilings, was like the interior of a cathedral. The enormous arched open-air windows provided plenty of light, and the steady sound of the falls wafted in to promote an atmosphere of relaxation. But Harmony couldn't relax since they'd been captured by the Forest Tribe. She looked around at the long tables that held platters of fruits and nuts. Fountains of spring water spouted into stone bowls near the food tables. Glasses were placed nearby, give the impression they had been set up for a convention. Benches nestled into quiet alcoves, but no other seating was offered.

As tribespeople passed by, they perused the food tables and then walked away with a delicacy. The women who had ridden back with them stood munching and chatting, their cats stretched at their feet. Harmony thought it was a lovely place for refreshments and conversation, but she felt like an unwelcome guest.

Harmony noticed the adorned and scantily cut clothing of the tribe. Unlike the coastal clan, the inland tribe's wardrobe consisted of more than tunics and pants. The undyed fabric appeared to be the same though. Several men were casually clad in sleeveless tunics with decorative trims that reached their thighs. They also wore belts, and an additional strap crossed their body, secured around one shoulder. Strapped to their belts were knives and various tools. They wore more sturdy footwear, primarily boots made of leather and fur, probably to protect their feet from the forest floor, in contrast to the coastal clan's sandals, which were easier to kick off for quick access to the water. Again ancient

Rome came to Harmony's mind; the tribespeople reminded Harmony of Roman citizens.

The hunting party wore much less fabric and more animal skins. The man were bare-chested but wore the same belts. The women wore a short fabric skirt cut high to expose their thighs; belts securing their weapons. Their halter-style leather tops exposed their stomachs and were skillfully stitched with intricate patterns. The young girls in the city that dashed by wore tunics that flowed to their knees. Each one of them was adorned with primitive jewelry, something the coastal people didn't wear.

"Do you think we can slip out before their chieftain returns?" Rio asked in low voice as they clustered together.

"It's too risky," Binda said, glancing again at the men who stood by the door. Harmony following her gaze, wondered if they were stationed there as guards. Harmony shifted her glance back to Catori, who stood posed with a hand on her hip, laughing with a group of women.

Kodiak blocked Harmony's view with his head as he swung in close to her. "We'll figure this out." When she flashed angry eyes at him, he seemed startled and arched a brow.

"What did you say to Cat Ears? You two seemed cozy." Her flippant tone and name-calling apparently were not lost on him. His expression changed, and he tried not to smile.

"I was flirting with her, to help things go our way," he answered honestly.

The roar of an approaching lion caught their attention. Kodiak took a protective step in front of Harmony, and Rio did the same for his sister. They watched the opening in the great hall's arch as twenty men jogged into the chamber. Several women followed, wearing mostly animal skins, and slowed their giant cats to open a wide path for their chieftain.

Entering the hall, the revered chieftain rocked to the rhythm of the big cat beneath her powerful thighs. Her air of authority commanded the bowed heads of everyone she passed by. She wore a crown Harmony thought was reminiscent of a Native American headdress. The chieftain slid off, and the cat followed her toward the fountain, where a girl handed her glass of water. The others follow suit, and soon the hall was filled with more people drinking and talking. Catori approached the chieftain and spoke, but it was too noisy for Harmony and her companions to hear.

The chieftain looked in their direction and gave Catori a nod. Catori clapped her hands, and the hubbub in the hall quieted. Catori summoned the travelers to approach. The onlookers were curious to see coastal people in their great city. Kodiak stepped forward ahead of his group and bowed. Rio stepped up beside him and did the same. Binda stayed a step behind her brother, as did Harmony. Both bowed at the waist to show deep respect.

"Welcome to our city. You are far from home." The chieftain's voice rang clear and loud. "I am Nakoma, the chieftain of the Forest Tribe."

Kodiak flashed his charming smile and led the introductions. "Thank you for allowing us safe passage into your city. I am Kodiak. This is Rio, his sister Binda, and Harmony. We are from the coastal region. We come seeking herbs grown only on your lands. We don't have much to offer, but Binda is a Linker in training, and she also has a gift." He paused for dramatic effect. "She is an artist as well."

Binda pulled aside her tunic to reveal her sacred mark, but Nakoma's eyes returned to Harmony, who kept her head down. Binda spoke, drawing the chieftain's attention. "Perhaps I could be of assistance to your people for the afternoon or leave you some of my drawings in exchange for the herbs we seek."

Harmony felt a moment of relief; the chieftain seemed to forget about her as she listened to Binda.

"Where are these herbs?"

"A day's ride north of here on elk, in a grove alongside Big Bear Lake. Once we obtain them we will leave your land straight away. May we have your permission to pass through your lands?" Kodiak said humbly.

"You have come a long way for this herb. It must be very valuable to you." Nakoma shrewdly didn't mention the fact they had snuck into her territory when Catori's hunting party had spotted them.

Harmony listened to Kodiak's believable lie. "Our Linker, Calder, who is training Binda, has sent us along with her to gather herbs so she can become familiar with the varieties throughout our realm. We were journeying here to ask your permission when we unfortunately startled your people in the woods."

Nakoma seemed to consider his statement. Then she advanced quickly, brushing past the boys, to stand in front of Harmony. Her lion hunkered on the cool stone floor to rest, sensing no danger, joining his fellow felines.

Alarmed, Harmony tilted her head back to look up into the strong-featured face of the chieftain in her imposing feather headdress. Even without it she stood as tall as Kodiak. Harmony swallowed nervously as Nakoma's eyes appraised her. Tucking a lock of hair behind her ear, Harmony imagined the dash through the woods had ruffled it. She felt the golden strands waving at her cheekbones like flags of distraction.

"And you? Why are you here?"

Harmony felt small. All she wanted to do was shrivel

into invisibility. Strangers stared at her, whispering. Her cousins and Kodiak too—everyone was staring at her.

"I'm visiting my cousins. They invited me along."

Nakoma, who had been waiting intently for her answer, broke into a wide smile that softened her features. Harmony released the breath she'd been holding. She looked to her friends and relaxed a fraction when she saw them nod.

"Since you were coming to my city to seek my permission and grant me something in trade, I will have you safely escorted to Big Bear Lake by my hunters." Several men advanced and gave an obedient nod. Her eyes never left Harmony. "However, Binda, your Linker, and this girl will stay here during your journey."

Rio, fearing for his sister, said, "But this journey is for her to gather knowledge. We need her to locate them. Surely after an afternoon or a day of Binda's service here, we all can be on our way." The chieftain's lion rose from its resting place at Rio's exasperated tone.

Nakoma smiled, although it didn't reach her black eyes. She turned to the other three. "Of course, I have many talented artists." She indicated the tribal tattoos on her face and the others that ran from her shoulders to her fingers and her waist to her ankles. No fabric covered her hips, only the thick strap of a belt. A scant loincloth rested like a miniskirt, showing off her powerful body. "So it is settled. Your sister will accompany you while Harmony remains my guest. When you return, Binda can spend a few days preparing salves and helping with injuries." Nakoma waltzed toward her immense cat to stand beside it, a fierce pair. "Naturally, you can all leave afterward."

Harmony felt panic rising. Her eyes were desperate and silently begged her friends to intervene. Before they had a chance to protest, Nakoma called to Catori.

"See that they have rooms for the night. They will

share the evening feast with us, and their party will leave at first light. I will arrange the escort. Place my guest in my suite."

The chieftain swung around and strode away, her posse falling in behind her as she left the hall. The lions silently joined their masters in the theatrical parade. As everyone bowed and watch the procession, Harmony hissed to her group, "Don't leave me here!"

Kodiak stepped close to her and brought his lips to her ear. "They will keep you safe until we return. Just don't tell them where you are from. It's only for a few days. We'll come back for you."

"We can't refuse," Binda whispered as the last of the chieftain's cohorts left the room.

Catori crossed the hall, a woman beside her. "She will escort you two to the west tower," she announced to Binda and Rio. The woman and her cat led them toward a corridor. Rio gave Harmony a reassuring look over his shoulder, and they disappeared from view.

"I'll take you both to the east tower. Your room will be near mine," Catori said to Kodiak. *"Harrrmony."* Catori pronounced her name harshly, rolling the *r*. "You will be an honored guest in Nakoma's suite. Be sure to follow her instructions," she warned.

"I think I would feel more comfortable in my own room," Harmony suggested.

"Nakoma has commanded you remain with her. Her rooms are very comfortable, I assure you." She led them down a corridor lined with tall windows until they reached the stairs. The stairs circled around a thick center column. At the landing, they advanced past two wooden doors and stopped at the third. "Kodiak, this will be your room for the night. Mine is just across the hall. I will fetch you for the evening feast in a couple of hours. Fresh clothes will be brought to you in the meantime. Also, someone will launder your items and have them returned to you by morning." Catori held the door open for Kodiak. He paused before Harmony.

"You are an honored guest, but it is best to do as Nakoma asks of you," he cautioned. "I will see you at the feast."

Harmony contemplated arguing, but his golden eyes with flecks of copper distracted her. He reached for her hand. What she mistook for a caress became his thumb brushing the surface of her pearl ring. They both looked down at it. Harmony's eyes flashed to his face, and her anxiety over their impending separation vanished. *He wants me to do as I'm told so they can get what's needed and he can collect his prize.* She yanked her hand away and raised her brows expectantly at Cat Ears.

Catori smirked at their exchange before she led Harmony away. Leaving Kodiak in his room, Catori and Harmony continued up a second curving staircase.

23

Nakoma entered her suite, and her attendant Amadahy greeted her. She informed the girl a guest would be arriving soon and a bed should be prepared for her in one of the antechambers. The chieftain's suite occupied the entire level of the tower and was guarded by a pair of women wearing weapons and their cats.

One of the guards soon knocked, and Catori waltzed in along with her apprehensive guest. Catori pointed to an open space on the floor, and her cat submissively lowered its bulky body to the floor.

Amadahy was removing Nakoma's headdress. When she stepped away with the bulky feathers, Nakoma turned to Catori.

"Catori, you have done well this day. I am pleased." Nakoma praised her talented huntress as she approached. Catori lifted her chin in pride. After a brief pause, Nakoma shifted her gaze to her golden-haired honored guest.

"Harmony," Nakoma pronounced. "Harmony…what kind of a name is Harmony? What does it mean?"

"Umm," Harmony eyeballed the lions and stepped closer to Nakoma, maintaining distance between herself and the beasts. "Umm, my name means *unity*. It's musical."

"Not named to honor our lord of the sea?" Nakoma smirked. Harmony's eyes flew to her face. Nakoma waved a dismissive hand. "I'm not named for his pleasure either. *Nakoma* means great warrior. *Catori* means spirit. Is the lord of the sea really flattered by babies named after the water he resides in? Foolishness!" Her attendant began to brush her chief's dark-chocolate-colored hair.

"Why do you want me to stay here, without my friends?" Harmony probed.

Nakoma raised her dark, arched brows at Harmony's candidness.

"I want you here because you are different. I want to get to know you. Why don't you tell me how you came to be traveling with the coastal clan?" Nakoma halted the girl brushing her hair. She unhooked the weapon-heavy belt at her waist and lifted it off over one shoulder. Handing it to Amadahy, she approached and faced the blond once again.

"What value do you bring them, Harmony?"

Amadahy returned after disappearing with the heavy belt and bent to unlatch the fur-covered boots on Nakoma's feet. She easily stepped out of them. Amadahy carried them into the other room.

"The Linker sent me along as another Diver, like Kodiak."

"A Diver. Hmm." Nakoma considered that but clearly wasn't convinced.

"What about your hair? It's an unusual color."

Nakoma studied her features: the rounder eyes, pinker skin, and bow-like, full lips that deepening the philtrum above Harmony's lip. Harmony's blond hair was a beacon crowning her head. The chieftain seemed to understand she was not from this realm.

Harmony looked her square in the eyes and did not falter when she answered, "Surely a gift from Suijin, our lord of the sea."

Nakoma's laugh was throaty, deep, and husky. She reached out to gather a handful of Harmony's hair, curling around her palm, appearing mesmerized by it. She lifted the hair to her nose and inhaled, her fathomless eyes never leaving Harmony's. Again searching her face, Nakoma could almost have been fooled by Harmony's amber-colored eyes, which were similar to the Aquapopulo, except not nearly as bright.

Dropping the lock of hair, she said, "You are just in time to join me in the mineral springs. I will have Amadahy assist you and wash your hair." The girl who'd removed Nakoma's headdress, belt, and boots gathered a basket of items and headed toward a staircase within the chamber. "Catori, you may join us as well."

"Thank you, Nakoma." Catori sounded delighted. Nakoma smiled at her trusted confidant, knowing she had bestowed an honor upon her.

They descended several flights of stairs; Harmony noticed no exits along the way. The sound of the falls quieted as they moved deeper underground. Finally the sound returned as they neared the bottom level, below the cliff.

Nakoma headed to a balcony supported by decorative arches that looked out into the falls. She loved the way the pounding vibrations could be felt in throughout her body. This was the best view, up close to the falling water. She beckoned Harmony to come closer and take a look. Harmony was required to oblige and walked up beside the chieftain. She craned her neck to look up at the towering falls, and then she gingerly leaned over the rail to look down at the rocks and mist.

"Wow. It's extraordinary!" Harmony said loudly, sweeping her eyes around in wonder.

Nakoma placed a hand on her shoulder, breaking the spell of admiration for nature. She felt Harmony's shoulder tense at her touch. Nakoma slid her hand down the length of Harmony's sleeve and clasped her bare hand, smiling when she felt the heat. Nakoma's assumption of where Harmony was from was making more sense to her now, and she had ways of testing her theory.

"The water is warm. You will enjoy it." Nakoma led Harmony away from the window, past the stairs, over to a large, softly bubbling in-ground pool. Nakoma let go of her hand and removed her own wrist guards and heavily beaded necklace, handing them to Amadahy. She stripped out of her halter top and loincloth, walking nude down the shallow steps into the pool. The pool leveled out just below her breasts. Nakoma walked across its length and then sank to her shoulders on a sunken bench.

***

Harmony attempted to avert her eyes from the naked woman, her lean, sculpted body adorned from head to toe with tattoos was spectacular.

"Disrobe and join our chieftain. It is an honor to share her private bath." When Catori nudged her, Harmony's cheeks turned red with embarrassment. Catori removed her clothing. Harmony turned her back while Catori entered the water.

The very idea of nudists added to Harmony's pulse rate. Her insecurities about her own body were ripped off like a bandage—exposed. *As if this realm isn't weird enough!*

She took her time unbuckling her sandals and kicking them away. Amadahy approached and held out her arm to hold Harmony's clothes. She slipped her tunic over her head, handing it over. Then her pants. Finally, reluctantly, Harmony removed her undergarments. Amadahy grinned before turning and walking away.

Harmony self-consciously hugged one arm across her breasts. Her other hand rested across her thigh as she scooted into the water, sinking to her shoulder as soon as she was deep enough. The water was very warm—so warm she felt beads of sweat form on her brow.

"Harmony, this is Amadahy." The girl nodded at Harmony as she placed her clothing into a basket. "She is my room attendant, and she will assist you while you stay with me." Amadahy's nose was pierced with a tiny black stone stud, and beads were woven into strands of her dark hair. Her hair was tied off at the nape of her neck, and the tip ended in a short braid. Amadahy knelt by the poolside and waited for further instruction.

"Come closer, Harmony." Nakoma voice was soft but held a commanding authority.

Harmony closed the gap between them, floating in the buoyant water. Suddenly, she felt a firm hand grab her ankle, vise-like, lifting her foot to the surface. She couldn't pull it free. She let out a surprised cry and bobbed on the other foot, keeping her head above the surface.

Nakoma, holding Harmony's foot tightly, slid her long finger between Harmony's toes. "Funny thing about the coastal clans. They didn't evolve like the Forest Tribe. They still have webbed toes—but you do not."

"There are mutations in evolution." Harmony's voice quaked in her throat.

Ignoring her comment, Nakoma faked a smile. "And they are known for their diving skills. You said you are a Diver... How long can you hold your breath?" Nakoma tugged Harmony's head under the water and held it under for several moments. Nakoma then loosened her grip, allowing Harmony to come up. She violently splashed to the surface, coughing and sputtering.

"Where are you from?" Nakoma demanded, but Harmony shook her head. She wasn't going to tell.

Nakoma yanked her foot again, forcing Harmony back underwater. No matter how hard she kicked she couldn't dislodge the chieftain's grip. She was trapped and might drown—it seemed inevitable.

Nakoma suddenly released the pressure.

Harmony broke the surface again. "I can't hold my breath! I'm not a Diver." Harmony howled.

Nakoma watched Harmony look desperately at

Catori, who was reclining with her arms draped over the edge, a smirk on her mouth. Then Harmony's eyes pleaded with her servant. Amadahy watched the exchange with interest.

Harmony coughed again into her elbow and held up a hand to Nakoma. She confessed, "I'm not from the coast. I'll tell you, but you probably won't believe me."

When Nakoma released her, Harmony swam away, putting a safe distance between them. Reluctantly she continued. "Over a week ago I came to your realm by mistake. I am from the human realm."

"Who brought you here? Calder, the Linker?" Nakoma apparently believed her. In fact, she didn't seem surprised.

"No, it was a mistake. I came over on my own. I found some herbs and..." She started coughing again.

Harmony shrank back at Nakoma's rumble of laughter. "You are a unique treasure indeed. Surely Calder knows that you are not of this realm?"

She nodded, sucking in deep breaths.

"What has Calder asked of you?" Nakoma asked with evident glee. "I must know, Harmony. Are the coastal clans planning to use you for a special purpose? Is that why you are really here?"

"No. We just came to gather herbs—that is all," she said.

"Is it your desire to return to the human realm?" Nakoma demanded.

"Yes, of course I want to return home. And I need to because of disturbances on the island. Calder thinks I can help somehow. I told him I would help any way I can once I return. I'm not going to say anything to anyone in the human realm. Who would believe me anyway?"

Nakoma nodded. "No one would believe you. And yes, I've heard about Calder's theories. Some say the lord of the sea is responsible."

"Look, I'm no one special." Although she had admitted she was human, she had not revealed that she was of mixed blood, Calder's descendant.

"We are not here to cause trouble. Just let us go," Harmony pleaded.

"Harmony I want you to consider remaining in this realm. Stay here with us, and we will send the others back to the coast where they belong. I can see there is potential in you to make a fine tribeswoman."

Harmony opened her mouth to protest, but Nakoma floated close and rested her hand on her flushed cheek. "Once you see how wonderful our city is, you will not want to go back with them. There is more for you here in this city, this realm, and I will take very good care of you."

Harmony seemed uncomfortable with her nearness and winced when Nakoma's hand slid from her cheek to her chin. Nakoma murmured, her breath fanning across Harmony's face. "Amadahy will wash your hair." Suddenly, Nakoma pulled away and called over her shoulder to Amadahy. "Harmony is ready for your assistance." As the chieftain left the pool, she slipped into a robe. Catori did the same.

"I will see you upstairs when you are finished with your soak. Take your time," Nakoma said, as if Harmony were an old pal. Then the tribeswomen ascended the steps, discussing the day's hunt.

24

When Harmony reached the dining hall, she arched her neck back to take in the impressive vaulted roof. Electric chandeliers and sconces illuminated the gigantic room. Extensive trestle tables stretched the length of the room, and several hundred people were seated. The wall of arched windows faced west. The sinking sun, now below the tree line, cast the sky in hues of pink and purple. Nakoma advanced from one end of the room, walking behind the seated guests and bidding them good evening and good health. Harmony and Catori followed Nakoma until they reached the center dais, where a circular table was raised above the others. There sat Binda, Rio, and Kodiak, all seeming relieved to see Harmony.

Nakoma turned to Harmony. "Please have a seat at my table." She swung her arm up toward the center platform. "I will join you shortly."

When Harmony was allowed to choose a dress earlier, she selected the one with the most fabric, although there wasn't as much as she'd like. The soft cloth hitched over one shoulder and clung to her form before it reached her thighs. Amadahy had wrapped a beaded belt adorned with small animal tails around her slim waist. A headband with delicate feathers pushed the hair off her forehead. Harmony was surprised her friends wore plain, comfortable tunics. She didn't like this game Nakoma was playing with her.

Her eyes connected with Kodiak's. He straightened in his chair at the sight of her.

Harmony climbed the few steps onto the platform. Rio had saved her a seat between Kodiak and himself, and she gave him a grateful smile. Seated, she noticed Catori slip into the chair on the other side of Kodiak, playfully bumping his shoulder in greeting. Harmony tore her eyes away, not wanting to watch Kodiak charm the tribeswoman. Instead, she observed Nakoma, who continue to stroll past each table, greeting everyone and stopping briefly to talk to those who flagged her down, her popularity among the crowd evident.

Harmony wrapped her arms around her stomach and leaned back against her chair. Her belly knotted in anticipation of what she needed to tell her friends. It had been confess or drown—would they understand?

"Are you okay?" Rio leaned over, speaking quietly.

Harmony noted Kodi was keeping Catori busy with conversation so she quickly whispered in Rio's ear, "She knows I'm from the other realm. She wasn't surprised, and she even asked me to consider staying here in this city. I'm sorry I told her, Rio, but she held me under the water... She is manipulative and dangerous."

Rio clasped her hand under the table and gave it a gentle squeeze. He leaned over to repeat Harmony's words to Binda. Binda crossed her arms, scowling at her.

On the surface this tribal community seemed hospitable, but Harmony wasn't blind to the underlying pulse that made them almost more like humans. For now, the four of them had to play the role of polite guests. As Nakoma approached, Harmony took a deep breath, adjusting her expressions to reflect that role. She resigned herself to getting through this—somehow.

Nakoma took her place on the dais, which signaled the servers to place platters of roasted meats and vegetables on the table, offering their chieftain the first serving.

Harmony's mouth watered. She'd lived off fish and vegetables for the last week, and this smelled heavenly. Her woes were momentarily forgotten.

Harmony dug in before she noticed her vegetarian cousins, who sat back, unmoving, staring at her. As the meat melted in her mouth, she allowed herself this small reprieve, this simple pleasure, with a soft groan. Spying Kodiak heaping vegetables on his plate, she grimaced apologetically as she licked the grease from her lips. He then placed the platter so Rio might serve himself some agreeable fare. Rio lifted a spoonful and held it over Binda's plate.

"Savages," Binda muttered under her breath.

Harmony heard her insult and shot a look at Nakoma, but the chieftain's attention was now on the council member beside her. Harmony narrowed her eyes at Binda in warning.

To Harmony, Nakoma's seemed distracted; her eyes swept the room and entrance occasionally as though she was looking for someone. Within the hum of voices and passing of platters, Nakoma asked questions about Calder. Binda answered as vaguely as she could.

Harmony could tell Binda was irritated by Nakoma's inquiries. Binda looked directly at Nakoma, a false smile on her lips. She said, "I'd like to meet your Linker. Would that be possible?"

When Nakoma's black, shrewd eyes bore into Binda's face, Harmony felt afraid for her cousin. Binda's seemingly innocent request sent flutters of distress jumping in her gut. *Something is amiss.*

"Our Linker was charged with an unethical deed and banished fifteen years ago when I was a newly appointed chieftain. It seems there are temptations in the human realm."

Harmony had to keep her eyes from rolling at Binda's remark. It was obvious by Binda's smirk that she already knew what happened to their Linker.

Just then there was a commotion at the entrance as a group of men arrived. The chieftain's tattooed face swiveled to the open doorway and her scowl was instantly gone. As the dozen men walked through the door the crowd roared in applause. The finely chiseled men dispersed to the lower tables. They were greeted with slaps on their backs by comrades and passionate kisses from women who clearly missed them. They tossed children in the air, who squealed with delight, before taking their seats.

One man made his way straight to the dais. "He has finally arrived." Nakoma's smile was genuine.

Catori jumped into his arms and gave him a possessive kiss. His brief acknowledgment sent Catori quickly back to her seat. Queen-like, Nakoma rose, and clasped wrists firmly with the newcomer.

"Welcome home, Finn. Visitors have arrived in your absence. I've been most eager to present them to you." She released him and introduced each of them.

Finn's eyes circled the table as he nodded at the group of coastal neighbors. Harmony smiled politely when his eyes lingered on her. She thought Finn stood out among the tribesmen. He was ruggedly handsome, and the wavy, brown hair that curled at his collar was sun-kissed with highlights. He took the seat next to Nakoma. The three other council members shifted down the table.

Nakoma praised the man who loaded his plate. "Finn is our lead hunter, as Catori is our lead huntress. Finn covers the northern territory. His specialty is bear trapping, and he has brought us back outstanding specimens."

Harmony noted the large teeth, probably bear teeth, woven into Nakoma's braided top. The open-weave top did little to hide the skin underneath.

As if on cue, four brawny hunters rolled in a cart heaped with bearskins. "It was a successful trip." Finn's chin lifted at the admiring murmurs in the room, and then he fixed his gaze on Harmony. "I'm glad I have returned."

Locking eyes briefly, Harmony quickly forced her gaze toward Catori, who'd watched their exchange as she noshed at her food.

Loud enough for the stranger's to hear, Nakoma said to Finn, "I'd like for you to spend some time with Harmony while her friends are escorted north. They've come seeking herbs on our lands. I've asked Harmony to stay as our honored guest until their return. I'm sure you'd like to get to know this lovely stranger. She's traveled a great distance." Harmony caught the knowing exchange between Nakoma and Finn at the last statements.

Harmony didn't dare defy a chieftain in a roomful of her subjects, her jumbo prehistoric lion lurking in the next chamber, but she was not planning to be abandoned here with these people. They were dangerous. Nakoma was scary. Harmony feared for her life.

25

The next morning Harmony awoke with a start, panicked that Kodiak and her cousins had left without her. She rose on her elbow and paused. Standing at the end of her bed was Nakoma, watching her. "Have my friends gone?"

Nakoma shook her head. "Not yet. They've been brought breakfast and are probably being escorted to the courtyard."

Harmony sat forward and sagged with relief. "Please, please let me go with them."

"I think there is more to know about you, Harmony. Humans are full of surprises, are they not?"

"What do you want from me, Nakoma?"

The chieftain ignored her question. "I'll be occupied with Finn this morning, so Catori will be at your disposal." As she turned to leave, she mentioned, "Your friends are about to embark on their journey. You'd like to say good-bye, wouldn't you?"

"Of course." Harmony scrambled to get ready and soon left her room to find her way to the courtyard.

Trotting down the broad outdoor staircase, Harmony was relieved she'd found them. She watched as the elks were led in and the saddles checked. She quickened her pace and rushed to Kodiak, who was loading supplies into a saddlebag.

"Kodi, thank goodness you haven't left yet!" she huffed, her breath was heavy after rushing.

He grinned and said, "I know you are worried, but you will be all right. Rio told me Nakoma knows you're human. Rio, Binda, and I have discussed what to do now that the chieftain knows who you are. I don't see why you being human is important to the chieftain, other than it makes you a novelty."

"I don't care! I want to go with you."

"We still think it's best for you to remain her guest. Calder said these tribespeople were a threat regarding collecting what we came for. That threat is removed when they escort us. We will be successful and return as fast as we can."

"Kodi, please don't leave me." She knew she sounded desperate, vulnerable.

He dropped his eyes to her mouth and stepped closer to her. He spoke in hushed tones. "I will come back for you no matter what."

Her mouth opened to protest against his departure again, but his declaration stalled her words. They sounded sincere, but what she wanted him to say was, "I won't leave here without you!"

During the awkward silence Kodiak cleared his throat, took a step back, and restated, "I'll come back for the ring. I won't fail my mission."

"Oh. Oh, right, the ring." Of course, he was doing all this so he could claim her pearl ring. *Why are my feelings hurt?* She turned away with a heavy heart.

"Take care of yourself, cousin." Rio came up to hug her good-bye. Harmony reached for her kin and hugged him tightly. She could feel tears well in her eyes. Rio had accepted her right away. He was kind and thoughtful toward her. She hadn't realized how much his presence made coping possible. Now he was leaving. *What if I never see him again? What if they don't come back? What if Nakoma is tricking them?* That woman had used scare tactics, to get Harmony to admit who she was. Nakoma scared her, and there was no way she'd ever trust her. With a deep inhale and one last squeeze, she reluctantly released Rio.

She tried not to cry, but she knew her eyes sparkled with tears. His expression softened when he'd noticed them.

"Be careful, and hurry back," she whispered.

Binda, Rio, and Kodi mounted the elk. Two male scouts mounted too. Catori walked up with her lion, which began sniffing at the other animals. She called a sweet good-bye to Kodiak, but to Harmony's surprise he looked only at her as they crossed the bridge and disappeared into the forest. Everyone had left the courtyard except Harmony and Catori.

Catori's skirt, made of fluffy animal tails, swayed as she approached Harmony. "Our men will make sure they come back." Catori started to walk away, much to Harmony's relief, but she then she stopped and turned. "By the way, you should stay clear of Finn. Nakoma may have plans for him, but Finn and I are meant to be together."

"Oh, really? Then why throw yourself at Kodiak?" Harmony was angry at being forced to stay behind. Everything seemed out of her control. And Catori's sassy warning was making her blood boil.

"I was having *fun*," Catori taunted.

Harmony was human, so she was used to bullies and assholes. Cat Ears didn't scare her. "Well, maybe I'll have a little fun while I'm here as Nakoma's *special* guest. I'm sure she'd have a laugh over this conversation. Maybe tonight in her private bath we'll joke about it. And as for Finn, he looked like he'd like to get to know me better... In fact, Nakoma suggested it."

Catori's mouth pinched with anger, and her lion was instantly beside her, its orange eyes fixed on Harmony. Harmony wasn't afraid of Catori, but her lion, Chaser, was another story. She managed with all her will to ignore the lion and focus on Catori, her eyebrows raised. *Bring it!*

Catori stalked away and her lion followed her, its nose sniffing the air, on to other things. Harmony exhaled a pent-up breath. *How am I going to survive the next few days?* If and when they returned, the group still had to trek back to the coast, wait for Calder to make the concoction, and pray that the combination returned her home. She felt alone in this realm, just as she'd been alone in her own.

Harmony meandered far enough along the river's grassy bank to take in the outline of the stone city. Catori had left her alone, and Nakoma was off with Finn, so she wandered in self-reflection. When the path diverged, either into the city or to the bridge, she chose the open air of the bridge. She leaned her elbows on the stone balustrade of the magnificent bridge that arched in several directions over and beyond the waters of Niagara Falls. She looked to the sky, empty save for the sun that climbed steadily overhead. As she listened for the sounds of the surrounding forest, she thought she heard singing past the constant noise of the falls. *But these people don't sing. They chant in meditation maybe, but definitely no singing.* She shielded her eyes.

Below her, the sunshine reflected off two heads in the water. As the heads glided closer their voices became stronger. Two girls, maybe fourteen or fifteen years old, waved to her. She waved back, and they giggled. They swam toward the grassy shore and beckoned Harmony over, laughing as they exchanged words of a song Harmony didn't know. Intrigued, Harmony ran her hand along the warm rail as she advanced to the end of the bridge.

"Hi," Harmony greeted them as she stood in the grass on the bank.

"Hello yourself," answered a high, young voice. The speaker swirled around in the water gleefully.

"What is your name?" asked the other melodious voice.

"Harmony."

"Harmony...Harmony..." they sang in unison. "Come into the water, Harmony."

Harmony kicked off the fur boots that were overheating her feet and leaped onto a large, flat boulder, its edge jutting over the water. She peered over the edge and noted the water was knee deep. Harmony sat down to dip her feet into the chilly river.

"It's too cold." The air temperature was pleasant enough, with no humidity, but the gusty breeze brought goosebumps to her flesh. "I like your song. I didn't think anyone around here sang."

"Come into the water..."

"Do you sing, Harmony?" One girl floated on her back, her complexion oddly whitish in the dark water.

"Yes. Would you like me to sing you a song?" They responded with gleeful squeals. Harmony couldn't think of any song they might know, so she decided on the popular children's song "Twinkle, Twinkle Little Star." It made her think of the enchanting night sky in this realm. As she sang they swam up and gripped the rock on either side of her. Their lips curved upward. Water droplets clung to the eyelashes surrounding their large juvenile eyes.

When she reached the second verse Harmony heard commotion behind her. Nakoma stood on the bridge, yelling for Harmony to get away from the water. Finn and the other hunters in their party, returning from the forest, surrounded Nakoma and watched in shock. At first Harmony thought the problem was her singing, but then she realized they were warning her about something as they waved their arms. Harmony's song died on her lips, and she felt tugging on her garment. She looked down. The girls, grabbing fistfuls of her tunic, were trying to drag Harmony into the water. Harmony pushed against the shoulder of the closest youth, touching her clammy flesh, and heat zipped down her arm. The girl hissed and withdrew.

Both girls suddenly opened their mouths unusually wide, revealing immense razor sharp teeth set in a row behind their normal front teeth. Their faces contorted ghoulishly. The girls' eyes, innocent and puppy-like moments before, turned black and evil. When Harmony pulled her hand away, she was shocked to see her handprint had left a scorched mark on the girl's shoulder.

Advancing, the second girl grabbed Harmony's bare arm—and quickly released it, as if she'd touched hot coals. The enraged girl's mouth opened even wider, as if she'd unhinged her jaw. She was about to sink her spiky teeth into Harmony's arm when Harmony shoved her head, repelling her second attacker. An agonizing scream ripped through the air. The girl pulled away, revealing the burned flesh on her face where Harmony's hand had touched for several seconds.

Harmony scrambled to her knees, preparing to run, when an arrow shot from the bridge whistled by. The arrow sank into the teen's neck, an arm's length from Harmony. The creature convulsed and slipped, arched and twitching, under the water. Before Harmony could scream, another arrow hit its target, and the girl with the burned shoulder joined her friend. Their bodies sank, slowly pulled away by the current. Their pasty skin turned gray as they disappeared into the darkness.

Nakoma reached the grass, glaring at Harmony. "Your singing brought the sirens! You are endangering us all. Singing is a siren's business and is forbidden to our kind."

"What the hell! Those girls...those *things* were sirens?" Harmony, still on her knees, bent forward, covering her face with her hands. Before she contacted her own skin, she drew back, contemplating her palms and their power. She'd felt the same surge of heat as when she'd blocked the sea serpent. She tried to wrap her head around this mythical realm and her new abilities within it. She knew strange and dangerous things swam in their waters, but never had she expected sirens! *And my touch burned them!*

She pulled herself up and stood before the chieftain. "No, my singing didn't bring them. They were already here. It was *their* singing that caught my attention."

Nakoma seemed to consider this. "I saw the burns you gave them. How did you do that?" When Harmony shrugged Nakoma demanded, "Let me see your hands. What did you use?"

Harmony stretched her empty palms forward, and Nakoma grabbed her wrists forcefully and examined them. Harmony glanced at the hunters who silently watched them. The cats hunkered down at their feet now that the danger had passed. Finn held a bow at his side. He must have been the one to send the sirens to their watery graves.

Nakoma released her and declared, "There is powerful energy within you. Let's go inside for refreshments and we can talk more." Nakoma's eyes revealed a triumph that cautioned Harmony to tread lightly.

Inside the city walls, Finn and the other men dispersed. Harmony couldn't keep her eyes from straying toward the man who killed those sirens. Finn nodded farewell to Nakoma and strode away with purpose. The hunters and their felines gathered by a pool fed by a cascading fountain. The female hunters removed their weapons belts and waded in the pool wearing their animal skin loincloths and beaded halter-style tops.

Harmony drank from the abundant fountain. Her hands continued to slightly shake as her adrenaline dissipated after her energy surge. She moved to sit across from Nakoma as platters of fresh-cut fruit were brought in. Nakoma sat studying her thoughtfully while she plucked at the fruit and ate.

"You would be a great asset to our people. As I said before, I want you to consider staying with us. I will make it worth your while." Nakoma sucked the juice from her fingers, watching carefully for Harmony's reaction.

Harmony nibbled what looked like cantaloupe. She hadn't eaten anything for breakfast. Kodiak and the others had been gone for a few hours that day, and she was constantly worried. *What if something happens to them? What if they decide not to come back for me?*

"You are special. Do you have these abilities in your world?"

Harmony shot her a look. "We don't have sirens or sea serpents sent by an angry god to kill me, so I haven't had a chance to try it out." Harmony lowered her lashes, realizing her sarcastic tone wasn't lost on the chieftain. Fear rose in her chest as she imagined the chieftain commanding her Amazonian warrior women to attack her, or worse, being torn to shreds by a gigantic lioness. "Sorry. I think it would be best for me to return to my realm. Perhaps then your god will be happier. Obviously he doesn't want me here."

"So, you have encountered a sea serpent?"

"Sort of." Harmony half-shrugged. "My ability or energy, whatever it is, seemed to hold the sea serpent away."

"Ha ha! You have managed to deter the lord's two most dangerous creatures." Nakoma laughed again, her chest shaking. "I wonder if your ability could affect Suijin. Can you deter *him?"*

Suddenly, something she said sent Harmony's memory zooming to a familiar thought. She had visions of herself underwater, her arms outstretched. A man…a

167

man with scales...reached for her, but she held him off.

"Our way of life is changing." Harmony returned her attention to what Nakoma was saying. "The time of relying on the water deity is over for us. We have found ways to get what we need and control our surroundings without his help. We use hydropower from the falls to generate electricity. We grow crops and hunt game. Birth and death ceremonies are the only traditional things left. If we could eliminate the threat of the sirens... Well, you see, don't you, Harmony?"

Nakoma's tattoo zigzagged from her left ear, then curved down her jaw in the shape of a sickle. The second zigzag from the same ear divided, one side stretching almost to her hairline, the other bracketed her cheekbone. Her dark hair was swept back away from her face and held by a band tied in an intricate pattern, emphasizing the dark clay color of her eyes. The tribespeople seemed to have lost the luminescent glow the coastal clan's eyes had.

"We are more advanced than the coastal clan in many ways. You could have a mate, a family, and be an important figure in our kingdom. Harmony, we *are* becoming a kingdom. You will see in time the value of my words." Nakoma leaned forward and declared, "Tomorrow Finn will show you around the city, but for now let's have a swim before the evening meal."

While the chieftain and her companions swam, Harmony was visited by a group of friendly young girls with a lion cub. Their curiosity about her hair made her grin. She was reluctant at first to warm up to the children, but they were clearly innocents. Eventually she lost track of time until Nakoma called her to dinner.

She was relieved that Finn joined friends at another table, although she found herself observing him from under her lowered lashes. She ate mutely and listened to the conversation Nakoma led about the upcoming harvest and the demand for longer hours in the salt mines.

The next morning, while they dressed, Amadahy came in to inform Nakoma that Finn was unable to join Harmony due to a disruption he was overseeing. Harmony saw the vexed look on Nakoma's face, but it disappeared with her audible sigh.

"Well, I will be escorting you around my beautiful city today."

Harmony faked a smile.

The city ran efficiently, its citizens athletic and merry. Frequent swimming was still popular with the tribe despite their changing ways. The men preferred the deeper pools in sections throughout the city. The city residents worked as blacksmiths, forging steel goods and hunting weapons. Builders added to their great city and maintained it. Some men toiled alongside the women in the fields growing crops, while many of them fished and hunted game. The women were in charge of making cloth and sewing, the men in charge of tanning the hides. Both men and women made unique pottery, applied tattoos, and created ornamental jewelry from beads, feathers, bones, and other materials. They traded cloth, spears, and rope for shell jewelry, soap, and sea delicacies. Harmony was awed by all that Nakoma showed her but was more certain than ever that this couldn't be a home to her. She had a house, a career about to launch, and a decaying hotel to save.

26

The scouts led Rio, Binda, and Kodiak up a steep incline to the crest. Looking down into the valley they saw a field of tall yellow flowers waving in the breeze. Just beyond was Big Bear Lake, fed by a mountain stream. Kodiak was thankful the guides had led them there rapidly; on their own they'd never have found the hidden trials.

"It doesn't look too steep going down," Rio surmised and prepared to plunge ahead.

"There is danger." A tribesman halted Rio and pointed to a sudden movement in the glade. Just as the group laid eyes on the animal, it caught their scent on the wind and stood to its full height, as tall as two grown men.

Binda sucked in her breath. "It's *arctodus simus* — a giant short-faced bear!"

"He knows we are here." Kodiak shook his head at the dilemma. Calder hadn't mentioned this obstacle. "Is this one of the bears Finn hunts?" Kodiak asked the tribesmen while surveying the area below. At their nods, he probed. "Any suggestions?"

The two barrel-chested, warrior-like men exchanged glances. "He baits a bear with honey. When it's distracted we take him down with our arrows or Finn surprise attacks him with this long knife."

"Honey, did you say?" Binda asked. They turned their attention away from the bear, which was advancing in their direction among the flowers in the valley below. "Look there." She pointed straight out, almost at eye level, in line with the trees. One tree towered above the rest. Hanging across two of its mighty limbs was an enormous bees' nest.

"Good catch, Binda! I have an idea." Kodiak calculated the time it would take the two tribesmen to sprint to the tree and climb to the height of the hive. He explained their roles to the tribesmen, who were known to be good tree climbers. He pointed to the tribesmen's hunting knives tucked in their belts. "Do you think you can cut it down?"

The men nodded, and one spoke. "We'll need a little time."

"Okay. While you are doing that, Rio and I will lure the bear away, toward the water, and occupy him until the hive comes down." He glanced at his boyhood friend. "Rio, once we are in the water, we'll be able to tire him by swimming under him, popping up a distance away, forcing the bear to swim back and forth."

The corner of Rio's mouth lifted. "You make it sound so easy."

Kodiak looked at the faces around him, exhaling his anxiety.

"Binda, go into the field and get what we need. Once you are safely back on this ridge, these two will release the hive. We'll make our escape while the bear is occupied with the mother lode of honey." He scanned each face intently. Everyone returned solemn, determined nods.

Binda cautioned, "Be aware that if the honey fails to attract the bear and he chases us—well, I read that he can run on his hind legs at great speed." Binda's statistics were confirmed by grim grunts from the tribesmen.

Kodiak and Rio raced into the water, and Rio's taunts ensured the bear followed them. They dove deep, able to stay submerged longer than the bear. Their game of catch-me-if-you-can with the powerful beast was relatively easy.

Kodiak observed as Binda collected a bag full of

leaves and then safely reached the ridge. She waved for the tribesmen to release the hive. However, he watched Binda start to run and was surprised to see a second bear behind her. Kodiak cursed.

The bear stood to full height, its nose raised, nostrils flaring. His growled warning sent Binda dashing along the ridge. She managed to find a hiding place and disappeared underground, away from Kodiak's view.

Binda skidded into a foxhole, the rocks underground biting at her skin. The bear pursued her. When he reached her refuge, he pawed at the ground and thrust his enormous head inside. Binda wiggled deeper. He pulled his head out of the hole, which was too small to allow him to reach his prey, and he circled, pouncing all around the hole, shaking the ground.

The first bear heard the intruder, a potential foe, and swam to shore, rising out of the lake. It shook, sending water sloshing across the grass. The boys swam quietly toward the shore. Just then a splintering, cracking sound echoed in the valley. With a loud swoosh, the hive, heavy with honey, fell from the tree. It burst open on the ground with a thud, and a flurry of angry bees whirled into the air.

Both bears rose on their hind legs, their nostrils flaring. As the bears were drawn toward the pool of honey, the tribesmen and coastal friends vanished from sight and left the valley.

27

Wandering the vast hallways and courtyards was interesting, but Harmony desperately needed some private time, away from prying eyes. As she stepped away from the fortress's walls, she paused, considering her choices. Harmony meandered away from the water's edge, not wanting another terrifying encounter with the sirens. She hadn't been told to stay nearby, nor was she under guard. Free to wander through the city and beyond its stone walls, she strolled along the hillside, admiring the view of the metropolis sprawled over the landscape. She wished she had a camera so she could capture her memories here. As she thought about modern conveniences, she marveled that the Forest Tribe lived without them just fine. They were a race more content than her own, and she understood the gravity of that.

Harmony followed a path away from the city that sloped downward under shady trees. She hadn't gone very far before she stopped to listen. *What does one hear in the woods if not birds?* She heard a snap in the underbrush that caused the hairs on the back of her neck to stand. Her eyes darted over her shoulder and focused on the brilliant green ferns. Standing among them was a lone wolf. Still as a statue, its eyes fixed on her.

Rapid-fire thoughts shot through her brain. *I shouldn't have come out here alone... No one will ever find me if this wolf takes me down. Should I stand still until he goes away or should I run?* Run!

Her flight reflex kicked in, and she sprinted back up the path toward the city, but the wolf dashed with lightning speed to cut off her escape route. She scrambled to a halt, and she teetered, struggling for balance. Spinning, she veered off the path, heading down through the brush, hoping to spot a tree with low branches to climb. Hearing the disturbed foliage behind her, she screamed. And suddenly the ground seemed to disappear beneath her feet. As she dropped, she clawed at the overgrown tree roots that stretched beyond the soil into the open ravine. Grasping one tightly between her hands, she felt the weight of her body jerk. Looking down, she saw her feet dangling above a five-hundred-yard drop. She looked up; she hung several feet from the top of the ledge. Her eyes stung with dirt, and she spat a leaf from her lip. Whining, the gray wolf paced on the solid ground above her. She debated: climb down and probably break a bone at best, or climb up and wrestle a wolf?

Her head snapped up at the sound of a yelp of pain, and then she heard the beat of four-footed running. Instead of the wolf's head above her, a man flashed his white teeth at her predicament. It was Finn. She had recognized him easily from the feast when he'd made that grand entrance and then sat opposite her at their table. Two days ago, his arrows had saved her from the sirens. "Are you okay?" he called.

"I think I can climb up." She pulled herself up and stretched toward a higher root.

"Good. One more before I can reach you." He lay flat on the ground and leaned way over, extending his arms to her. He clasped her hand and pulled her up. Back on horizontal ground, Harmony scooted away from the drop.

"Are you sure you are okay, Harmony?" He waited for her to catch her breath.

She nodded. "Thank you, Finn."

He handed her a container of water, and she thanked him again. She was sure she'd swallowed at least a handful of dirt. After finishing every drop of water, she admitted, "I shouldn't have left the city alone." She swept the dust from her eyelashes but kept her amber eyes locked on the man before her. Nakoma treated Finn with a respect she didn't show other men. Harmony wondered how he'd happened upon her now.

"It appears that you have saved me twice now." She crinkled her eyes and added, "What are the chances?"

"I think you could have taken out those sirens on your own. And as for today, I was following you. I should have stayed closer though," he said.

Suddenly there was rustling in the woods. Swiftly, Finn slipped a slingshot from his belt and a small stone from a pocket. In one swift motion he aimed, shot, stood, and repeated.

Harmony was on her knees searching for his targets when she spotted the wolf. He had returned with two buddies. Finn fired off a couple more shots, and the wolves ran off, whining.

"They won't come back now." He returned the slingshot to his belt.

Harmony stared after the canines until Finn curtly asked, "Are you hurt?"

She noticed she instinctively cradled her hip.

"Just a scratch, I think." She continued to watch the forest for other danger.

"Let me look…" He waited for her permission. She slowly turned her attention to him and regarded him with curiosity before nodding affirmatively. He lifted the tunic to reveal a puckered, red line that snaked from her ribs to below her trousers. "Just a surface scratch. I'll put something on it." He twisted to reach a large pouch hanging from the back of his belt and pulled out a round tin, like the one that held her lip balm at home. She leaned back on her elbow as instructed. Finn smeared on a pinkish cream, explaining it was an antibacterial salve.

"Why were you following me? I'm glad you were, don't get me wrong." It made sense that Nakoma would have her followed, after all. "Why you?"

Finn rubbed the medicine into her skin and slid her pants down to access the injured skin there. Harmony stayed his hand, and his eyes locked for a moment with hers. She adjusted the fabric to allow him access without exposing too much of her intimate flesh. He silently chuckled at her modesty.

Harmony couldn't get over how much Finn looked like a young Clint Eastwood: narrow eyes, sloping nose, and lips that stretched to reveal dimples. His abundant hair waved back from his forehead and curled at his neck. What was most notable about him was his facial hair—a couple days of scruff, which she had not seen on any other man in this realm.

"Nakoma asked me to seek you out and speak with you." He finished and tucked the tin away. "I was waiting for the right moment to approach you, but..." Harmony glanced toward the drop-off and nodded. "Why don't we start walking back? We can talk." He stood and offered her his hands. When she faced him, his hands in hers, she realized his hands were warm—very warm.

"Oh my... Your hands... You're warm," she exclaimed. "But how?"

"I'm human." He had a way of stretching one eyebrow, daring her to question him. Her lips parted, but no words came out. His eyes roved over her face. "I knew you were human the moment I saw you.

"But how did you get here?"

"I was taken from our world by a Linker when I was a boy. I have been in this realm for fifteen years."

Harmony found her voice. "I am told that I am the first human to come here. I can't believe the clans don't know about you. You are human—completely human?"

"My past is not a secret here, but no one speaks of it."

Shock and disbelief sent chills through Harmony. Their clasped hands connected them physically, but she immediately felt an internal connection with him—a fellow human from her world. "Fifteen years—fifteen years!" She searched his face, recalling that Nakoma had mentioned a Linker from fifteen years ago. "Do you remember our world? How old where you when you crossed?"

Finn nodded. "I was twelve. I remember."

"And they've kept you here? Against your will?"

"At first I wanted to go home. I had a family." There was sadness in his voice. "Once the tribe found out Linker named Gale had broken the sacred rules and brought a human into their world, they made him pay the ultimate price. He was sent into exile. But with him went the knowledge of the herbs to cross back over, so I was stuck here. I learned to adapt, and now this tribe is my family."

Harmony stood on her tiptoes and flung her arms around him. "I'm so sorry, Finn." He'd had a human family—that was more than she had, and she was confounded to find herself in an alternate realm. "Finn, you are a lost soul, like me," she mumbled into his ear.

"At one time I felt like a lost soul indeed, but I'm well respected, and this life is what I know. Don't you worry about me, kitten."

She pulled away at his indifference.

She stepped back. "If you could go back…back to your human family, would you?"

"I've always known it was possible. When I was young I often prayed another Linker would come recue me and take me home, but it has been so long. I wouldn't even know how to find my parents."

They waded through ferns to get back to the path. "We have a Linker who was born into the tribe with the mark eight years ago. It will be some time before he is

177

schooled in the herbs of the traveling Linkers. The funny thing about Linkers is they are very secretive about their knowledge. They claim they share their journals in the library, but much of our world is left out. Gale, our old Linker, told Nakoma I would be special, and because of my achievements she's given me a position on her council. She has afforded me many privileges."

Nakoma's words rang in Harmony's mind: *You are a great asset to our people. I want you to consider staying with us. I will make it worth your while.*

Harmony related the story of how she had accidently crossed, omitting the part that Calder was her great-great-grandfather. Finn grunted and confirmed his crossing experience was similar. He explained there were only six Linkers in their realm, some of them children still. Being born with the mark from Suijin contributed to an affluent life for Linkers. The Linkers guarded their knowledge of the herbs. Not all were allowed to cross over. The leaders ran the councils and were schooled in the library. "Nakoma is a strong leader. She is making many changes, and she's needed my help to do so. If you can't return to the other realm, then stay here with me. You wouldn't be the only human. I would look after you." His smile was sincere.

"I don't know what's going to happen, but I'd really like to go home, Finn."

He didn't press her further; he only asked, "May I hold your hand? It's nice to hold."

Harmony found herself smiling. And she allowed it as they walked back. Passing under the city gate into the courtyard, she was startled when she heard Rio call her name.

***

Kodiak dismounted, relieved their mission had been

successful, eager to see Harmony. He'd pushed his mates to travel late into the night and then to travel at first light. He'd thought of her constantly and wanted to know she was all right. Her distress over being left behind alone had tugged at his heartstrings. Kodiak heard Rio call her name and turned, smiling. But his smile quickly tightened into a thin line when he saw her hand-in-hand with the tribe's famed bear hunter, Finn.

Whatever she'd been telling Finn died on her lips. She beamed at her cousin. "Rio!" She rushed into his arms, and tears of relief filled her eyes. "You are safe! And you came back." Kodiak heard the crack in her voice. Rio lifted her off her feet and spun his cousin in his arms, her flowing mane catching the attention of onlookers.

"I missed you, cousin."

When Rio set her on her feet, she turned to Binda, who smiled proudly. "We did it. We have everything we need." Kodiak noted the relief in the girl's voice, realizing Binda had carried a large weight on her shoulders; as the Linker, they'd relied on her expertise.

"Thank you, Binda—for all that you've done for me."

Kodiak watched the girls' exchange. They seemed to finally accept one another.

Finn walked up, and the two tribesmen ascended upon him, excitement in their voices. None too quietly, they boasted about tricking the bears. Finn congratulated them on a job well done, considering they'd outwitted *two* giant bears. "I've seen a little action today as well. In the woods...with her." Finn gestured to Harmony.

When Harmony moved to Kodiak next, he shifted his stance, glaring at Finn and what he'd just suggested. Apparently, she'd made herself at home here while they'd made the long, tiring trek to collect the last ingredient.

"You were successful, Binda said. Thank you." Kodiak's eyes dropped to her lips. Harmony's sweet smile almost melted his resolve. Her next words expressed a deeper meaning. "I'm so glad you are back."

Her face was smudged with dirt, and he reached to pull a leaf from her wild mane. She looked like she'd taken a tumble. His eyes, glowing fireballs, probed hers before they bore into Finn's back. Finn was turned away, talking quietly now to other hunters, laughing and jesting. Kodiak rolled one shoulder, trying to alleviate the tension in his neck.

"Me too." He continued to stare over her shoulder at Finn. He said in a monotone, "Now I can collect my prize." His copper-flecked eyes sought hers. He read the shock there as he'd expected. Getting back to her, making sure she was safe, had driven him. When he'd seen her holding hands with Finn, with leaves in her hair, what could he think? He'd gone cold with jealousy.

"Oh." Harmony scarcely glanced at the ring before slipping it from her finger. When she rested it on his open palm, her eyes bore into his. "Take good care of it. It means everything to me."

Kodiak hated himself for making her look at him like that. It wasn't about the ring anymore, but he remained stoic, his jaw muscles flexing.

She turned away, trailing her warm fingers over his palm.

Kodiak glanced up. Nakoma stood on a balcony, watching the scene below. They owed the chieftain three days of service according to their bargain, and that was three days too many as far as he was concerned.

28

Finn offered the weary group a swim in his favorite pool. Harmony's cousins and Kodiak were willing to accept his hospitality and followed him along a corridor and down several flights of steps. A cavernous room housed a private pool.

"Enjoy the water. I'll see you at dinner." Finn excused himself.

Kodiak was the first to strip and enter the water. Stopping Rio and Binda, Harmony spoke in hushed tones. "There is so much to tell you."

"We have a lot to tell you too." Rio removed his shirt and kicked off his sandals. "Let's talk in the water."

"I need to swim. Kodiak made us leave without one this morning," Binda said with emphasis.

Harmony understood their need for soothing water.

She stripped to her underwear as the others had done and slipped under the water. When she surfaced she noticed the muddy water rising from her skin. She'd forgotten she had kissed the dirt when the wolf chased her. She spent several minutes running her hands over her face and arms and through her hair. The pool was deep. When she went under, her feet never came close to touching the bottom. She swam to the wall and waited for the others to surface.

Binda and Rio joined her first and began telling her about the encounter with the giant bears.

"It seems we've all had some crazy experiences." Harmony watched Kodiak reluctantly swim to them before she continued. "The day you left, I came into contact with two sirens. They swam up and called me over to the water's edge. I thought they were young girls out for a swim. I didn't realize people here choose not to sing because sirens do. Anyway, when they tried to drag me in, I touched them, and that strange ability came back, the same as with the sea serpent—except my touch burned their flesh." She paused as the horrible thought of what her touch had done to them filled her mind.

"Did you kill them?" Binda asked, baffled.

Harmony shook her head vigorously. "No, Finn shot them with his arrows. Nakoma saw what I did to them."

"Wow, I've never even seen a siren," Rio declared. "I've been told their beauty and their hypnotic voices lured even the strongest of men to their deaths."

"Yes. Well, there is more. But it's about Finn. It turns out he's human."

Binda pursed her lips and looked doubtful. "That can't be. Maybe he is lying to you?"

Harmony gnashed her teeth. Binda would believe the tale of sirens over humans. She insisted. "No, he is quite warm-blooded—there is no denying that."

"And just how did you discover that he is warm-blooded?" Kodiak's tone was flippant. "Did this come up today while you two had a tryst in the woods?"

Harmony was taken aback by the sneer in Kodiak's tone, surprised to hear what sounded like jealousy. "Yes, it was this morning. I was lucky Finn followed me into the woods, because I was chased by a wolf and dropped off a cliff. I ended up hanging from roots over a ravine. Finn saved me."

"Are you hurt?" His hostile tone changed to concern.

"Cousin, they let you wonder in the woods alone?" Rio asked with surprise in his voice.

"I'm fine." She waved away the boys' concerns and looked at Binda, whose expression hardened.

"I know what the unethical deed was. Their Linker must have brought Finn over." Binda sounded enlightened. "That has to be it."

"That makes sense, I guess," Rio said in support of

his sister's theory.

"You are right, Binda. Finn told me Gale the Linker brought him over when he was just a kid—twelve years old. He was taken from his family."

During a yawning moment of silence, the four pondered what would possess a Linker to bring over a human.

Harmony's hollow voice echoed in the cavern. "And what is even crazier, to me, is they want me to stay here. Nakoma said so the morning you left. But now that the chieftain and Finn saw what I can do to the sirens, I assume they want me here because they think my abilities are valuable. Nakoma said something about maybe my ability could affect Suijin, your god."

The light in Kodiak's eyes darkened, and he nearly growled. "You are not staying here. You need to go back."

Rio and Binda gave Kodiak a curious stare. It was one thing for him to state the obvious, but they raised their eyebrows over his desperate tone. Harmony felt just as confused as they did. She glared across the pool at him.

Exasperated, Harmony replied, "I know! Of course I'm going back, but I think we should take Finn with us. We can help him return home to the human world."

Binda floated back, clearly taking a moment to let this idea sink in. Copying his sister, Rio did the same.

Kodiak's nostrils flared. "Does he want to go back with you? Did he say that?"

Harmony shrugged her shoulders, her voice softer. "No, but I told him there might be a chance he could go home." She pleaded for their understanding. "He was taken when he was boy, against his will, by their Linker, who's in exile now. Finn didn't ask to come here—like me he was a victim of circumstances. Calder can send us both back—if Nakoma will let us go."

29

The gathering for the evening meal was a small one in an intimate room. Nakoma observed the unique blend of invited guests: Finn and Harmony, the two humans; Kodiak, a Diver; Binda, a Linker; Catori, a renowned huntress, and Rio. Nakoma was at a loss over what Rio's significance was, other than the brother of Binda, grandson to Calder. *How could he be useful to me?*

After the food had been laid out on small platters by a serving man, she nodded for them to partake. Kodiak and Rio gave her an appreciative nod when they saw the variety of grains and vegetables. Binda remained guarded, and Nakoma knew she was the one to watch. She'd learned Binda was Calder's granddaughter, and she knew from experience the influence of Linkers. They were not to be trusted.

Kodiak thanked Nakoma for allowing them passage with her scouts. He confirmed they'd been successful in their journey. "Binda will get started on her services first thing tomorrow."

Nakoma surveyed the young Linker, who was quick to agree with Kodiak.

Binda reassured her, "I was planning to mix salves and tooth polish. Also, I gathered some flowers along the paths to Big Bear Lake, and I can make scented soap with them."

Nakoma nodded at Binda in approval and turned her attention to her human guest. "Have you enjoyed our city, Harmony?"

"It's lovely." She sipped her tea. "I enjoyed visiting the women working on the looms. Watching the process of making cloth was interesting." She glanced at the faces around the table. "Even the little daughters worked alongside their aunts and mothers."

Nakoma could practically feel the energy in the room, an altogether negative vibe.

"Finn told me the two of you enjoyed exploring the forest together." Nakoma made her expression impassive. She watched the others stare at Harmony because of her suggestive words. Harmony shot Finn a questioning glance.

"Harmony was curious about what lurked beyond the city. We share human curiosity. Isn't there a saying— curiosity kills the cat?"

Catori hissed under her breath at Finn's insulting comment while Binda and Rio stifled their laughter. Nakoma enjoyed watching the dynamic playing out in the group that surrounded her table. Curious why Kodiak's gaze flashed from Harmony to Finn, watchful and seemingly cross, Nakoma sought clarification on what drove him.

"Finn, you make it sound as if humans don't like cats." Nakoma wasn't amused at his comment, her tone warning. She adjusted her regal head, and pointedly said, "I assume Harmony has informed you that Finn is a fellow human."

"Yes, and your Linker was responsible," Binda blurted. Nakoma's mouth twitched as the others gasped at Binda's impoliteness.

"Mmm, he's been punished. It is unfortunate we currently don't have a Linker. It's been fifteen years since we've had to get along without one. I'm sure Calder has trained you well—perhaps you are ready to take on a more esteemed position." Nakoma hoped her hint would appeal to the young Linker, as the girl's rebellious nature was plain as day. Influence and manipulation were clever tools in Nakoma's arsenal.

Harmony spoke up, attempting to break the tension. "I love cats. Well, small cats. We have smaller cats in our realm." Her voice trailed away and she took another sip of tea. No one seemed to hear her.

"Finn is human, not that it's a secret to the citizens of our city. We have chosen to keep this information local. It doesn't concern the outlying villages." Her tattooed face hardened. "There is a more important issue I want to discuss. As you know, there has been struggle for some time regarding Suijin. He is an unstable god who sends his sirens to cause multiple deaths every year, even our children."

Binda nodded. "Yes, our people have been affected too. We have built other temples..."

Nakoma's sharp laugh silenced Binda. "Temples will do no good. He has to be stopped. Our people have relied on him for too long, but we don't need him any longer. We can sustain ourselves. Frankly, we probably never needed him." She turned to Harmony. "Your ability to fight the sirens is fundamental. With the energy the two of you possess, we could defeat Suijin." Nakoma's eyes blazed at the humans, who returned vastly different looks. Finn grinned triumphantly, while Harmony scoffed.

Binda spat, "You can't defeat a god!"

"We can now. Finn has the ability to control the weather. And with Harmony's help we could test our theory for containing him. You see, this is not the first time this has been discussed. For many years Gale, the Linker who brought Finn to me, has wanted to achieve this ultimate freedom."

"It's impossible!" Binda's eyes became round. "A crazy idea... Your people may be faithless, but the true Aquapopuleans of the coast won't stand for your insane meddling."

Nakoma held up a hand to stop Binda from stating what everyone knew about the faith of the coastal clans.

Finn supported the chieftain. "We can't allow this

god to wreak havoc on the people any longer. Until now this has remained in the planning stages. We now have an opportunity to see this through." He turned to Harmony. "We'd like your help, kitten."

Nakoma keenly observed their interaction. Two humans outside of their realm, both lost souls. She controlled Finn easily enough. He sought acceptance, and she used that to her advantage by giving him the honored role of lead huntsmen.

Gale had given her Finn, assuring her this boy would be someone special one day. Too bad Gale had been found out by the last chieftain. Nakoma was young then, just stepping into the chieftain's role. Although Gale was sent into exile, she'd been in contact with him throughout the last fifteen years, unbeknownst to Finn. Gale's hideaway was just up the river in an abandoned power plant, where lived and continued to serve his chieftain.

"I don't see how I can help. I don't know how to control my abilities—they just happen. And Calder said the destruction on the sacred land in my realm contributes to the quakes felt in this realm. Therefore, I must go back to do what I can from the human realm."

"Perhaps, but it only seems to effect the island. That is, after all, the closest land to the portal. Why do the clans stay? Isn't it time the coastal people have the freedom to move away from the island. Why be held by the bonds of worship?"

"That is our home." Rio's gentle tone implored the chieftain to understand.

Nakoma offered him little in the way of a smile, more like a grimace. She set down her utensil and nodded at Finn, who kept silent, waiting for her to continue with their plan.

"Stay here Harmony," Nakoma said, her dark eyes gleaming. "Finn would like to take you for a wife. It will be the greatest union in our history. Your children will be strong, possess great abilities, and someday rule in this realm."

Finn smiled at the honor she'd bestowed upon him. He placed his hand over Harmony's. Her mouth went slack with shock.

The quiet gasp from Catori told everyone that she had no knowledge of this. She lowered her eyes when Nakoma shot her a look.

"That's not possible." All heads turned toward Kodiak, who spoke calmly. "Harmony and I are together."

Nakoma's brows lifted.

Binda confirmed, "As long as she remains in our realm, she is spoken for."

"Well, this is a surprise." Nakoma watched Harmony pull her hand from under Finn's. Harmony met her gaze without faltering. Nakoma calculated: if Harmony had feelings for Kodiak, then he'd be an asset. The way she saw it was that people would do anything to protect their loved ones. However, she had to probe for a reaction. "I wouldn't think a human woman would be interested in a man with Aquapopulo blood."

Harmony didn't look at Kodiak but kept her focus on Nakoma. She shrugged and said, "The heart wants what it wants."

"Poetic and romantic." Nakoma's lips stretched back into a smile. "I've read in the library your human tales of love."

"I'm sorry, Finn," Harmony whispered sincerely.

"Well then, I insist you have a marriage ceremony here." Nakoma had no intention of letting her valuable weapon go. She'd find a way to persuade the happy couple to stay in her city.

Binda's eyes widened. "But Harmony will be leaving, so there is no need for a marriage ceremony."

Nakoma waved away her concern. "In two days we will perform the ceremony." She swiveled her head toward Finn, who hadn't said a word about this change of plans. "Finn, I hope Harmony hasn't hurt your feelings by choosing our race over yours, but love conquers all."

Finn's jaw was set. "As you command."

Suddenly, Nakoma's chair scraped against the floor. She stood. "Catori will join you, Finn. I'm sure she can comfort you." She laughed when her command prompted Catori to smile wickedly. Finn and the others rose out of their seats.

Nakoma hesitated, enjoying watching them squirm. She'd seen through their little scheme. If they'd married, where would the happy couple live? Kodiak wasn't a Linker, and there was no guarantee he'd make the crossing alive if he was foolish enough to try.

"Come, Harmony, we will bathe and discuss your big day."

***

What could Harmony say that would change this dictator's mind? She thought saying she wanted Calder and others to be a part of her wedding day would result in her sending for them. Harmony couldn't take that chance. They were safer where they were—far away from this extremist group. Besides, now that her friends had returned successful, maybe they could all escape before this got out of hand.

They filed out of the dining room. The cats rose to accompany Nakoma and Catori. Harmony followed behind the chieftain's proud, straight back, stealing glances at each of her cousins and Kodiak. Before she knew it, Binda and Rio detoured, waving a solemn goodnight. Soon, the remaining group reached the residential tower.

Finn and Catori reached his suite. "It stays outside," he ordered, indicating Catori's lion.

"Of course, like always." Catori purred to Finn, and then she pointed to the ground. "Stay," she commanded her lion as Finn strolled into his room.

Harmony glimpsed Finn removing his belts, dropping them on a bench, and reaching to tug his shirt off. Catori waited for her cat to obey and turned to blast her gaze at Harmony. She bent her fingers like claws and gave Harmony a silent hiss followed by a sneer, before she closed the door behind her.

Harmony's brows drew together. She wondered about Finn's relationship with the feisty girl. When Kodiak chuckled beside her, Harmony whipped her head around, narrowing her eyes at him. *What is so funny?*

Nakoma was ahead of them, and she stopped several steps from Kodiak's door. "Would you like to bid your beloved goodnight?"

At the word *beloved*, Harmony glanced at Kodiak, knowing they were playing a dangerous game. She didn't know what this fierce chieftain might be capable of. She needed to make this convincing, so she rushed into Kodiak's arms. Their eyes locked. His earlier glare gone, his glowing eyes now shimmered in the dark hallway. He'd spoken up to save her, save all of them. But if they went through with the ceremony what would that mean? Was this just part of a bigger scheme? Harmony slid her hand along the taut column of his neck and urged him to lower his head. When his soft lips lingered on hers, she pulled him closer. For a moment Harmony forgot they had an audience. His gentle kiss was convincing to her as he captured her lips!

At Nakoma's subtle throat clearing they parted. Harmony slid her hands down his arms, knowing he'd feel a heat trail. They whispered their farewells, and she slipped from his hold. Nakoma raised a brow and smirked as she swiveled and advanced toward the stairs. Harmony followed, but she couldn't resist a glance over her shoulder at Kodiak. His arm was propped on the doorframe and a smile lingered on his lips. He looked gorgeous. *The flirt!*

In the bath, the women's conversation stayed on the topic of Harmony's wedding day. Nakoma's councilwoman, a spiritual guide in residence, would perform the ceremony. Harmony played the polite game as she tried to analyze her adversary. Nakoma was smart. Her dark eyes intensely computed information, making Harmony fearful. Everyone in this city not only followed Nakoma's every command but seemed to admire and even worship her. Nakoma was like a celebrity. The more she engaged her subjects, the more the people adored her. She reveled in this power, and Harmony began to understand why the people would follow her. Nakoma promised them freedom from a god that punished them and took away their loved ones. She played the savior well.

Amadahy, Nakoma's room attendant, led in a broad-shouldered man who strutted into the bathing chamber wearing a scant loin cloth. Harmony swallowed at the sight of his amazing physic. His dark hair hung to his shoulders, and his smile promised pleasure. His eyes were on Nakoma, whose face softened with desire. She excused herself and slowly padded out of the pool. In her naked glory, her tattoos circled one of her shoulders and wrapped like a sleeve of scorpions down one arm, then circled around both hipbones before finally scrolling down to the calf on the opposite leg.

Harmony was fascinated by the two tight, powerful bodies before her, and she watched Nakoma pause with her hand running seductively down this man's barrel chest before she caught his hand. Without a backward glance Nakoma led him up the steps.

30

"Hey, kitten!" Finn called as he fell in step alongside Harmony. He'd been watching for her, anticipating she'd come down the main corridor. It was just after breakfast, and they walked among the crowd. "Where are you heading?"

Harmony tilted her head to look up at him, never breaking her stride. "I'm going to the infusion rooms to find Binda. We spent all day there yesterday making soaps and a bunch of other stuff."

"That's where you were. I was looking for you yesterday. I think we need to talk." He noticed she looked reluctant, and there was something else. Finn said, "You look tired. Didn't sleep well?"

"Nakoma has had company the last couple of nights...and they were noisy." She lifted her brows.

He got her meaning and smiled at the pretty blush that glowed on her cheeks.

"And besides that, I have a lot on my mind."

"Is it true what you said the other night? About Kodiak—the heart wants what it wants?"

"Kodiak and I are...complicated," Harmony demurred, but he reached for her hand.

"You don't want to stay with the coastal clan, believe me." He guided her into an alcove with a window that overlooked the shimmering river. The sun was peeking through the treetops. "There is so much we could have together here. You could still change your mind. There is much at stake that you don't understand."

"I'm not staying with the coastal clan for long—I'm going home, to the human realm." Seemingly annoyed with him, she grumbled, "Don't tell me what to do. I know what I need to do. And Finn, *you* must understand my *abilities* aren't going to defeat anyone. You wouldn't gain anything from marrying me. Besides, you already have someone to warm your bed. Good luck with Cat Ears!" Harmony stormed away.

Finn, on her heels, chuckled at her name-calling. He knew the two females clashed. He also knew his huntress could be cruel and unforgiving, and he hoped Harmony would watch her step while she was around her. However, Catori was loyal to their chieftain and a dedicated lover to him.

He snatched her elbow to slow her. "Let's take a ride so we can talk."

Others lingered nearby, eyeing them openly.

"I'm not going anywhere with you," she huffed.

"Yes, you are." He clasped her hand and led her none too gently down to the elk paddocks. He strapped a saddle on an elk while she sulked.

"I'm not riding that thing." She crossed her arms over her chest.

He swung onto the animal's back. When she tossed her hair and turned to leave, he lifted her off the ground and planted her in front of him. At her grunt of displeasure he spurred the animal forward, so she crashed backward against his hard chest. He held her in his vice-like arms. She eventually stopped wiggling when he dramatically moaned in her ear. When she pinched his forearm hard he chuckled.

They galloped across the bridge and into the forest before he finally stopped. In a clearing, he helped her down, but she smacked his hands away once she was on her feet.

"How dare you!"

Finn leisurely tied the elk's tether to a tree branch, observing Harmony. She stood facing him, feet apart, and lifted her arms, palms flat. She seemed to concentrate, heaving a deep breath as she pressed her palms at him.

"What are you doing?" He grinned, knowing she was trying to blast him with her ability.

Harmony marched up to him and pressed her hands against his broad chest. Squeezing her eyes closed, she held her breath.

"Harmony, what are you doing?" he repeated, unaffected. "You know you can't use your ability against me."

At his comment, she opened her eyes and blew out all her air. With it went her gusto.

"Finn, how can you want to stay here?" Her voice was gentle, pleading. "Nakoma is a dictator. I know you don't see it that way, but from what I've seen…I think she will cause more harm than good."

"She's trying to make changes for the people. The peace is disrupted, the coastal clans are resistant to advancement, and Suijin's actions are taking their toll. Something needs to be done."

"Even if I wanted to stay here with you, you'd be asking me to start a war!" She dropped her hands from his chest. "Calder is counting on me to return to our human realm so I can try to maintain peace. War is awful, Finn. Our realm has been devastated over and over by it."

Finn suddenly had a flashback to his former family life when he was a boy, and his mouth tightened. He fought the demons inside all too often, but he'd hardened himself. He'd stopped asking the *what ifs* long ago, yet they surfaced again with this girl in front of him. The possibilities! If they mated he could have children. He'd been with many of the tribal women in the past and more exclusively with Catori in recent months, but no children had been conceived.

"Hold on to your humanity—you'll lose it here," he bit out. In this pinnacle point he questioned what was right. Since the early years when he was brought here, he wanted to achieve leadership—prove to the council and the tribe he was worthy, even if he was human. He'd challenged authority and fought hard against other hunters to obtain the position he had today. He'd done things he wasn't proud of. His demons came back to haunt him now, and he told himself if he could be leader someday then he could make the right changes for the good of both the tribes and the clans. *Maybe Nakoma is wrong?* Harmony made him question the risk. Nakoma had strung him along on the one thing he'd asked from her. He'd wanted Nakoma as his bride and to rule beside her. Instead she'd offered him Harmony, and it wasn't a bad trade-off. Harmony had mentioned Nakoma's nighttime visitor. He knew she had many lovers, and being with her in that way never really interested him—but the power to rule with her got his blood boiling.

He spat out, "You should go. Run far from here…and from me. I may be human, but I'm a changed man. I've adapted to this life. I've worked hard to prove myself worthy in Nakoma's eyes. I've earned the respect of the tribespeople. I am a valuable member of their society." He was still holding out, but when Nakoma had told him it was best if he married Harmony his faith in her faltered. She'd promised him eventually they'd rule together. She'd either lied or she was using him.

Finn caressed the waves of Harmony's golden hair and spoke gently. "Nakoma said I deserve to have you as my mate." He held her chin. "I've thought about what it would be like to lie with you. These women are all the same, cold-blooded. It would be like igniting fire with—"

"Stop!" She pulled away. "We can't go down that path. Finn, you don't have to do this. You can come back with me to the human world. It's not too late. Calder will help you. And besides, Nakoma shouldn't battle a god—that's insane."

Finn shook his head. "You don't understand." His hand returned to her hair, rubbing the strands between his fingers. "Nakoma will never let me go... *us* go. My ability is vastly different from yours. Nakoma told you I can control the weather. I will show you."

She shook her head, afraid of what he was planning. Finn circled a finger, and a strong breeze kicked up, flapping Harmony's hair all around. Dark clouds started to gather, and there was a distant rumble of thunder. She placed her hand against his chest as her head swiveled side to side. She watched the mounting cloud mass.

Thunder rumbled, and the smoky-looking clouds lit up with flashes of lightning.

"Finn, stop," she whispered, and he stopped the movement of his hands.

Harmony slipped her arms around his chest and pressed her cheek against his heart. "Oh, Finn, I fear you are right about Nakoma, and we will never get out of here."

He had compassion for this girl from his homeland and hugging her warm body flooded his memories of other times long ago. His hands were buried in the lavish cascade of her blonde hair—he hadn't seen the like in over fifteen years. Nostalgia set in, and suddenly his interest toward her began to stir. Finn held Harmony in his arms.

He remembered the day Catori had happened upon him lying in a grassy field. He hadn't known then that she'd watched as he twirled his fingers skyward. An invisible force twisted the clouds into funnels, and he kept several of them spinning. He'd heard her bid her lion to stay while she stalked him, inching closer, staying low in the waving reeds. Suddenly, he'd sent a gust of wind that nearly knocked her back on her heels, catching her off guard. He plowed her to the ground, landing on top of her. Catori's startled cry brought her spirit animal, sprawled and yawning in the tall grass at the hill's edge, to land feet away from the couple, snarling a warning.

"Down!" she'd commanded the cat, who licked away excess saliva produced when the call to fight had sent her to her master's side. At Catori's giggle, the cat trotted off, giving them privacy.

"Are you spying on me?" Finn's handsome face was inches from hers. His weight pressed her into the sharp grass.

"I came to find you," she challenged, arching her back, but she couldn't dislodge him. "What were you doing?" she asked, her curiosity piqued.

"What did you see?" he asked nonchalantly, tracing his finger up the bridge of her nose, across the arch of her eyebrow, down the curve of her jaw, and then across the fullness of her lips.

"Ouch!" He yanked his finger from between her teeth, shaking it a couple of times.

Catori licked the blood that dotted her lip. He growled at her and captured her lip between his teeth. She sucked in a sharp breath and locked eyes with him. His teeth released, and his tongue lashed out, dipping into her mouth. Then he kissed her. Her eyes fluttered closed. She made a growling sound deep in her throat as his hands roamed her body. He felt her nails dig into his backside as she drew her knees up around his waist.

Feeling the splat of fat raindrops, Finn rolled Catori on top of him. He lifted his arm and circled his wrist.

Catori paused from kissing him to see what was so distracting. The rain fell around them, but they lay in a perfectly dry spot. Through the clouds, like the eye of a storm, they could see blue sky. They were in a pocket; the air gently swirled around them, keeping the rain out. Before she could comment, Finn turned her face back to his, recapturing her mouth and making her forget about her surroundings.

Just months after his initial tumble with Catori, the tribe was concerned they'd not had rain. The crops planted in outlying fields were turning to dust, and they were forced to manually water kitchen gardens. This was a clear sign that their god was angry. But why?

Finn suspected it was because of what he'd done that day in the tall grass with Catori. He had altered the weather around them. Suijin wasn't the only god-like being in this realm!

He'd been secretly learning to use his ability. He wasn't sure what he was capable of. No one else seemed to have this remarkable gift. He'd only toyed with his power—he'd drawn in distant rain clouds, summoned a fog, and made fun, but dangerous, funnel clouds—just small ones. He didn't dare unleash a tornado if he wasn't sure he could control it. So on that day, when the people were preparing to pay tributes to the water god, asking for rain, Finn strode onto the bridge's highest point. With his energy, he gathered rain clouds, and as the crowd watched in awe it began to rain and continued to do so for the rest of the day. They celebrated with arms stretched out and faces lifted as the deluge of water poured on the thirsty city.

Later, in Nakoma's rooms with Catori at her side, he'd confessed that he'd known of his strange ability for some time. That was when he'd found out that Catori had already told their chieftain about what had happened months earlier, when he'd shielded them from the rain all afternoon. He'd never forget Nakoma's words. "Gale has truly given me a gift."

Finn forgot about giving Harmony a demonstration of his abilities as he held her. Her warmth strangely comforted him. He dropped a kiss on the top of her head. "I'll take you back. We will figure something out."

31

Binda helped Harmony slip into a gauzy white dress. It fastened at her neck, halter style, the empire waist supporting her breasts, and flowed down to her ankles. Binda braided and coiled her hair like a golden crown on her head, tucking tiny white flowers in its folds. Harmony watched her cousin's face, inches away, while she worked the flowers into just the right places and then leaned back to be sure they were disbursed evenly. Binda's almond-shaped eyes showed pupils of tranquil blue, darker shades stretched in a starburst pattern from the iris to the edges. Her thin lips were pressed together in concentration, and she smelled of wildflowers.

"You look beautiful."

"Thank you. So do you." She smiled at Binda, who was nicely dressed in an embroidered tunic.

Binda hesitated a moment, her eyes cast down. "Harmony, I want to say I'm sorry about how I've treated you. Now that I've gotten to know you... Well, if you had grown up in this realm I think we would have likely been close. Also, although this wedding is born of necessity, rushed, and without Calder to share his wisdom, I think Kodi will make a good husband, in case you can't return to your realm."

Harmony's smile waned. "Do you think we are making a mistake? When Kodi started this, I don't think he had any intentions of going this far. We haven't had any opportunity to escape. He's making a big sacrifice by allowing this ceremony to happen."

"Kodi knows what he is doing. Besides, I've known Kodi since boyhood. I know his nature, and I know he feels something for you. But understand, Harmony, it is forbidden for Aquapopulos to cross if they are not a

Linker."

"I understand," Harmony said solemnly. She dared ask, "Once I go back...will I, maybe, see you someday? Will you come to the human realm?"

"Maybe it would be a good thing, having a friend from beyond this realm. I'll definitely find you if I decide to cross." Binda nodded, the corners of her mouth turning up. Harmony wrapped her arms around the smaller girl, who patted her back awkwardly. Amadahy entered, and Binda stepped back from their embrace.

"These are for you." Amadahy handed Harmony a bouquet of exotic white and violet flowers.

"You remembered! Thank you, Amadahy!" Harmony hugged the servant girl. During her bath in the pool last evening, she'd explained traditional human weddings, and Amadahy had said she loved the idea of carrying flowers. Since this wasn't a traditional item among the tribe, which preferred a ceremonial arrow and dagger, it meant so much to have something small from her human traditions. This was just one more reason Harmony liked the gentle-natured girl, which made her realize not all tribal members were aggressive. Amadahy cheerfully told them it was time for the ceremony.

Harmony's tension grew when it was finally time to head to the ceremonial pool. Nakoma paused to speak with her in the outer chamber. The chieftain's dress was a patchwork of animal hides, and her headdress emphasized her strength with a crown of horns. She glanced down at the flowers but said nothing. Instead she nodded her approval of Harmony's appearance.

"You will honor our city today. Having a human and an Aquapopulo marry is monumental. You will be written about in our history books." She flashed Harmony a toothy smile that sent chills down her spine.

Harmony swallowed hard as the chieftain and her cat strolled away. The others followed suit, glancing over their shoulders at the human who was making history in their city.

A great gathering of onlookers crowded around the ritual platform, and others filled open windows above, all curious to watch this event. At the pool's center, a floating stage attached to a stone bridge. An appointed councilwoman stood there wearing a ceremonial headdress, Kodiak by her side. Kodiak's tunic was edged with fur and elaborate stitching. His eyes shone brightly, almost glowing in the twilight, and he shifted his feet as he watched Harmony approach.

Never had she imagined even being in another realm, and getting married in one felt dreamlike. She looked down at the bracelet her aunt had given her before this fantastic journey, and she wished Nami was here to witness this. Harmony stepped next to Kodiak, her recently discovered cousins seated behind her. Standing by his shoulder, she cocked her head to the side, looking up at this fairytale prince. She allowed her thoughts to drift... *If only this were a true marriage, Kodi and I in a loving relationship...* She had no one, and he made her feel something.

Their eyes were locked, but his flitted away as the officiate spoke.

She was nervous, and her gaze dropped to his chest. She focused on the rapid rise and fall of his chest. Harmony began to doubt herself: should she go through with this? She was planning to leave him and return to the human realm. She told herself it didn't matter that he was just doing this to get them out of this city. Her feelings had to be put aside, though a longing for more from him was brewing in her heart.

Even though the words were different, the ceremony was similar to the human version. The joining of souls, the blessing of offspring, and of course eternal love... When Kodiak slipped her grandmother's pearl ring onto her finger, she gasped. Her amber eyes sparkled with tears. It was symbolic, even if it wasn't for real.

Binda, who sat on the outer ring of the platform along with the chieftain and the other high-ranking council members, stood. She took Harmony's bouquet and handed her a gold band to place on Kodiak's finger. Once she slid it into place they observed one another, feeling the gravity of the moment.

They were pronounced Mr. and Mrs. Kodiak Night. *Huh, I'm Mrs. Night. Mrs. Harmony Night.*

After they were announced, he bent to kiss her. *Damn, his kiss feels real.* Harmony was slightly overwhelmed.

As cheers and well wishes rose, she couldn't help but smile. Everyone smiled. Rio slapped Kodi on the back. "Treat my cousin well," he said.

Kodiak led her to a secluded lagoon beyond the ceremonial pool as the others left them alone for their water joining.

"Where is everyone going?" Harmony wondered aloud. When Kodi stripped off his clothing, Harmony's eyes widened in panic. "What are you doing?"

"It's time for our water joining." He flashed a smile at her, his eyes mischievous. "It's the custom after a wedding ceremony for the newlyweds to mate in the blessed waters. It's good luck, helps you conceive your first child."

She shook her head and started to protest, but he pulled her close. "It's okay. We will swim for a while."

"How deep is it?" Her voice was shaky.

"Harmony, I've got you." He reached behind her. With two quick motions her dress fluttered to the ground. She clamped her arms as best she could around her naked body. Then she quickly advanced into the water, giving him an exasperated look. He finished stripping and followed her with a wolfish grin.

They swam far enough out so no one could overhear them, although the thick brush gave the illusion of privacy. Harmony soon realized the lagoon was man-made and the walls were stone. She could touch the bottom if she stood on her tiptoes. This bonus helped her relax, but Kodiak kept swimming right up to her, so she was forced to keep moving. She played the cat-and-mouse game well, until he simply disappeared underwater.

Damn him! It was the twilight of a long summer night, and she felt naked, exposed to his viewing underwater. She swam to the farthest edge and backed against the wall, waiting…waiting. She had just resolved to swim the length of the lagoon and get out when he surfaced before her, blowing air out of his nose and shaking excess water from his dark hair.

She splashed him, squeaking, "You startled me. What were you doing under there for so long?" At his devious smile her cheeks flushed. She regarded him, remembering the last time they were in the water alone together, when he'd washed her hair, massaged her skin, and then intimately grabbed her bottom.

"I was thinking." He glanced beyond her shoulder at the thick foliage behind her, as if searching for movement.

"About what?" she asked. She had been thinking about him and being alone with him, not only now in the mating pool but later in their honeymoon suite.

His copper eyes returned to hers, their coloring reminding her he was otherworldly.

"We need to come up with a plan to get away, in case Nakoma tries something. I don't trust her, or Finn."

After tomorrow their debt would be paid. Binda would have served her three days of services and they were free to leave, supposedly.

"Right. I don't trust Nakoma either, but I wish you

would reconsider about Finn. He is innocently caught up in her plans."

"Finn is not innocent." He stood and pulled her chin up. "Forget him."

The jealous demon was rearing its head again, and the thought made Harmony tingle. What was it that drove him so crazy when she defended Finn? Could he truly be jealous, thinking she might possibly choose Finn over him?

"He deserves a chance to go home, Kodi."

"With you?" he asked hoarsely.

She pulled her chin from his grasp and answered, "No, not as you think. My feelings are not for him."

His palm cupped her cheek, and she leaned into it, despite herself.

"I wish you didn't have to return. I wish..."

She wished he hadn't said that, and she was relieved that he didn't finish his sentence, because it caused her deep anguish. Damn it, she wasn't going to like him, but she couldn't control how she felt. Her body temperature acclimated to the cool water. Stretching her hand out to touch him, her fingertips tickled at his waist. His skin felt smooth under the water's surface. She glided her hand up and down his torso.

"Kodi, you could return with me." She dared to put her thoughts out there, but she hated what his answer had to be.

"You know I can't go. I'm not a Linker. It's not permitted."

"If you want to go, I know Calder would help you. Especially now that we are married. And," she tried to entice him, "there are many pearls and treasures under the human seas for the taking."

"You tempt me." His smile became a laugh, and she giggled. He cupped the nape of her neck and drew her to him.

His kisses grew ardent and she responded. She opened her mouth to him, and he dipped his tongue in, tasting her. The rolling of his tongue seemed to control the stirring at her core. The tightening of her center made her thrust her hips against his, and she came into acute contact with his need for her.

He broke their kiss with a growl.

The darkness surrounded them, and she knew the brilliant stars were shining overhead, but she couldn't look away from the light in Kodiak's eyes. They captivated her. What she felt for him was more than desire, but in this moment the craving from his mouth scorching hers was her lifeline. "Kodi, kiss me."

He obliged. She pressed her body against him once more. At her moan, he clutched her shoulders and then ran his hands down her back to once again claim her behind. He kneaded and squeezed, and she lifted her legs and hooked them around his hips.

He had full and easy access to her, but he broke their kiss once again. "Oh, Harmony. What do you want?"

Their breathing heavy, they just held each other for several moments. "I want to go inside."

"Okay. There is a feast for us." He slid his hands to her waist.

"Oh, right, a feast. I guess we should go to that." She had meant go inside to the bedroom, but she didn't elaborate. Instead, she dropped her legs and let her arms float away from his torso.

"I think I need a few minutes to swim around and cool off." He bent to kiss her briefly before releasing her and swimming away.

Harmony swam across the pool, dressed, and waited quite a while for Kodiak to join her. Their evening meal was waiting in the dining hall, where the rest of their guests also waited. Harmony tried to keep her eyes from straying back to the man she'd earlier held intimately between her thighs. During the celebratory meal, she functioned as a polite bride, but she couldn't shake the anticipation. She knew a night alone with Kodi would prove interesting.

32

The nuptial suite featured a large bed draped in opaque fabric; the same fine cloth framed the tall windows that offered sweeping views of the lake. The sound of the falls far below rumbled through the open windows. The chamber featured a pool surrounded on three sides by walls of intricate tiles.

Kodiak leaned back against the windowpane, his long legs braced. The cool night air, fragrant with pine, tugged at the curtain fabric, sending the panels floating into the room. Sipping a tall glass of water, he observed the girl attending Harmony. His thoughts returned to earlier, when he'd waited for his bride. She was a vision of loveliness, her swept-up hair showing off the delicate arch of her neck. Her shoulders were drawn back, emphasized her youthful posture as she glided across the ceremonial bridge, abundant flowers covering her slim hands. He thought she was comparable to a goddess straight out of the sea, and Kodiak's heart had hammered in his chest. The circumstances that brought her to him were unbelievable, yet now she was his—she could be his.

He ran his hand through his hair and eyed Harmony. There is no way a siren could be more tempting than the woman before him, or more dangerous to his heart. While he debated how to handle the evening, she sent him a seductive smile. He noticed her usual shyness at her exposed body was gone. She cast a level gaze at him, and he shifted. In the ceremonial pool, kissing her had been intoxicating. Just the thought of the taste of her mouth sent his internal heat churning.

The attendant bid them goodnight, and his wife stood before him, waiting. Her golden hair had been released, but the ringlets remained. His fingers twitched with expectation. The ceremonial gown had been replaced with a negligee of sorts, a near-transparent tank that reached the top of Harmony's thighs; its slits extended to either side of her breasts.

His breathing speeded up, his gaze fixated on the transparent fabric—what was underneath the transparent fabric—as she tiptoed gingerly toward him.

"Kodi, why did you do it? Why did you marry me? We didn't even try to escape... I mean, if we'd escaped then you wouldn't have had to go through with this."

Kodiak stood, and drew his brows together. She was dousing the flames of his desire with her questions he didn't feel comfortable answering. He slipped off his ceremonial robe, tossed it onto a nearby chair, and stretched his bare chest, released from the confines of his finery. He stepped close to her and grasped her hands. "Harmony, there was no way I could have let you marry Finn. He is a savage, just like the rest of them." She pulled away from him, but he plowed on. "I know you think that just because he's human, he's like you."

Kodiak recalled Finn's congratulatory hug in the dining hall. It had lingered too long as he'd whispered in Harmony's ear. And he'd made some comment about human love being different from the love between the Aquapopulo, which made Kodiak's blood boil. What did Finn know of human love anyway? He was unique in this world, and why was he deliberately throwing the word *love* around? He knew nothing about Kodiak's relationship with Harmony.

"Is that what this is about? If you married me only because you think I'd have let Nakoma marry me to Finn..." She yanked her hands from his and angrily planted her fists on her hips. "Argh!" She winced and pulled her hand back. She'd just smacked the scratch she'd gotten during her fall in the woods.

Kodiak advanced for a better look. "Are you hurt? When did this happen?"

"It was that day in the woods, the day you got back. I told you I was chased by a wolf and I fell. Then I was hanging over a ravine. That's when I got this." Her anger seemed forgotten, and she sounded dismissive.

"When Finn rescued you?" He sensed her hesitation.

"Finn scared those wolves off!"

"Wolves? I thought you said one wolf. And he's responsible for you getting hurt in the first place." Kodiak's eyes trailed the red line from her ribs to the crease of her thigh.

"It wasn't his fault, and he applied some salve."

"Finn should stay away from you, and you should forget him," he said through his clenched jaw.

"Kodi, have compassion. He's already told me to get far away from him...and from this place. He said he has demons. I know he is suffering from what he went through all those years ago. I have demons too." Her expression told him an intimate story, and he could somewhat understand her connection to a fellow human. Her next words were small. "I hope he wasn't the reason you married me."

Ignoring the pout on her irresistible mouth and the high arch of her brows, he reached to caress her cheek. "That is not the only reason." His voice gruff. His mind raced. Her *I hope he wasn't the reason you married me* rang in his ears. Legally Harmony was his, but that wasn't satisfying enough. He wanted more, but a warning bell clanged loudly in his head. *This is one treasure you can't keep.* He'd never considered crossing to her realm; then again, he hadn't planned on being married to a human. As uncertainty churned in his gut, he lifted his head and rested his lips against her forehead. She leaned into him, her hands braced on his ribs. The combination of heat and her palms sliding up and down his torso was driving him mad. He dropped kisses across her brow and down the curve of her cheek. She stretched up to give him access to her mouth. He captured her lips, and she tugged him closer, slipping her arms around his back and stoking the flames.

Never had Kodiak felt this all-consuming heat. It stimulated his very core. The thrill of possibly having her, of experiencing all of her, left him trembling. His head jerked back, and they both gasped for breath. "Harmony, you agreed to marry me." He eyes searched hers. He needed her to want him as much as he wanted her. "I don't know how long we have together in this realm before..." He couldn't finish saying *before you leave me*. "I want you."

***

His magnetic eyes with their copper flecks imprisoned her. She was mesmerized by them. His nearness had a way of dispelling her troubles. When she had touched him earlier in the pool she knew that she wanted him— all of him. He was her husband, and she didn't want to hold back. She could allow herself to let go of inhibitions and roam wherever her hands would take her. It seemed long ago when she'd decided to dislike him; it seemed silly to her now. She'd been fascinated by him the moment she'd seen him. She'd used the excuse of her grandmother's ring to put a wedge between them, but now it rested on her finger as *her* wedding ring. She was his, with the ring on her finger——a neat package. She wondered how he felt, but she couldn't ask. *If I leave – no, when I leave – I'll be leaving my husband behind. He said he couldn't come with me because it isn't allowed, and the thought of saying good-bye is killing me. Why, Kodi? Why have you made this harder for me?* This might be her only opportunity to experience the level of closeness she desired, but she knew it would cost her. Was she willing to pay the price—one more loss in her life?

"Harmony, give yourself to me." His command was laced with anguish.

A smile spread across her face, and a laugh bubbled out. Everything that had happened to her so far was plain crazy! Could she have fallen in love with him so quickly? She'd never had these feelings for anyone else, and she couldn't resist him a moment longer. "No matter what happens," she said between heated kisses, "know that tonight belongs to us, Kodi. Make me your true wife!"

33

It was their final day in the stone city on the Great Falls, and the newlyweds walked into a gathering room, where Binda was bandaging a hunter. During a recent bear hunt, the man had received a nasty claw wound that had become infected. Finn stood nearby with other hunters, giving their companion grief.

Harmony and Kodiak approached hand in hand, and Harmony raised her brows as she watched Binda. Binda turned away from the man she gave a sweet smile to, a rosy blush staining her cheeks. Harmony recognized this look from back in the trader's village when Binda had eyed a fruit vendor. The bandaged man ignored his teasing comrades and murmured a grinning thanks to Binda. He seemed to leave the table hesitantly.

Rio waved at them from just outside the open-air gathering room where he ran with some young boys kicking a ball in a field of grass. Kodiak was quick to join them, leaving Harmony to talk with Binda after her patient reluctantly left to join Finn and his friends.

The girls watched Rio and Kodiak at play, running and laughing as if it were a carefree day. Binda said casually, "Looks like things are well between you two."

Harmony mooned at her husband, and wistfully she sighed. "Yeah, but I wish things weren't so complicated. If only I didn't have to go back." Her words about not going back to her realm surprised her as much as they did Binda.

Binda, alarmed, blurted, "But you must go back. You must do everything you can to stop the destruction of the sacred land. We are all counting on you—even Kodi."

Harmony swiveled her head, pinning her gaze on her cousin. "Right, I know! You can count on me." The girls exchanged a silent nod of agreement, trust, and understanding. They let that subject lie and moved on to other topics. Harmony raised her eyebrows and asked, "Who is that man you were helping? He couldn't keep his eyes off you!"

The atmosphere that afternoon was relaxing until Nakoma and Catori joined them. The big cats found shady corners to rest in. Their riders advanced into the room, settling near the large windows that were open to the mist from the falls. It wasn't long before Nakoma sent Catori was over to gather Binda, Harmony, Rio, and Kodiak.

A crowd filled in the room, as people always seemed to follow their leader wherever she went, and everyone settled around to observe her queenly commands. Reclining on cushions plumped on the stone bench, Nakoma called Binda and Rio to come forth. Harmony practically held her breath in anticipation. *This could easily become a power struggle.* She prayed Nakoma would uphold her end of the bargain.

"Binda, I want to commend you on the items you've completed to fill my coffers and for mending the needy, as was the deal in exchange for the herbs you've collected on our tribal lands. You and your brother, Rio, are free to go. However, I'd like Harmony and Kodiak to stay longer. You can tell Calder they will remain with the tribe." Tension was high, and Harmony rushed forward to reason with Nakoma, hostility mounting within her. Finn moved closer.

"Thank you for your hospitality, but we want to return with them." Harmony sensed Kodiak at her back and immediately felt his hand on her shoulder.

"You will remain here." Nakoma turned her head, her sickle tattoo a menacing sight as she scanned the faces of her loyal subjects.

"You can't keep us here. I know why you want me to

stay. I won't use my abilities to start a war," Harmony declared.

"I did as you asked, and we *are* leaving!" Binda raised her voice, her chest heaving. Harmony and her cousin were united.

"Our people will be freed from that deceitful god, and you *will* help us." Again Nakoma's wild, dark eyes scanned the crowd. Murmurs of concern radiated through the onlookers. Catori shot her leader an odd glace at the mention of war.

Binda growled, "This isn't just about our god. This is about you, Nakoma! You want to take control. Just over a week ago in the trader's village I overheard men boasting about the soon-to-be-increased price of salt. And just who is going to mine the vast quantities of salt? Your tribesmen alone are not capable of it. Everyone knows that for years you've asked the council to have coastal clansmen assigned to do the mining, but your wishes have not been heeded. And since I've been here, I've seen the extensive weapons training the tribespeople have been undergoing." Binda turned, speaking to the crowd. "Harmony cannot stay here. She is human and must return to the human realm. Nakoma's greed will only cause you suffering!"

"Silence! You fool!" Nakoma stood, fists and teeth clenched. The giant cat stood several feet behind her, its yellow eyes fixed on Binda.

Harmony tried to hush Binda, knowing that angering Nakoma could be disastrous, but Binda stepped forward fearlessly, shaking her head and raising her voice another octave. "You will not succeed. Our realm is peaceful! You don't know what you are risking. You don't know what you are doing! Suijin is powerful in this realm. I've read about war in the other realm. You are putting their lives at risk!" She swept her arm to encompass the crowd, and then she goaded, "Besides,

Suijin will stop you. And the clans will never accept you as their leader nor worship you. You are insane to believe it."

"Ha!" Nakoma spat. "Suijin cannot stop me with these weapons." She pointed to Harmony and then at Finn, who seemed to be poised, ready for action.

"Look around you," Binda challenged. "They don't want to replace worshiping one idol for another. A leader has the privilege to lead her people and help them exist in a peaceful world. We must preserve our race—not destroy it!"

Nakoma stomped her foot like a child. Her cat jumped forward and landed menacingly at her side. Her breasts heaving, she raised her clamped fists, shaking them. She shrieked, "The clans will worship me! I am different, born to rule and given the gift of power to wield as I see fit. I will rule over the people, and if they resist... You will be the first to know my wrath." Nakoma reached for the hunting bow and quiver of arrows on her cat's back and swiftly loaded an arrow onto the bow. She pointed it at Rio. Before further negotiation, she let the arrow fly. Binda jumped in front of her brother, taking the arrow in her chest.

As screams and surprised gasps erupted around the room, Rio crumpled to the floor, the weight of his sister in his arms. Harmony dashed to Rio's side and dropped to her knees, willing everything in her to summon the heat to her hands. Something—she had to do something!

Nothing happened, no heat. Binda reached for Harmony, clasping her wrist. A tear trickled from the corner of Binda's eye, and Harmony smoothed the salty drop into Binda's hair, crying softly. "No, Binda! Stay with us." Harmony watched her cousin take her last breath; Binda's grip loosened and her hand dropped to the stone floor. Harmony heard the moan rise from Rio's throat, and she probed the pain in his teary eyes. *This can't have just happened! Oh, Binda, I'm so sorry! And Rio, I'm so sorry!* Harmony couldn't speak; she was too dazed. Her throat burned from the tears.

Harmony dragged herself off the floor, not even noticing that everyone stared in shocked silence, stunned at Nakoma's act. Kodiak grabbed her arm, to keep her from suffering the same fate as Binda, she knew.

Catori was the first to come forward, her pretty face contorted, scolding Nakoma. "Why did you do that? You can't do that!"

Nakoma was frozen, until Catori's harsh worlds seemed to send another crazy jolt through her. She loaded a second arrow and let it fly. Again screams erupted, and people took cover. Catori sank to her knees, disbelief in her eyes as she looked down at the arrow protruding from her chest. She convulsed in pain and slid to her elbow. Catori's lion, poised steps from her body, fixed his gaze on his dying master.

Nakoma looked down on her in disgust and then addressed the crowd. "This will be your fate if you don't follow me."

Harmony gaped at Finn. How would he react to the chieftain killing his lover in cold blood? Finn's face remained impassive as he watched Catori's eyes flicker, her last glance at him before she sagged to the floor, her eyes blankly stared at the ceiling. The lion crouched to the floor and tentatively sniffed her hand.

Her attention on Catori, Harmony didn't see Rio gather up his sister's body. When she heard his ragged breaths she turned, and she saw tears rolling down his face. Harmony bit her lip, holding back a sob.

Suddenly, Rio ran toward the open arched window with a burst of energy, and to everyone's shock and disbelief, he jumped with his lifeless sister in his arms into the roaring falls below. Harmony and Kodiak sprinted to the window and leaned over the railing.

Harmony screamed his name but saw nothing but rocks and churning water.

Kodiak gathered her to him, and she sobbed into his shoulder. He nodded at Nakoma in defeat.

"Take them out of my sight. Guard them!" Several women and their big cats escorted Harmony and Kodiak back to their room. When she caught Finn's eye, Harmony couldn't read his expression. If this didn't prove Nakoma was out of control, nothing would.

Harmony and Kodiak helplessly walked alongside the felines who eyed them like meat. Harmony shuffled along, unable to control her crying. Binda was dead, and probably Rio too. What was she going to tell their mother, Nami? And Calder…? He would surely regret placing those herbs in the walls of the Wentworth-by-the-Sea so long ago.

Harmony sat on the bed rubbing her puffy eyes, lost in thought. Binda was finally starting to accept her. Just yesterday, she'd worked alongside her, laughing together at the children who wanted to learn about tooth polish. Binda showed them how to rub it inside their mouth and then rinse and spit out the water. Their sweet faces beamed when their mouths foamed with white bubbles. Moments later they'd spit, sticking their tongues out at the bad taste while pointing and laughing at each other's reactions.

Harmony had burst out laughing at Binda's comment: "These little carnivores truly need the stuff!"

Before that, when Binda helped her prepare for her wedding, they'd come to an understanding. They were becoming friends. Harmony's shoulders began to pump, and she couldn't hold her grief in. She started crying and continued until there were no tears left. Kodiak sat by her side, holding her until the last few hiccups subsided.

"What about Rio? Do you think he survived that jump?" Her saturated eyelashes clumped, and Kodiak move the curtain of her hair over her shoulder.

"I believe so. He'll head for home and warn Calder. Right now, we need to figure out how to get out of here."

34

Finn watched the chieftain stare at Catori's body after Harmony and Kodiak were taken away. The crowd had evaporated. The few remaining councilmembers shuffled behind her, clearly afraid to speak. He wondered if Nakoma felt remorse. Why would she kill her most trusted friend? What had caused her to snap? Nakoma turned her muddy, wild gaze to Finn. He blankly returned her stare. He wouldn't allow her to read him. Catori was his lover and *she* killed her.

"No one will oppose me, Finn," Nakoma warned. She inhaled deeply, her nostrils flaring. Her eyes dropped again to Catori, her mouth grimly set. Abruptly she turned and left the chamber, her councilmembers reluctantly following.

Finn squatted next to Catori's body. The lion was the only one to witness his actions. This animal had spent a fair amount of time in Finn's presence. He wrapped his hand around the arrow at her breast feeling the sticky moist blood against his skin. A quick jerk freed the arrow and he tossed it aside. He lifted Catori in his arms, holding her cradled to his chest. The lion stood also but didn't follow them. With his broad shoulders and strong arms, he swiftly carried her out of the city and into the forest.

Just downstream from the falls, Finn emerged from the woods and waded into the river. His eyes caressed the face of the huntress in his arms. Catori was a spirited vixen in life but looked like a sleeping child in death. She'd been spiteful at times and took other lovers to try and make him jealous, but he enjoyed their relationship for what it was—lustful sex. Still…there had been something about her that Finn found appealing. Perhaps her independence or her teasing smile or how she loved to sneak off with him…

"You didn't deserve this, Catori," he whispered. He was up to his elbows in the river and the current was pulling at her body. He lifted her back, bringing her mouth close to his, and he pressed a kiss to her cold lips before releasing his hold. She floated in a spiral pattern until the swifter currents dragged her under.

Finn dragged his eyes from the spot where Catori disappeared under the water and forced them to look across the river, unfocused at the tree line. Eventually, he trudged from the river only to glance down at his vest, stained with blood. He pulled the fabric from his body, maneuvering it through his heavy shoulder belt, and tossed it into the river. His pulse was racing as he headed back to the city, because it was time to take action.

35

Hours later Harmony jumped to her feet as the door to their chamber opened. Finn slipped into the room, closing the door behind him. Kodiak sprang from his seat and stood between Harmony and Finn. She shoved Kodiak's protective arm out of her way.

"What are you doing here, Finn?" She didn't trust him. Kodiak was right. He'd done nothing to stop Nakoma. He stood by without a word after she killed Binda—and Catori! Harmony knew there was something between them, but he showed no emotion at her death.

"I've come to help you escape. I've given the guard and her cat their food containing a sleeping herb." Finn held up his hands in surrender.

"How do you know about sleeping herbs? You don't have a Linker in this city," Kodiak challenged, skeptical that Finn would help them.

"I've learned things traveling in these enchanted forests. How do you think I bait bears and live to tell about it?" The men locked eyes, testosterone pulsing.

"Okay!" Harmony broke their standoff, pointedly saying to Kodiak. "We are already dead in the water." She saw his eyes narrow in confusion at her statement at first, but the corner of his mouth pulled, and he gave her the teensiest of nods. Harmony knew Kodiak only agreed to let Finn help them because there was no other way.

"Finn, what's your plan?" Maybe she didn't completely trust him, but he was their best hope for escaping.

"It's already in motion." He pointed toward the window. They turned to watch the sky darken. Thick, gray clouds were rolling in at a rapid pace. "We'll take the corridors and stairs along the weaving galleries, all the way down to the base of the falls."

Through hydropower, the falls generated the energy to run the larger looms; the galleries were located adjacent to the falls. There were woman and children in those areas. Seldom were the hunters nearby. Harmony recalled her tour of the area and agreed it was a good escape route.

"Once we are at the base, I have hidden a canoe there."

The clouds were above them now, the rain as loud as the falls. Finn had to raise his voice. "The heavy rain will disrupt their arrows, and once we are in the river, the cats won't be able to catch us."

Harmony snatched a headband adorned with long feathers to cover her hair while Kodiak gathered his satchel. Cautiously opening the door, they stepped over the sleeping cat, which sprawled like a rug outside the door, and they left the tower.

The driving rain was sending people indoors. They had to duck into niches or behind doorways until the path was clear. They were soon below the lake; they heard the clacking of the looms, and the rumble of the falls vibrated in their chests. They descended to the floors below the looms where supplies were held. The final floor led to a doorway. Finn stopped them. "Five hundred yards away, in the bushes, is the canoe. They will probably see us."

They nodded at each other before Finn opened the door. As they stepped out, the pelting rain drenched them in seconds. Dashing across the spongy grass and sucking mud, Finn and Kodiak reached the bush and worked to untangle the canoe from the saturated limbs. They flipped it and shoved it into the water. Finn reached for Harmony and pulled her in. It was impossible to hear anything above the roaring falls and driving rain. Kodiak scanned the sheer cliff of the city to see if they'd been detected. He held his arm above his forehead, blocking the stinging drops from his eyes. Through the mist he saw hunters gather, pointing down at the escapees.

"They see us!" he bellowed, and he shoved the canoe off, jumping in as the current sucked it away.

They paddled toward the distant clear blue skies while Finn manipulated his hands to send lightning and gusting winds down upon the city. Harmony felt the temperature plummet and soon heard the smack and ping of hale nearby. Finn wielded his ability superbly, and Harmony wondered what *she* could be capable of. She sat in a puddle on the floor of the canoe, hunched down, peeking over the rim. Despite the raging storm, cats raced along the banks in pursuit. Finn deflected the warriors' arrows with wind. The swollen waterways swiftly moved the canoe downstream, away from their attackers.

Eventually, they drifted out of the storm. Finn pointed to a cove. "There. We need to get to the bank."

They paddled out of the current toward the shore. Once on land, Finn sent the boat back into the churning waters with a hard kick, certain the hunters would be looking for it. "We need to head east, and we can only do that over land. Come." They dashed after him. He slowed as they approached a cave not easily detected by man.

He sent a low whistle, and they heard a rustle and the shuffle of a large animal. Finn smiled, and Harmony followed his gaze. A woman stepped out from behind lush vines, and Finn rushed to clasp her shoulders. "You made it. Thank you, Amadahy."

Harmony's eyes widened in surprise at the sight of Nakoma's room attendant. Harmony whispered to Kodiak, telling him who the girl was, and that she'd been kind enough to provide a bouquet of flowers for her wedding ceremony.

Amadahy smiled shyly up into Finn's face. "The herbs worked as you said. She's asleep."

Finn stepped away from her and disappeared into the opening of the cave. A moment later he led out three elk.

He handed Amadahy one of the leads. "Hurry back before Nakoma awakens." He stepped close and lifted her chin. "I won't forget what you've done for me." The girl's face softened, adoration in her eyes as Finn bent and kissed her pretty lips. "Be safe." He turned, leading the elk toward Harmony and Kodiak.

Kodiak swung his leg up, but before he could reach for her, Harmony ran to Amadahy.

"Thank you!" Harmony slipped off the bracelet Nami had given her and offered it to Amadahy, who accepted it with a smile. The two hugged good-bye before Harmony ran back to Kodiak, who offered his hand. Mounted on the elk, Harmony waved over her shoulder at Amadahy and smiled in gratitude.

Finn steered the elk east. They picked through the thick forest, careful to hide their trail. By nightfall they made camp under a thick hollow of trees and rested on a bed of leaves. They dared not make a fire and ignored the grumble in their bellies.

Kodiak excused himself and wandered into the woods. Harmony took this opportunity to thank Finn for rescuing them. And to ask, "Finn, will you come back with me? What could Nakoma accomplish without your ability?"

The whites of Finn's eyes reflected in the moonlight that shone through the trees. He sighed. "It's not an easy choice for me, Harmony." There was a long pause. "I never wanted innocent people to die. Battling a god for the good of the people is one thing, but Nakoma killed her own." The anguish in his voice remained raw.

"Catori was loyal... It was senseless."

"I'm sorry about Catori. I know you had feelings for her," she said, squinting to read the expression on his face, but darkness shielded him.

They remained silent as they heard Kodiak return. After Kodiak sat next to Harmony, Finn said, "I must explain to you both that there is more to all of this than you know. Nakoma's tired of the trading laws and wants to obtain riches by upping the bargaining power with salt. The revenue from the quarry would allow the empire to expand by building beyond the falls, and she needs workers to carry out her plans. She plans to persuade the clan's councilmembers to entice the clan people to work for her. But she would only pay the laborers slave-wages."

"She can't force them to leave the coast," Harmony said, skeptically.

Finn confided, "Nakoma has been training her hunters to use as an army against the coastal villages if they resist. There is a tribal village south of the city were the training is taken place. I have met with the warriors from that village."

Harmony felt Kodiak's form stiffen at the mention of the coastal villages, and she hugged the arm he'd wrapped around her shoulder. Finn's leaving with her wouldn't stop Nakoma from waging war on the defenseless villagers.

Kodiak barked at Finn. "You knew this, and you were still going to help her. You wanted power and wealth, just like she does. You human scum!"

As the men scrambled to their feet, Harmony did too, and she turned to holler into Kodiak's face. "Stop! Kodi, stop!"

Kodiak's fist was cocked and ready.

Harmony grabbed him around his neck with one hand and slid her other hand through his hair, guiding his head so he looked at her. The moonlight reflected across his furious face. "Please, he's here with us now. Finn has changed. He's helping us."

She prayed their trio would make the long trek back to the coast in one piece. Considering the way Kodiak and Finn fluffed their feathers at each other, she felt right to be concerned.

"Fine," Kodiak snarled, "but when we get to the village you need to talk to Calder and the council, Finn, and tell them all that you know."

"Of course," Finn agreed.

After a few moments, the energy around them settled, and they returned to their makeshift beds.

***

Finn struggled with his demons once more. He had wanted to rule at Nakoma's side, and he knew the stakes. Now, everything was in chaos. Where was his place in all of this? Nakoma would realize it was him who helped Kodiak and Harmony escape. He considered Harmony's question. Was leaving this realm a possible solution? He felt compelled to help the people, be a true leader. If he pursued this path then he knew what to do first. Kill Nakoma. Kill her, and take her place as leader of the tribe. His dark side wrestled with the notion. *What will that make me? A conqueror or a hero? Or can I go back with Harmony to the unknown?* He forced his breathing to slow. He needed to sleep now. They'd need to leave well before dawn. The hunters were expert trackers. He knew because he'd trained them.

36

Harmony stood on the bank looking down the hill at the Hudson River. The air was fresh and still; it was a beautiful day. They'd made record time reaching this point, but their urgent pace had proven grueling. The trio was scarcely averaging four hours of sleep each night, traveling in darkness, and eating only the nuts and jerky Finn had packed in his satchel left them grouchy and short-tempered. She brooded about the upcoming river crossing. *The elk kept me above the surface the last time, so why worry?* She tried to reassure herself. Something upstream caught Harmony's eye. She watched a young girl frolic and heard her hum a tune. A siren.

When Harmony heard underbrush snapping and fast-moving footfalls from the woods she rushed to meet her companions, who'd gone to scout. They were followed, despite trying to hide their trail.

"They're here!" Finn yelled.

Kodiak grabbed her hand and ran with her through the grass to where the elk grazed. They mounted and picked their way to flatter ground, where entry into the river was possible.

Harmony nearly jumped out of her skin at the roars from the big cats that thundered out of the underbrush south of them. There was a considerable distance between the two groups, but crossing the river could be slow going and Harmony wondered how fast the cats could swim. Suddenly, Harmony formulated a plan. Recalling the siren, she started to sing as they entered the water. The elks sank to their backs, submerging the riders in the cold, swift-moving current. The cold snatched at Harmony's voice, but she shivered once and then sang louder.

"What are you doing?" Kodiak asked over his shoulder.

"You'll see!" she whispered in his ear. Then she sang the next line. As her song echoed along the river to the north, several heads emerged from the water, and soon other, more ghostly sounding voices joined Harmony's.

Arrows started to fly around them. Finn slid off the elk's back to get safely underwater, allowing the beast to swim faster. The warrior women with their cats and the tribesmen riding elk now entered the river, simultaneously sending their arrows north toward the dozen sirens that closed in on their intended victims.

Harmony and Kodiak slid into the water and their elk swam faster. They were about halfway across the river, in deep water. Harmony turned to the boys and yelled, "Go!" She treaded water, continuing to sing.

Finn had seen what she was capable of with the sirens and plowed on, but Kodiak had only heard. He stopped when she did. He wouldn't leave his wife, who hated deep water.

"Go, Kodi! I will lure the sirens closer. They won't come near me, but they will go after the tribesmen."

"No, Harmony, keep swimming!"

His concern for her safety touched her, but it was her turn to protect him. She turned her back to him, continuing her song.

The warriors advanced, and the sirens cunningly picked them off. A few were hit by arrows.

When Harmony's song ended she started to swim toward the riverbank with Kodi. Finn was already on solid ground with the two elk, waving his arms at them to hurry. Harmony looked back and noticed that not even one warrior had made it to the middle of the river. The riderless cats returned to the safety of the shore, roaring for their lost masters. Harmony turned toward the shore with a triumphant smile and found herself face to face with a siren. The siren, young and lovely, peeled back her lips and opened her mouth, revealing razor-sharp teeth. Suddenly the siren's eyes glazed over in pain, she screamed, and blood gurgled from her mouth.

Kodiak reached the shore and turned to help Harmony out of the current to discover she was missing. Finn grabbed his arm, holding him still, not letting him return to the water. He exhaled in horror. They watched a siren swim in front of Harmony and heard a scream. Kodiak thought the scream came from Harmony, whose face was contorted, but he watched Harmony thrust the siren away and swim freely toward them. The siren's torso bobbed above the water, the skin of her chest and shoulders burned and steaming as she convulsed.

As Harmony reached the grassy bank Kodiak lifted her out of the river, pulled her several feet away, and hugged her tightly. She arched, turning her head to watch the other sirens abruptly slip under the water, out of sight. The one she burned lay dead, tangled in the brush along the river's edge.

"I killed her! I killed them!" Her tiny voice shook. She had literally killed the creature who was trying to kill her.

***

"It's okay. It's okay, Harmony. You did what you had to. You saved us and probably spared the coastal villages from an assault. You gave us a big head start. Come, we must go." Kodiak knew she felt remorse that she'd called upon the sirens to attack the tribespeople, resulting in their deaths. Kodiak coaxed his wife upright. The trio mounted the elk and were quickly trotting off into the foothills.

Kodiak had been astonished to witness Harmony's ability to incinerate the siren. She'd harnessed her powerful energy to save Binda from the sea serpent before, but today she'd sent the tribal attackers to their deaths. Kodi heard her softly crying behind him during their hasty retreat. He knew the tender heart of his human wife was good; her remorse wasn't lost on him.

37

Past the Hudson River and well north of the dreaded swamp, they traveled into the hills. After making camp by a stream, Kodiak waded in to find them food while Finn used his slingshot to acquire some meat. Feeling safe after the hunters were taken away by the sirens, they dared to make a fire. While Finn spun a skewered squirrel over the flames, Kodiak laid the gutted fish, wrapped in wet leaves, onto the embers.

Harmony had looked to Finn after they'd mounted the elk and left the Hudson River behind them. He'd given her a nod and in that moment she understood his demons. He'd warned her to get away from here, that it would test her humanity. And it had. Without thinking of the consequences, she'd summoned those sirens to attack the tribal warriors. They died because of her.

She stared into the fire, lost in thought. *What is this ability? Why has this happened to me? How could I have done that?* She sensed Kodiak and Finn exchange glances.

Finn said, "Harmony, they may have told you this is a peaceful world, but it's not. We do what we have to, just like you did what you had to. If you hadn't stopped them, we wouldn't have a chance to return to the village to warn the coastal people."

"Maybe this is entirely my fault," she cried miserably. "If I hadn't been snooping around in that old building I wouldn't have found those herbs or crossed over. We wouldn't have crossed into the tribal lands in search of the ingredients to send me back, and Nakoma would never have discovered my ability. Binda would still be alive. And Rio… Maybe this whole mess could have been avoided. Maybe you could have worked out peace negotiations."

Finn shook his head.

Kodiak caressed her shoulder, and said, "None of this is your fault. There are greater powers at work here. You just got caught up in them. Calder said you have a special connection to this place. You are the only human with Aquapopulo blood in your veins. That has to mean something."

Finn's voice rasped. "What did you just say?"

Harmony swallowed, unable to tell her fellow human that she wasn't completely human. That secret had been safeguarded, but now she felt like she'd deceived him. He was the only full-blooded human in this realm. She was glad when Kodiak gave him a summary, explaining she was Calder's great-great-granddaughter.

"I had no idea! You look completely human to me—well, your eyes are a little unusual." Finn studied her face, and she felt her cheeks turn pink.

Over their meal, both men emphatically agreed none of this was her fault. They made her feel a little better, though she wondered how she would live with herself after what she'd done. She murmured, "All right." She ate silently while they argued over the best strategies for dealing with Nakoma and her warriors.

A couple nights later, wrapped in the arms of her husband in the mountain forests of Vermont, Harmony stirred.

She was small. Her red-and-white-mitten covered hands stretched upward, holding onto her mother's. Her mother's blue-gray parka was zipped tight against the cold, her hood over her head. Wavy brown hair streamed out the bottom and hung down the front of the parka. The day was hazy, bright, and Harmony squinted up to see her mother's face. The sunlight winked like flash photography, but then the hood shifted, blocking the sunlight, and she saw golden-brown eyes smiling back at her.

The cold wind blew across her rosy cheeks, but she didn't care. She was happy. That happy feeling evaporated when they heard cracking sounds. Panic and fear set in, and then she plunged into the wet darkness. Icy fingers worked their way into her jacket, bloating it, causing her skin to go numb. That was when his face appeared.

He came toward her, bare arms extended. His expression changed as she held her hands out. Her mittens drifted away. Heat built in her body, replacing the numbness. He came at her, but she was deflecting him.

Suddenly he was gone, and she spied him dragging her mother away. She opened her mouth to scream, but it filled with icy water. At that moment she was yanked from the depths...

"Harmony! Wake up!" Kodiak shook her, and she shot up to a sitting position. "Harmony, you were moaning. You were having a dream. It's okay."

Finn lifted himself onto an elbow in the early morning light. "Is everything okay?" His hand was on his hip, hovering over his knife.

"I remember. I was there." She swallowed hard, blinking at the images in her mind.

"Remember what?" Kodiak coaxed.

"The day my mother fell though the ice and drowned. I was there. I fell in with her. I saw him, Suijin. I know it was Suijin! He came after me, but I used my ability to hold him off—like with the sea serpent. He was confused at first, but when he couldn't take me he turned and took my mother." She choked in horror.

"You saw Suijin in the human world?" Kodiak leaned back on his hands. "He knows you have a unique ability, Harmony—and that you've used it in both worlds. There are no such abilities in your realm. Not any that I've heard of." He looked to Finn for confirmation, but Finn shook his head. "This interwoven connection you have to both realms is astounding, unprecedented."

She nodded grimly. She tried to make sense of her surfacing memories. She whimpered, "I was there, but they never told me."

My five-year-old brain must have blocked it out. I've suppressed the horrible memory of my mother drowning before my eyes, and no one spoke of my involvement. It was not even reported on in the newspaper clipping.

The year she'd spent with her father before he died was vague. While he was away at sea for months at a time to support her, she'd stayed with her grandparents. So it was a natural transition after his death for her to live with them. Her grandparents never talked about the day they lost their daughter. When she'd asked about it later in her childhood they said it was an accident. Harmony cast a level glance at Kodiak. "It all makes sense now—why he's taken everyone I love so he could single me out. Your god wants to destroy me." She said bitterly to Finn, "I see why Nakoma wants to terminate Suijin." Harmony felt terrified for her life. A god who wanted her dead was after her!

Kodiak attempted to reason with her. "Harmony, you can't make this personal. There is too much at stake. Calder says if Suijin is appeased then the peace will remain in balance. It's better than starting a war, as you yourself have said."

She jumped from the blanket shouting, "That was before I was sure he'd killed my whole family! He is responsible for drowning all of them! It finally makes sense. Kill off any Aquapopulean bloodline in my realm so he can control the people of this realm. Well, I'm not staying here. Argh—I hate this place!" She didn't want to hear what Kodiak had to say, even if it made sense.

She was still healing from old wounds.

In the predawn light, they packed up. Harmony tossed her words over her shoulder at Kodiak: "I'm riding with Finn. I want to talk to him about Nakoma." Kodiak immediately stepped in front of her. His sudden movement caught her off guard, but she noticed his concern.

"Harmony!" His eyes pried into hers with an intensity that made her inhale sharply. "I want you to know I will do whatever I can to ease your suffering. While you are here, while you are my wife, you are a part of me."

Her eyes fluttered closed as his head dipped down, and at the brush of his lips she reached for him. His vow obliterated her doubt about his feelings for her, and she let him know with her response how she felt about him. The long sensual kisses left them both breathless.

Caressing the angular curve of his cheekbone, she said, "I'm still riding with Finn." Backing away, she hid her smile. He stood with his hands on his hips, head cocked to the side; a line appeared between his brows.

***

Kodiak saw there was no use in protesting. He was learning that Harmony could be determined when she wanted to be. Maybe Finn could talk some sense into her. No one wanted a war, especially Harmony, but Kodiak knew so little about her and her human life that he felt at a loss to help her. He watched Finn reach for her elbow and hoist her behind him, and then he returned Kodiak's stare with raised eyebrows. Kodiak turned away, momentarily focusing on the task of mounting, not wanting to look at Finn's smug expression.

Kodiak led the way to the north road. The rough mountain paths were abandoned as the ground leveled and the road led them closer to the clan village.

On a flat roadway, Kodiak mulled over his feelings for Harmony. When he heard her brief laugh, he jealously glanced over his should at the pair on the other elk. Rolling his eyes, Kodiak labeled Finn egotistical. The fact that Finn had plotted to take over the clan in his village left a bad taste in his mouth. Even now, Finn's very existence irritated Kodiak. He didn't want Harmony sitting with him, or including him, or especially not traveling back to the human realm with him. All Kodiak wanted to do right now was be with his wife. He hungered to strip away her clothes and make love to her. They'd had only one night together, their wedding night. The burning desire to be with her again consumed him. He wanted more of her, the taste of her, the heat he felt. Kodiak rubbed his neck trying to quell his building arousal. Looking down the road, he sighed. *And here we are, on the run to a place she'll leave soon after we arrive. Damn you, Finn!*

38

Harmony silently pondered her impact here as they picked their way off the mountain path. If she went back to the human realm to her old life, pretending none of this had ever happened, she could move on. She would fight to preserve the Wentworth because it meant a lot to her and her family—that would never change. What more could Suijin take from her? If he came after her again she knew she could protect herself, as long as her ability still worked. What about the Aquapopulo? Even if she managed to stop the tearing down of the Wentworth, somehow restoring balance, what about their safety from Nakoma? Who would protect them? Would their god intervene? Supposedly, he was a god who sent his sirens to drown innocent victims. He didn't seem like someone who cared about their welfare.

"Finn, tell me about Nakoma and the Linker Gale. It seems to me like Gale planted the seeds of a takeover when he brought you to this realm."

"When I was brought over it was a time of transition for the tribe. The former leader was in his final stage of life, and Nakoma had trained to take his place. She was in full control while he rested during his last couple of years. Nakoma was young then, and Gale was constantly at her side. As you know, he was banished shortly after bringing me over. I'm sure he wanted to keep my existence a secret, but let's just say I wasn't very cooperative." The elk's movements on the sloping forest floor while gaining steady ground had Harmony tightened her arms around Finn's square waist. Realizing Kodiak's brooding glances meant she was clinging entirely too intimately to Finn, she sent Kodiak an apologetic smile. His grim mouth and darkened eyes told her he wasn't happy.

Harmony refocused on her conversation with Finn. "So what was Gale like?"

"I will never forget his face or his words to me. He told me I was special. Apparently he's very smart, knowledgeable of many things human. He passed into our world more often than any other known Linker. But I think that is what made him dangerous. And the elders thought so too. Humans are considered a destructive, all-consuming race. It was forbidden to bring a human into this realm, and yet Gale had done so."

"So where does someone who's cast out go? Is he still alive?" Harmony wondered. With no one to stop Nakoma, she could allow Gale to return.

"No one has seen him in many years. Nakoma's predecessor advised her to take harsh action against Gale to appease Suijin. Everything defaults to *pleasing* the god." Harmony understood his confusion over what made religious sense and what didn't. She didn't have the heart to tell him that the various religions in their birth realm were far more complicated.

"It was the first time someone was cast out of tribal lands and prohibited from the coastal villages in generations. Word was sent throughout the villages that the Linker Gale was in exile, the charge: unethical deed." Finn glanced over his shoulder at her. "I remember when Gale spoke to Nakoma about the *gift* he had brought her, which was me." He snorted. "Neither I nor Nakoma knew I had abilities at that time. I don't know what Gale suspected I could do. Nakoma was conflicted about sending Gale away, but she had no choice. That was what the people wanted. She took Gale's advice to assimilate me into the tribe. Eventually the tribespeople treated me like one of them. I might have been brought to this realm through less than ethical means, but once Nakoma knew about my abilities she was unwilling to set *this* asset free. She needs me."

"Finn, that is just one more reason for you to come with me. I can't promise anything, but I'll help you assimilate back into our society." At Finn's silence, she glanced at her husband. If Kodiak returned with her, she'd help him adapt to her realm too. Both men seemed reluctant to join her.

39

Finn conjured a thick fog to reduce visibility to a minimum as they made the arduous journey to one of the roadside trader's posts. Since leaving behind the Hudson River, the site of Harmony's deadly attack, they'd slowed their pace a bit, taking time to hunt and cook a meal each day. Kodiak had suggested they spend this one night at the post to get a decent meal and sleep in a bed. Finn guessed Kodiak wanted a night alone with Harmony before their inevitable separation. Admiring Harmony's stamina, Finn could tell she'd benefit from some rest, and he had to admit even he was drained—mentally drained, as he'd still not decided whether to go with her to the human realm or not.

The trio claimed a dark corner in an establishment that served both meat and vegetarian dishes. Finn chuckled when Harmony gave Kodiak an apologetic look while she sank her teeth into hot, greasy pork chops. He swiftly dug into his plate, piled high with meat, and his mouth thanked him by lighting up all his taste buds. Once their stomachs were full they would come up with a plan.

Finn washed down his meal with brew and placed the mug down on the wooden table. He flagged a server to order another. "Harmony, do you want a brew? Kodiak?" She nodded and Kodi wrinkled his nose, so he ordered two. Finn had let her taste his brew earlier when it came to the table. After smelling it, and taking a sip, she'd laughed, and said it was beer. "It figures you'd like brew!" she'd scoffed good-naturedly. Finn couldn't help but smile at her. Once the frothy mugs were delivered, they turned to dire matters.

"So your Linker, Calder, thinks if you return to the

human world you can somehow restore balance or appease the god? How are you planning on doing that?"

Harmony shrugged and sighed. "Honestly, Finn, I don't know. There's a building at home, Wentworth-by-the-Sea, that resembles the temple in this realm—you know, the one they built in honor of their god on sacred land."

Finn nodded. "I know about the Aquapopulean evolution on that island. What does Suijin have to do with what happens in the human world?" He knew more about the human race from the library than from his own childhood memories. And he served no god.

"Right. So anyway, in the human word the building is set to be destroyed. According to Calder, if the sacred ground is disrupted it will have adverse effects here…on that island, I'm guessing." She shrugged. "I've already been working with others to preserve the building, so if I'm successful, then the crisis is adverted. As far as Suijin is concerned… I don't even know what he's capable of besides drowning people. Appeasing him—I couldn't guess."

"Harmony, he is different from the gods in your realm," Kodiak answered. "Suijin may be able to travel to both realms, but he is earth-bound and cannot return to the sky." Kodiak placed his elbows on the table, speaking quietly to both of them. "He's looks like a man, but he has scales. They say at one time he walked among us, and he has an island fortress of his own in the sea. In fact, long ago, the Aquapopuleans lived there with him, but not anymore. He's distanced himself from our kind physically, but I think he is always watching."

"After I make the crossing into my realm, I'll be sure to stay away from the water." Terror overtook her face, and she blanched. "If I survive the crossing." Her fingers massaged her temples.

"Of course you'll survive!" Kodiak reproached,

plucking her hand from her face.

"Are you going with her, Kodiak?" Finn asked. Kodiak's sudden discomfort told Finn that his taboo question was a sore subject. Either the newlywed couple hadn't discussed it or Kodiak wasn't going.

"Are you, Finn? Are you going to return to the human world, where you belong?" Kodiak shot back, not answering the sensitive question.

Finn snorted. "Where I belong?" He leaned over the table. "I've been here more than half of my life. I'm a skilled hunter and trained warrior of the tribe. They call me the fearless bear hunter!" He held his hands up in mock praise before he bitterly went on. "I'm counselor and right hand of the chieftain. And I can control the weather." His eyes narrowed. "But I can barely remember what my own mother looks like, although she was blond, like Harmony."

Harmony reached across the table to rest her hand over his. Kodiak pressed his lips together at her intimate gesture.

Finn noticed the light from the candle on the table reflect in Harmony's amber eyes. They glowed like the Aquapopulos'. Finn froze at the eerie coincidence. She'd told him her great-great grandfather was an Aquapopulean Linker, and the evidence of her bloodline was in her eyes.

"Finn, I'm sorry for the circumstances of your crossing, but you can make a life for yourself in the human realm. You wouldn't be the only one *alone*. I've lost my whole family too."

Finn connected with her; they'd both been through so much. Two humans thrust into a realm via a violent crossing. He took her warm hand, feeling kinship with her. Kodiak glared at him. After a moment, Finn let go of her hand and he sat back, crossing his arms. "Still, if I leave, what can Calder and the coastal villages do about

Nakoma? I fear I may have to take measures to protect them."

"Yes, I agree Nakoma must be taken out of her leadership role, one way or another. In the meanwhile, we will have to prepare the villages for an attack," Kodiak reasoned, slinging his arm around Harmony's shoulder.

Finn watched her sag against him. He saw the way she looked at Kodiak—clearly she was in love with him. Finn said, "We will figure it out with the coastal council. It's getting late, we should get some sleep."

***

The inn's small room offered a step-down bath. While Kodi stripped down, his pulse pounded in anticipation of being alone and intimate with his bride. First into the waist-deep water, he scanned her every naked curve as she swayed into the water. They dropped under to wash away the dust from their eyes and bodies after the long day's ride. The soft water eased their aches. Soon they were in each other's arms. Kodiak braised kisses on each of her eyebrows, on the tip of her nose, and then he captured her lips over and over, coaxing her to desire more. Even knowing she was exhausted after the grueling ride down the mountain road over the last few days, he couldn't let this opportunity pass. Her hands began to roam frantically around his body, and his head dropped back as a half-cry-half-groan tore from his lips. He wanted to go slow and enjoy her, loving her to his fullest capability.

On the road two nights ago, they had finally had a window of opportunity to be intimate when Finn left them alone to hunt. The moment Finn was out of sight, Kodiak had pinned Harmony against a tree, pressing against her, ravishing her mouth with his tongue. Her taste was so exotic and intoxicating he thought he'd complete his release just from kissing her.

When she shoved him away, he was lost until she advanced with a bold and hungry look in her eyes. She lifted her hands to his shoulders and pressed him down until he knelt before her. He lifted her tunic and placed wet kisses along her belly, inhaling her scent. He'd yanked at her clothing and explored until she grasped his wayward locks and tugged his head back. He looked up at her, her prisoner. Then she knelt too, kissing him and leaning him back onto the leaves. She moved against him, avoiding his plunging efforts. Just when he thought he'd burst, she'd clamped down on him. He bit hard on his lip, stifling his pent-up roar.

That memory had burned in his mind until this very moment. With her there before him, again he couldn't wait. He lifted her under his arm, and she squealed as he strode from the pool, carelessly splashing water over its sides. He tossed her, slippery and wet, on the sheets. With her arms open to him, he laid against her, pressing her into the soft mattress. Swiftly dashing his tongue across the column of her neck and down the valley of her breasts, he inhaled, unable to get enough of her sweet, intoxicating scent. He could hardly wait a second longer; his arousal was nearly at its pinnacle. He clawed the sheets as his mouth worked up her torso delivering soft kisses until he reached her mouth. On his elbows above her, his hands, fistfuls of sheets at an attempt to control his desire, he paused from kissing her. He used all his strength to wedge his knee between her legs, but she wouldn't budge. Instead, she reached down and stroked him. He sucked in air through his teeth as he dragged his gaze to hers. Her brow was raised, questioning his next move, but he was frozen, barely able to hold back. Together they paused. She caressed his face, and her amber eyes spoke volumes. He knew from her playful smile the satisfaction she felt as she drove him mad with her touch. She sensed when he was ready and relaxed her legs.

Once tightly joined, he gripped her hands and drew them over her head, lacing their fingers together. Their eyes locked. Their noses touching, he stretched into her, invading and occupying the deepest part of her. The intense heat of her grip was like nothing he'd ever experienced. She squirmed beneath him until he began his rhythmic crusade, taking them both to a gratifying end.

Rolling on his back holding her, he pressed her heated skin to his. Her damp hair tangled around his arm and under his back. With her shoulder wedged in the crock of his arm, her head rested on the pillow, touching his. Although every ounce of him had physical invaded her moments ago, Kodiak's heart both ached and rejoiced at the realization that it was she who held a much deeper penetration. His heart was totally consumed by her. Kodiak thought of himself as a treasure seeker, and he thought he might have found his greatest jewel yet.

40

Harmony stroked the elk's soft fir and silently bid the animal good-bye. They'd reached the final trading village and traded the elks for a canoe. They settled in the boat and skimmed the water's surface not much past noon, which should put them in the coastal village that evening. Finn and Kodiak's powerful arms moved the canoe efficiently along the course, and she thanked them for getting her back safely when she recognized where she was. With overwhelming relief, she smiled when they pulled up to the dock, her cousins' dwelling in sight.

Stepping out of the house into the darkness of the evening, Rio waved, his smile sad.

"He made it!" she whispered, relieved, pressing her hand to her heart as if she was feeling the loss of Binda all over again. The last they'd seen of Rio was when he'd jumped out the window in the tribal city with his sister's lifeless body in his arms. No one knew if he'd lived through the jump into the falls.

Harmony climbed onto the dock from the canoe and ran to Rio. She hugged him a long while. "I'm so happy you are alive! And I'm so, so sorry about Binda." She sniffled. She felt semi-responsible for Binda's fate. If Harmony hadn't crossed over, they never would have made the treacherous journey, and Binda would still be alive. Rio assured her he'd given his sister a proper water burial before returning to the village.

Nami and Calder emerged at the commotion, and Harmony was quickly folded into her aunt's embrace, both women with tears in their eyes. The boys climbed the steps, and Kodiak clasped Rio in a bear hug.

Harmony knew Kodiak had held his feelings in check

about whether or not his childhood friend had survived the jump. She could see the clear relief on his face now. Harmony introduced Finn, who was eyed with curiosity. Calder greeted each of them, offering them a seat inside.

Once they were settled, Calder commented, "I hear a joining ceremony has taken place."

Harmony warmed at the smile that perked up Kodiak's face. Her heart squeezed at Calder's next comment, however.

"I was surprised to hear that my great-great-granddaughter had married a man of this realm when she is destined to return to her own realm. You do understand that you must go back." Calder's voice was gentle, but firm. He added, "Rio told me you've managed to gather the remaining herbs. Do you have them with you?"

Harmony mutely nodded.

Kodiak's said, "She has what you need. And we did what we had to regarding our marriage."

Harmony understood Calder's underlying question—what were they going to do now that they were married? She couldn't speak for Kodiak.

Calder brows lifted. "I will prepare the mixture and you can cross soon. You will have to say good-bye to your spouse. He is forbidden to cross."

"We understand." Kodiak remarked, curtly.

"About that," Harmony spoke up, "I've offered Finn the chance to return to our realm—with me—if he wants to. He is human after all." She glanced at Finn; it would be like taking Tarzan out of the jungle. She dared not look at Kodiak because she knew she'd crumble in tears.

Calder's bushy brows snapped together, but he nodded. "I cannot guarantee your safety, Finn, if you choose to cross."

"Understood," Finn replied.

"Right now, we need to warn the council of what's

developing." Kodiak injected. "Time is of the essence."

Harmony calmly recounted all that had happened in the tribal city: how Nakoma made her stay behind while the others gathered the last ingredient, forcing her to tell who she was. And how she'd met Finn, and what his ability was. Then she confessed she'd used her ability again with sirens, twice.

Finn spoke up, when Harmony became distressed about the sirens, turning to another dire problem. "The tribal council became agitated when they heard about Nakoma's murderous acts and wild ideas. But she has become powerful and no one dare oppose her." Finn held up his hands. "She's built an army. We know your clans have no weapons, generals, or skills to combat renowned hunters. She will come and take full advantage of you."

"I see. I hoped it would never come to this." Harmony thought Calder's wrinkled brow and wise, bright eyes showed his age. He looked tired.

Kodiak slid his arm around Harmony's shoulder. She turned her head to take in his copper-flecked eyes. The gravity of his home being threatened undoubtedly weighed on him. Would he stay here and be forced to engage in a possible battle? If Nakoma brought her hunters with their bows, it would be a massacre—the clan wouldn't stand a chance. Kodiak could lose his life! Harmony felt the rush of emotion, and tears moistened her eyes.

Calder stood, and her eyes shifted to him as she blinked back her tears. "I will arrange a council meeting at the Wellness. In the meantime, I'll start drying and preparing the herbs. Why don't I take you along with me to Wellness? There are plenty of rooms where you can stay until all this is sorted out."

The council members met the next evening at the Wellness after a light dinner was served. Finn was instrumental in advising them about what to expect and offering strategies for neutralizing the situation. He told them Nakoma wanted coastal workers for her salt mines, and she wanted premium prices for the salt. Both would make her rich and more powerful.

The hour grew late. After stifling several yawns, Harmony slipped from the room and climbed two flights of stairs to her room.

When she entered, she didn't bother to turn on any lights. Crossing to the window, she gazed at the black, moving ocean, knowing she'd be in it soon enough. Once the herbs were ready, she needed to leave. She'd said she hated this place, but in truth she felt she was part of it. She had family and a husband here, the very people she wanted to protect by leaving.

In the silence, she heard the door open. The hallway illuminated Kodiak's outline before he closed the door. He advanced toward her in the dark.

"Are you okay? I turned around and you were gone." The concern in his voice was making this situation harder.

"Sorry. I was tired and I...I can't stop thinking about leaving." She slid her palm up his arm. "I can't stop thinking about leaving *you*."

He cupped her face in his hands and whispered, "Only Linkers can cross. They are marked. I could try, but..."

"I know, I know! If I didn't need to return, I'd just stay."

"Oh, Harmony!" he said, grief-stricken. His mouth rushed hers; his kisses were desperate and urgent.

They tugged away each other's clothing never moving more than an inch away from the other. Backing toward the bed, Kodiak supported her back until she rested against the soft blanket and his smooth skin pressed against hers. Sorrow flooded her. Tears seeped from her eyes while he made love to her. She had crossed an ocean, a realm, to find him. As fate played its cruel hand, she'd have to give him up.

Several days later, Harmony met Finn in a private room in the library, hoping to convince him to return with her. Before she could say all she wanted to, Calder appeared in the doorway. "Here you are. I've got something for you, Harmony." He handed her a tin similar to the one she'd found in the wall at the Wentworth. "Whatever you can do to keep this land at peace is greatly appreciated, although I fear this may all be in vain. We will pray to Suijin to help us if Nakoma decides to strike our villages."

When Kodiak enter the library, Harmony sensed the tension in the air. Kodiak walked up to her and looked at the tin she held up to him.

"It's ready. I need to go soon." Harmony gulped, melancholy bubbling inside her. She needed to say good-bye to her only living relatives. And what of the man she married? She'd ask him to go with her, and he affirmed that he couldn't cross. Would he try? And what of Finn—where would he ultimately feel at home?

Calder said, "The council has agreed to establish negotiations with Nakoma's council. We are preparing to send a messenger. Our citizens are organizing a tribute to appease Suijin. Prayers are already underway." He turned to Finn. "What have you decided? Do you want to return with Harmony?"

Harmony cringed at the desperation in her voice when she asked, "Calder, is it true only Linkers can cross? Has any non-Linker ever done so?"

Calder's smiled sympathetically. "I'm sorry, Harmony, but I have never read about a regular citizen crossing realms. I do not know if it's possible."

Finn glanced at Harmony's disappointed face. Her brokenhearted husband loomed at her side. "I will return with Harmony. See what the other realm has to offer. I can always journey back here, right?"

"These herbs do not burn away and can be used again, many times," Calder confirmed.

Harmony's eyes grew round at this news. This left her options open, even if the crossing wasn't something she ever wanted to experience again.

Calder cautioned, "Traveling through the portal is dangerous. It shouldn't be done too many times. I know from experience. I have gone through more times than anyone I know, and several times I suffered physically with massive headaches for weeks, to the point of being bedridden."

Harmony's stomached cramped in fear over her impending crossing. Although she hadn't experience any physical symptoms as Calder described, her fear of deep water was enough to paralyze her.

"Well, I'll gather the others to say good-bye, if you are ready." At her nod, Calder shuffled from the room.

Finn, who was leaning against a table, straightened. He thumbed toward the door. "I'll wait for you out there." The door closed quietly when he exited the room.

***

Turmoil expanded within Kodiak as he tried to decipher his feelings. He pulled her into his arms and planted a soft kiss on her mouth. She opened to him, but it was like a knife twisting in his gut, forcing him to admit what he was really feeling. He didn't want her to go, but it was out of his control.

When he'd lied to Nakoma, pretending he was involved with Harmony, he'd thought, *This is just a lie.* When he'd gone through with the ceremony, he thought, *This is just pretend.* When he was overcome with passion for her, he thought, *This is just desire.* When she stood here before him, about to give him his freedom back, he thought, *I love this woman.*

41

In two weeks' time, Nakoma efficiently moved an army of two hundred of her best hunter-warriors east to the coast. These hunters had been secretly training in combat for years. During their sequenced hunting excursions, she'd rotated the units into an underground facility just up the falls, where they were instructed by one with knowledge of war: Gale the Linker. Although Gale never showed himself to the tribesmen who had ultimately banished him, he used the hunters from the southern villages to instruct them. The elite trained there, many others trained in the southern village. Gale's trusted warriors, Umiko and Taura, helped orchestrate the training and the correspondence between himself and the chieftain. They played a critical role and they were close friends with Finn—designed to spy on him.

Once Finn had revealed his ability to control the weather, Nakoma sought the old Linker. He had been right; Finn had turned out to be quite special, and it was time to move forward with his old plans to give her ultimate rule over all the Aquapopuleans.

Nakoma mindlessly stroked the neck of her giant lion as the advancing tribe made its way into the coastal town. She considered how Finn was instrumental in her future plans. Over the years, Nakoma became wise to what Gale had seen in this boy. He was smart, a fast learner, and capable of handling himself in a variety of situations. Taken from his home and brought into an unknown culture of big cats and water god worshipers, Eventually, he found comradeship with tribesmen who taught him their trades and skills. Finn advanced, making and bettering hunting spears. He excelled in tracking and communal hunting. But it wasn't until he reached manhood that his spectacular ability began to blossom. Finn was a force to be reckoned with, but she was confident she could control him. She couldn't let Finn just abandon the tribe. His control over the weather allowed them access to rain for crops and replenishing the lakes and pools, making their lives comfortable; he was essential. His ability alone was vital in convincing the people to desist worshipping the water god. And Harmony's abilities to combat the god couldn't be timed more perfect. If they leave this realm together, Nakoma thought with malice, I will be powerless to change anything. They are the tools we need to enact our vision of a new world.

The coastal villagers watched in fear as Nakoma and her legion of tattooed warriors and big cats paraded into town. The men carried hunting weapons and rode elks, the animals decorated with war paint. The elaborate head adornments worn by the tribal women gave them a mythical look as they sat astride their snarling felines. Upon seeing the invading Forest Tribe, villagers took their children into their boats and rowed a safe distance into the harbor. The clans had never seen a battle or experienced war, which they had only read about in the library, but they sensed the danger from the trespassers. The coastal clans didn't have weapons, only fishing spears and knives, which they gathered instinctively before escaping into the harbor.

The occupants of the Wellness dashed inside for safety while Morie, the keeper of the sacred temple, rushed out to defend her territory, Wellness-by-the-Sea. Nakoma crossed the bridge to the island, and her cat leaped up the hill to take a menacing stance in front of the grand vestibule. The tribe members fell in around her, filling the road and spilling into the grass.

"I am Nakoma, chieftain of the Forest Tribe. I want to speak to Calder the Linker," Nakoma demanded.

"I am Morie, the keeper of Wellness. Would you like to come inside?" Morie's posture was rigid, and her voice sounded sharp, her fear barely hidden.

Before Nakoma could respond, Calder stepped out with hands held up in peace, his face grim. Nakoma raised a dark brow. She hadn't seen Calder in a very long time. He'd aged significantly since then, but she knew this old man held knowledge he'd kept from his own people about the human realm. Gale and Calder had served the same master; her Linker had enlightened her on many things. When she had told Gale about a human girl in her city with the ability to burn sirens with her touch, his wicked smile was followed by a master plan.

Calder faced the chieftain. "Nakoma, there will be a consequence for your actions. You're responsible for the murder of my granddaughter Binda, the next-generation Linker for our clan. And Finn has informed us about your expectations for a high salt price and labor adjustment. I've spoken to our council, and we will negotiate, but only after you've been punished."

"The time for negotiation is over. And as for crimes—I have the authority to decide what must be done. I demand that Finn and Harmony are returned to me immediately. Turn them over, Linker, and your people will not suffer." She swung her long, muscular leg over her lion's back and sprang down. Her fur-clad knee-high boots crunched on the pebbles and broken shells that surfaced the road. Her narrowed eyes scanned the windows, and she glared at the white faces, which all withdrew when her eyes probed them.

***

Harmony stood with Finn and Kodiak before a window, watching Nakoma intimidate the gentle population. Finn growled, "If we leave she will destroy them. I can't create a storm to ward them off without endangering the coastal families."

Harmony watched Finn's handsome face darken with determination. His eyes narrowed, calculating. Indeed he looked the predator. Finn's earlier words returned: "Run from here… You'll lose your humanity."

"I will go down and do what I can to help," Kodiak announced, catching Harmony's attention. "You need to go. Harmony, I want you to be safe."

It seemed Kodiak was preparing to let her go, but Harmony felt only panic at the thought of leaving him. Was this really it—was her time here over? She wouldn't get to say good-bye to Rio, Nami, and Calder—another family lost?

"No, Kodiak, I will go down, and I will agree to travel back with Nakoma—*if* she lets Harmony go without further destruction. When the time is right—I will do what I have to."

Finn's unselfish words drew Harmony to his side. She yanked at his arm. "What? Finn, no!" she cried. "There must be another way."

He pulled her close and forced her to look up at him. "Go through the portal and do what you can." His eyes roved over her face. "Harmony, the tribe is my family. I'm needed there. I will do what I have to do to protect everyone."

What did that mean for Finn's humanity, Harmony wondered. How would these people be safe unless he eliminated Nakoma *and* her followers? He'd admitted his soul had darkened. But surely there would be no coming back from killing them all. She knew—she'd killed, and she still struggled with it. Harmony's stomach churned. Had her coming here ended the peace and driven Nakoma to act? Although hating what Finn said, she understood. Slipping her arms around his waist, she hugged him fiercely. She felt him drop a kiss on the top of her head.

"Be ready." Finn pulled away and indicated the herbs safely tucked into her bag. And then he turned to Kodiak and said, "You should go with her. She needs you." He left them alone in the room.

Harmony moved back to the window, tears in her eyes. Kodiak was behind her within a moment, his hands on her shoulders.

Harmony was infuriated. "This was Finn's chance to go home. Nakoma is taking his life away—again!"

42

Finn stepped out into the sunlight. He noticed Calder's surprise at his arrival. Nakoma flashed a triumphant smile, but it faded. He knew she was waiting for Harmony to appear. Finn strode toward her, waving to the others, hoping his relaxed approach would put them at ease.

"I'm willing to stay and do as you bid, if you let Harmony return to the human realm and not cause these people harm."

Nakoma seemed to consider his words.

"Finn, I did not see you as a hero, but I never did understand the human condition." Nakoma lowered her voice so only he could hear. "I want to rule the Aquapopulo. I want the people to worship me, not the water god. I want you to help me secure a workforce in the salt mines." She paused, narrowing her eyes. "If you do this, I will take you as a mate. You will be exclusively mine, and in time you will rule with me."

His face was impassive. "Agreed."

"Ride with me," she commanded.

Finn read Nakoma easily. She was threatened by Harmony and ultimately willing to let her go. He, on the other hand, was respected and revered by the tribe, an asset. Agreeing to her demands reconciled their differences. He knew his willingness to return with her offered her hope.

He turned to Calder and bellowed, "Send Harmony home. We will not disturb you further today. In the future we will negotiate on what Nakoma sees as essential to moving us into a new age."

Before they could mount, the ground began to rumble and then shook violently. Screams filled the air. Calder and many others yelled, "It's an earthquake! Take cover!"

They had felt rumbles before, but this was powerful. The earth's plates shifted, creating tremendous vibrations. The ground split open and stretched out like the roots of a tree. Warriors on the backs of their beasts teetered on the edges, the animals shifting their feet, trying to escape being swallowed by the ground. Warriors on foot scattered, heading toward the bridge, hoping to get off the island.

Nakoma drew her lips back in a snarl and glared at Finn. "You've ruined everything, Finn—do something!"

Finn's atmospheric ability had no effect on an earthquake. "There is nothing I can do. You need to lead the tribe to higher ground—go now!" he commanded Nakoma.

He turned to leave, but her shrill voice rose above the din and destruction around them. "Come with me!" Her distressed lion hunkered down, pawing at the grass while Nakoma mounted.

Before Finn could reply the ground beneath his feet cracked and the earth tore open. He jumped, scrambling to snatch the root of a bush; he felt his legs dangle above nothingness. Suddenly a lion yowled beneath him. Finn twisted. His eyes widened in shock when he saw Nakoma at the bottom of the jagged chasm below. He hauled himself over the broken edge and kneeled on the grass, sucking in a desperate breath. He looked down and watched the cat twitch once before going still. It sprawled, broken and dead, on top of the tribe's chieftain. Nakoma was a threat no longer.

He wasted no time hopping to his feet and looking around to assess the damage. The water in the bay rapidly receded, and he watched boaters frantically trying to row farther out to sea, trying to outrun the approaching swell. Then the building behind him groaned, and nearby trees toppled over, loudly cracking before thudding to the ground.

Above the shrieks of terrified beasts, the wails of trampled tribespeople, the screams of others racing for safety, the blast of the sea serpent's warning drew the attention of every breathing thing. The serpent thrust its horned head from the retreating ocean. Terror-filled shouts from the boaters carried toward Finn on the wind.

43

"Oh no, Kodi! They must be destroying the Wentworth in my realm, disturbing the balance! I'm too late!" Harmony despaired, believing all their struggles, all the deaths, were now meaningless!

Violent vibrations sent the pair toppling against a nearby table. Regaining their balance, preparing to make their escape, Harmony and Kodiak dodged books that bounced free from the shelves. They stumbled down the stairs, hanging on to each other and the railings. Another tremor sent her freefalling down the last flight of stairs. Kodiak called after her, trying to reach her. She landed in the Wellness's lobby. Through her tears, she saw Calder on the floor, blood oozing from his temple. Harmony crawled to the doorjamb.

"Calder, you're hurt!" Harmony looked around and realized many were hurt. When she looked out onto the lawn that sloped to the sea, it appeared several more were dead, held in the arms of their loved ones.

Harmony watched the water in the bay before her withdraw and saw the sea serpent thrust its head from the sea and blast a cry as loud as a hundred Mack truck horns.

Kodiak reached the ground floor at last and lurched toward Harmony as the floor began to buckle. He pulled her up and dragged her away from the open doorway.

Kodiak gripped her hand tight, keeping her steady, keeping her from running off into danger. She skidded and staggered, trying to break free.

The sea serpent! I need to get out there and help them! She knew she was too far from the sea serpent for her ability to work. She needed to get out there, closer to the sea. But through a window she saw the deep, churning water was now rushing back toward the island. *A tidal wave!* The temple, even up on the bluff, was going to be slammed by wall of water. She and Kodi dove behind the counter.

The sounds—splintering, glass shattering, and then seawater bubbling, gurgling—lasted but a moment before a wave ripped her from Kodiak's hand and dragged her underwater. Her shoulder thumped against something hard; something else struck her leg. The water carried her out through a broken window. She flailed and kicked until she resurfaced and took a huge gulp of air. The back side of the Wellness loomed before her—she was in the bay, drawn out by water's force in moments.

Suddenly, Harmony was yanked under the surface. Pawing against the current, she fought to resurface, but she felt hands grasp her just above her knees. She looked down through the roiled water—it was him!

Suijin, the water deity, had trapped her!

He looked just the same as when she was a child under the ice, that fateful day in the river with her mother. She observed the handsome face, his dark hair flowing downward as he thrust upward until they were face to face under the water. His eyes caressed her face, and he smiled at her. His hand slowly reached to touch the golden strands of her hair that haloed around her head. As he did, she drew back her elbows before shoving her hands as hard as she could manage underwater into his chest. His face contorted in pain. His bare skin blistered where her fingers touched. He reached out; she saw the flash of a blade. Then she felt the yank of her hair. Suijin swam away with a lock of it in his hand. She struggled to rise to the surface and drew a lifesaving breath.

"Harmony!" Her heart sang at Kodiak's voice. He was okay, and there he was, swimming toward her. His strong arms supported her head above the surface, and their lips met briefly.

Relief overwhelmed her. The Aquapopulo could hold their breath and survive the flood! The tribespeople could not. But now the tribe was no longer the main threat.

"Get me to the beach! I can drive the serpent away from the villagers. Their boats must have gone ashore with the tidal wave," she yelled above the loudly fizzing water around them. From what she could see, Wellness remained intact, although heavily damaged.

"Please, Kodi, hurry!"

She adjusted the satchel strap, sure the herbs were still safely tucked inside, and slung her arms over his shoulders, and then he turned. He soon swam under the bridge, toward the beach. His powerful arms eventually towed her close to the shore. The water pushed far into the landscape, over the grasses, past the trees, into the fields beyond. Soon their feet touched solid ground once more.

Boats had been driven ashore by the tidal wave, and many lay smashed on the beach. As the serpent closed in for the kill, families pulled their loved ones from the wreckage. Harmony ran to the water's edge, arms stretched upward, feeling heat course through her hands.

"Get behind me!" she screamed toward the last of the survivors. They scurried to comply, looking with terror offshore, where the sea serpent was fast approaching. Kodiak lifted two little children, carrying them to safety. Screeching in fury, the sea serpent burst through the waves, twisting to pluck a running man from the shore. Harmony's energy force momentarily faltered and she dropped her exhausted arms. Her knees threatened to buckle. An oncoming wave nearly knocked her down. She watched as the man was consumed by the beast before her eyes and shook with despair. *How can I defeat this thing alone?*

"Run! Take shelter!" a loud male voice bellowed behind her shoulder, and Harmony glanced sideways to see Finn, his hands extended, his wrists twisting.

"Finn!" Relief washed over her at the welcome sight, his muscular shoulders bulging with strength, his handsome face dark with concentration. Black clouds rumbled in, blotting out the horizon. Storm clouds, intensely ominous, gathered above the rising beast. Suddenly lightning struck the serpent. The beast lit up like a candle; the air puffed and sizzled. The sea serpent wobbled, its throat exposed and tongue lolling, before it sank like a freight train straight down into the lapping waves. The tremors went dormant and the clouds evaporated, allowing the sun and salty wind to return to normal.

Harmony flung her arms around Finn. "You did it! I couldn't do it..." She realized he was truly the *special* one. He was right; he was needed here. Both the tribes and the clans would benefit from a strong leader and protector. She was going to miss him.

Many Aquapopulo gathered on the shore, assessing the damage. Finn and Harmony made their way to the temple.

"Finn, your tribe! There are so many..."

"Dead," he finished. "Nakoma is dead, crushed to death by her lion when they fell into a deep, narrow chasm the earthquake opened."

Two tribesmen called to Finn. Finn seemed to know these men. Harmony stood numbly at his side while the men informed them that the tribe had been wiped out except for a sixteen remaining men and women. Finn told them that with their support he planned to claim the chiefdom. Both tribesmen Umiko and Taura swore allegiance on the spot.

Finn and Harmony passed through the devastation

toward the muck-covered steps of the battered temple. The Wellness residents moved quickly to provide any help they could, bandaging wounds and offering aid to those in need. Harmony noticed Calder sitting on the outdoor steps, a woman applying a bandage to his forehead. He shouted instructions to passers-by.

"Harmony!" He waved his arm when he saw her.

"Thank goodness you are all right, Calder. Have you seen anyone from the village? Rio or Nami?"

"Yes! I spoke with someone who saw them. They are all right. Do you still have the tin?" he asked urgently.

Harmony felt comforted that she wouldn't need to worry about her relatives. For a brief moment she panicked, then was reassured when she patted the satchel that hung across her chest. Miraculously it hadn't broken loose when the tidal wave swept her away and she'd confronted Suijin. She nodded, relieved.

Calder exhaled. "Good! Good girl!" He took a calm breath. "I think the time has come. You must return immediately. This wooden structure, perhaps this very island, may not survive another earthquake. I'm reluctant to say that I'm relieved, but the tribe is now reduced to nothing, that threat avoided. But I have not seen Nakoma."

"Finn told me that Nakoma is dead." She looked at Finn for confirmation. He nodded and smiled at Calder. "And he wants to step in as chief." Harmony's expression became solemn. Her heart was torn. She wanted Finn to explore life in her realm, but being chieftain here was what *he* wanted. Perhaps she wished too strongly for a companion, a friend to ease her own loneliness in her world. She had grown fond of Finn.

Calder rose and nodded at Finn. "We will call a council meeting as soon as we are able." He held up his webbed hand to emphasize his next words. "First, Harmony must return to her realm! Finn, take her inside, light the herbs, and send her home."

Frantically, Harmony scanned the devastation before her. Kodiak was nowhere to be found. Calder leaned forward to half-hug her, patting her shoulder kindly. "Good luck, Harmony."

Finn clasped her hand and pulled her inside the temple and found the nearest room, a birthing room, the pools now filled with debris, the floors covered in puddles. The wall of seawater had smashed the windows and flooded the entire lower half of the building.

Finn said, "It's too humid in here. No match will light in this room. We must go up."

Clasping her hand again, he opened the door and led her down the corridor to a staircase. They ascended until they reached the library. It was chaotic, books all over the floor, shelves overturned, but it was dry.

"Hand me the tin," he instructed.

She wrestled with the buckle and then pulled out the small tin. Finn righted a knocked-over table and scooped up a container that once had held bookmarks. He popped the lid off and dumped half the herbs into the container. "Is that enough?"

"Yes, but where is Kodi? I can't leave without saying good-bye." *This is too soon. I need more time!*

The floor shook for a moment and then stopped.

"Something is happening—you've got to go now! Where are the matches?" She held open her hand to reveal them. "I'll tell him good-bye for you." Finn brushed a kiss across her cheek and then plucked the match from her hand. He struck it against the leather band that circled his wrist. The match ignited, and he tossed it into the container holding the precious herb blend. He dashed from the room.

Harmony snapped the lid back on the tin and stuffed it into the satchel. As the smoke rose she tightly gripped the satchel around her torso.

All she could think about was Kodiak. How could she leave without saying good-bye? She started to cough. She imaged his beautiful copper-flecked eyes, his lazy smile, his voice… She coughed again and again.

In her mind she could hear his voice… She could hear him calling her name—

He is calling my name!

Kodiak burst into the room, waving away the smoke as he reached her. She was beyond coughing and couldn't say anything. She was happy to see his face one last time but knew he was in danger if he inhaled the toxic smoke. Wanting to keep him safe, she tried to push him away, but she had no strength left and dropped to her knees. He tried to catch her, but he was overwhelmed by a fit of coughing.

She fought to keep her eyes open, even a sliver, to be able to watch him for as long as she could, but it was little use. Her eyes flooded from the herbs. She reached blindly for Kodiak as the blackness engulfed her.

44

Awareness surged through Kodiak's body, waking his senses. He was under water, his lungs tight, like when he stayed under too long. He was in the ocean. He remembered inhaling the herbs, and he realized this wasn't his ocean. He swirled around, looking for Harmony.

He saw her struggling nearby, her body slowly sinking. He swam to her, grabbed her hips, and propelled her up. Breaking the surface, they each sucked in deep gulps of air.

Treading water with her in his arms, Kodiak called her name, anxiously waiting for her to respond. Her eyes popped open and focused on him. A surge of relief washed through him.

"Kodi! You made it through!" She wound her arms around his neck and kissed him, the kind of kiss rooted deep in gratitude and reverence. They were together; they'd made it this far.

Kodiak lifted his eyes away from his beautiful wife's face to see a boat speeding directly for them. He quickly pulled Harmony under the water. Seconds later the boat zoomed over their heads. The dangers of this realm suddenly overwhelmed him. He was a fish out of water.

Bursting to the surface again, Harmony coughed several times, expelling seawater. Kodiak gasped and said, "Let's get out of the water." He was unnerved by his need for air so soon. The thought of losing his ability to remain underwater in this realm scared him.

Harmony swiveled her head. "This way," she said through blue lips. He noticed goosebumps on her arms as she began to swim toward an island.

Following her, he noticed a building on the bluff that

resembled the Wellness. "Is that where you found Calder's satchel?"

"Yes, that's Wentworth-by-the-Sea. But something's not right." She raised her arm to begin to swim again.

He swam alongside Harmony underwater and surfaced, inhaling heavily, after a couple moments. He tried again and again until his suspicion was confirmed—he could no longer hold his breath for an extended period of time. This human world suppressed what he loved most about his race, what made him special. Kodiak Night was a Diver, a treasure hunter, but now he felt disconnected. *I'll have to figure this out later. Right now I must focus on what caused the earthquake. Is there anything we can do to prevent another one from happening?*

Winded from the long swim, they reached the beach. She immediately turned to him. "You came back with me! I'm glad you did, but I thought it wasn't allowed. We didn't know if it would work."

"I wasn't ready to let you go," he admitted.

"You risked your life…"

Kodiak, not ready to analyze his actions, looked at his surroundings, trying to absorb the strangeness of her world. He had realized as soon as the herbs began to choke him what was going to happen. And he was here now. His priorities were to figure out what to do about the disturbances and get Harmony to a safe place. "Harmony, we will figure everything out. Right now we need to know what is happening. Did something here cause a disturbance on the sacred site?" She nodded, wild-eyed. "Do you know the way?"

"Of course." She slicked her sodden hair back from her eyes. "Of course," she repeated. She looked around until her eyes rested on the setting sun. "It's strange, but the day and night are slightly off kilter somehow. Maybe it takes hours to pass through," she commented. "It's up

271

there. There are steps." She waved for him to follow her.

Reaching the crest of the hill, the Wentworth before him, Harmony several yards ahead, Kodi turned to look out to sea. The familiar moving dark waters calmed him. He tensed as a strangled cry emerged from Harmony's lips. He jogged over to stand at her side. Her hands covered her mouth, and tears shone brightly in her eyes as she stared at the devastation before her.

So this was her precious building she said she'd worked to preserve: Wentworth-by-the-Sea. Rubble littered the ground. The breeze kicked up dust. No one was around. It seemed the army that took this place down had moved on.

"Oh no," Harmony moaned. "Look at how much they tore down. They've taken most of it...maybe eighty percent of it. At least they left the original structure intact. That must mean something!"

Kodiak wiped dust from his eyes and squinted at the vast wasteland of wreckage. Large, yellow contraptions loomed in the dwindling light. "What are those?"

"Those are what brought this place to ruin," she snarled, but she continued more softly when she remembered he'd never seen such things before. "Sorry. That's the construction equipment." She named each monster.

"I'm sorry, Harmony. I know you care about this place."

"I was just here! Well..." She seemed to calculate. "I guess that was five...six weeks ago. It must be April by now." She rubbed her arms against the cold, a faraway look in her eyes.

"This teardown must have caused the disturbance which in turn caused the earthquake in my realm. The portal is just there, very close," Kodiak speculated. He watched her dash a tear from her eye.

With a sniff she said, "Let's go. It's getting dark."

***

They walked awhile before arriving at her house. She had no other option but to lead him down the paved road. The beach was not accessible because many properties sloped toward the rocks and sea, and swimming was not even worth considering. Harmony was relieved that the evening traffic was light; only a few vehicles passed them. She had to tug Kodiak along after each went by, because he'd stop and stare in wonder.

"This place is wild," he repeated a few times.

They soon walked up Harmony's driveway. He followed her around to the back of the house to the porch. The door screeched on its hinges, and they stepped on the Astroturf floor. He reached down to touch the fake grass. Harmony shook her head, thinking fake grass was silly. How could she explain it? Inside the screened porch, Harmony lifted a vase and retrieved the key from its hiding place.

Harmony was dying of thirst after swallowing her fair share of salty water, and the long walk had magnified her parched state. In the kitchen, she opened a cupboard, reached for two tall glasses, and filled them with tap water. She looked in the sink at the lunch plate she'd left there so long ago, before she'd found herself in the other realm.

Kodiak gratefully accepted the glass of water and downed it twice as fast as she did. She set her empty glass on the counter, and he did the same.

"I was in my grandpa's den when the herbs caught fire. Let's check it out." She still carried the satchel; her hand had instinctively checked for it when she'd reached the beach. The tin Calder gave her remained safely inside.

She opened the den door gradually, sniffing for that acrid smell. *Nothing.* Crossing to the desk, she inspected the letter tray that still held the paper and herbs. They didn't even appear burned. *Wow, that's strange.*

She carefully cupped the paper nesting the herbs and returned it to the original tin. Tucking the tin into her satchel, she paused, scanning the room for a place to keep the satchel safe. Pivoting toward the desk, she decided the desk drawer would at least hide it.

She closed the drawer and addressed Kodiak, who was examining a model ship inside a glass case. "Let's get out of these wet clothes. Then I'll fix us something to eat."

She led him through the living room, past the half-filled boxes, to the stairs. She flicked on the stairwell light, illuminating the framed photos hanging on the wall between the first and second floors. Kodiak stalled on the steps, a smile tugging at his lips. Harmony could tell he recognized her at various ages.

She cleared her throat at the landing and said, "I have something for you to wear. Some of my grandfather's clothes are still here. He was tall, like you."

"You grew up in this house?" His hand was on the newel post when he stopped. She stepped back, suddenly feeling too close to him in the tight space.

"Yeah, my grandparents raised me here. Now that they have passed on, I own this house." She pointed her chin down the hallway, signaling the direction she wanted to go.

She felt his eyes on her back. Sighing at the surreal feeling of returning from another realm, she entered her grandparents' room and opened the closet. Luckily she hadn't gotten around to giving away all her grandfather's clothes. Several of his shirts and pants hung next to her grandmother's things. Harmony selected appropriate garments and led him to the tiny bathroom off the bedroom that her grandparents had converted from a guestroom closet, with a basic shower, toilet, and sink, in 1982.

The bathroom remained stocked with supplies. Harmony pointed out various soaps and handed Kodiak a towel. "My room is down the hall. I'm going to take a shower in the other bathroom. Do you have everything you need?"

She knew exactly how he felt to find himself in a strange world, but her world had so much more in the way of modern conveniences. His world was simple, almost ancient. She would explain what he wanted to know soon. Right now she needed the basic comforts of her home—a shower, clean clothes, and hot food.

Kodiak raised his eyebrows and blasted her with his luminescent amber eyes. "Stay close by. Don't leave this house without me."

"I won't leave. I promise." She thought at first he was panicky about being out of place in this world, but then she realized he was being protective of her. He didn't feel she was safe here, but in truth she felt she owed him protection. He was here because of her, and there were dangers here.

"I won't leave you, Kodi." She stepped close to him and reached for his hand. His face tilted down. Those strange, beautiful eyes seemed brighter in the dim room. "You are safe in this house. We can rest here while we figure out what to do." She reached up, touching his chin and running her finger along his angled jaw. "Are you okay?"

His eyes fluttered closed for a moment, and he rested his cheek in the heat of her hand. "I am fine. It is you I am worried about." His whispered words were filled with anguish. "Back in the Wellness library, when I saw you choking, I didn't realize they were sending you back." He clasped her hand and drew it to his chest.

"And you were going to leave me without saying good-bye," he accused.

Harmony shook her head. "That's not what I wanted. Calder was rushing to send me back to see if I could intervene with whatever was causing the earthquakes in your world. I'm not sure what I can do to help. Kodi, the thought of leaving you without saying good-bye haunted me—and then you showed up and tried to save me." They stood together, familiar, and Harmony wondered how two such different people could have such strong feelings toward one another. It wasn't as if they were born on different sides of the tracks, they were from completely different worlds—they weren't even the same species. She might carry some of his genes, but she was mostly human. But Kodiak could pass for human—and a fine-looking specimen at that.

Kodiak responded after a long pause. "Okay. Well, I am here with you now. I will do what I can to help you." He released her hand. She nodded a thank you, turned, and left the room.

Harmony needed some time alone to think. Kodiak's presence was distracting, and she had important things to figure out. In her bathroom, she stripped down and climbed into a steaming shower. Opening her shampoo bottle, she inhaled deeply. The coconut scent was deliciously familiar and comforting. She'd experienced a fantastic journey and come away with a husband. But was he here accidentally? After all, it wasn't like he'd made an active choice to come with her. Instead, he'd seen her choking and came to her...rescue?

After her shower she toweled the steam from the mirror and gazed at her reflection. *Why me? Why my family? I'm the only mixed-blood freak in two realms!* Placing the towel on the sink she raised her hands and examined them. Here in this realm, she wouldn't need her strange ability to repel sea serpents and water gods like a Jedi knight or lethally burn sirens—unless Suijin came after her again. But she wasn't planning on ever going back into the ocean or any deep body of water. She hoped that he'd stay away from her since she'd burned him when he tried to drown her during the tidal wave. She hoped he'd remain in the other realm.

The devastating scenes played out in her mind: the invasion of Nakoma's army, the quake and tidal wave, the return of the sea serpent and the water god. And finally Finn's determination to help the people. What had become of everyone?

She pulled on jeans and a tee-shirt and mindlessly wandered into the kitchen. She explored the cabinets for food. She opened two cans of Campbell's vegetable soup, dumped them into a pot, and set it on the stove to heat. Scanning the familiar room, Harmony noticed the answering machine on the counter. The red light was blinking. *Gosh, I've been gone for almost six weeks. Someone might think I've gone missing!*

She hit the button and leaned in to hear. Four calls from Samantha, who by the last message sounded worried. Harmony picked up the receiver from the wall. As the dial tone sang its stale tune, Harmony was motionless. What was she going to say to her dearest friend Samantha? *Remember those tea leaves? Well, I burned them, and they took me to another realm, where I met family and fought off sea serpents and sirens... And by the way, I'm married.*

She hung up the phone and returned to the stove to stir the soup.

45

Kodiak leaned against the doorjamb, filling the frame, while he watched his wife make dinner. "Smells good."

Her smile was apologetic. "It's vegetable soup from a can. It's not exactly the first choice of food I'd like you to try in this realm, but I'm afraid it will have to do."

As she opened a cabinet and reached for bowls Kodiak raised his brows at how the fitted pants hugged her behind. He certainly liked the clothing she wore. In fact, even with all the other interesting things to look at in this room alone, he couldn't keep his eyes from her. She set their meager meal on the table, flashing him a shy smile, and opened the refrigerator. She took out two bottles of dark liquid and set them down. As if an afterthought, she breezed to the sink and returned with a glass of water. She handed Kodiak the glass.

"Your welcome to try what I'm drinking, but if you don't like it, you don't have to drink it," she said, sliding into her chair.

He sat and then mimicked how she twisted the cap off the Pepsi bottle. She took a long sip that ended with an "Aahh!" He lifted the bottle to his lips. The effervescent liquid filled his mouth. The carbonation burned his tongue and the taste was sharp and long lasting. After he swallowed, he tried not to make a face, but he could tell his efforts were unsuccessful when Harmony cracked up laughing.

Kodiak grinned back at her, noticing a new sense of ease about her. He ate spoonfuls of soup, still smiling at her in the silence. This wasn't so bad—a cozy dwelling and a woman who he believed could make him happy.

With their bellies content, they moved into the living room. Harmony knelt down and dug around in a pile of books. She brought one over to Kodiak, who sat on the sofa.

"This is something my grandmother put together—photos and newspaper clippings of our family and local events from years ago. I think there is a picture of Calder in here," she said. She flipped through the newspaper articles until she found what she was looking for.

Kodiak leaned in to look at a clipping about the peace treaty signed at the Wentworth-by-the-Sea in 1905. Harmony was excited over one photo of a group of men on the veranda. "Here it is! When I met Calder, I thought I'd seen him before. After mulling it over and discovering that he'd been here for the Treaty, I immediately thought of this very photograph. Look, I think this is him." She pointed, and both their heads bent forward.

"He looks younger, but it's definitely him."

"I can't believe he broke the law and took up with my great-great-grandmother. Then he left her pregnant!" Her voice became small. "She must have been heartbroken when he left. I wonder why he didn't just stay. It sounded like they loved each other."

"It was his duty to return to his people. He's a valuable Linker." Kodiak knew there were only a handful of Linkers alive then. Supposedly they were the only ones who could cross back and forth between the realms, and yet here he sat, in the other realm.

"You're a valuable Diver. Do you want to return, Kodi?"

Kodiak confessed, "No. I can't go back…not without you. And it's not about the lavender pearl ring. Well, it was at first, but then it was about you. Harmony, you are the treasure." Pulling the scrapbook from her hands, he set it on the table at their knees. He placed his hand on the fabric of her jeans. "I basically lost my family when my mother died. I have nothing to hold me in that realm.

It doesn't matter where I am as long as I have you by my side. I'm of the Aquapopulo and you are mostly human, so I don't know if or how this will work, but we have to try. I need it to work because I've fallen in love with you."

Her eyes grew enormous and she blinked back tears. "Kodi, this seems so soon. We haven't known each other that long, but I feel the same way. When I gave myself to you, it was as your loving wife. I love you too."

His mouth was on hers, his kiss driving out any doubt she might feel, though they both knew that odds were against them.

Holding her in his arms his whispered passionate promises. "I'm not going to leave you like Calder left your great-great-grandmother. I won't repeat history. We will work together to help protect both our realms. And I will always treasure you."

***

The unlikely couple clung together. Beyond their window, far out into the sea, a man with scales broke the surface of the water. Suijin could cross between the realms because he was a god, but throughout all the years he'd spent in those realms he'd only ever desired one thing. Harmony Parker.

Author's Note

My imagination is continuously weaving plots whether I'm folding laundry, walking the dog, or driving the kids to practice. One of the fun things about being an author is when one of my many creative ideas comes together, especially when a particular idea develops into a story. In *The Rare Pearl* for instance, I had already planned the Aquapopulean race in my mind but wanted to give validity to the origin. When I searched the internet for information on evolution I came across the Aquatic Ape Theory. As I read through this fascinating theory I was thrilled to build the factitious Aquapopulean race I had conceived on the support of a concept already studied by scientists in the field of anthropology. This set the foundation for the Broken Water Series.

Another fun aspect to writing is where the inspiration comes from. I'm often inspired by historic events and the diverse locations I travel to. I like to use authentic places to help the reader better connect to the story. I used the Wentworth-by-the-Sea hotel in this story because it's inspired me for decades. This building has an amazing past and has housed many famous guests, my favorite being the sharpshooter Annie Oakley who was hired to teach female guests to shoot. This hotel closed in 1982 when I was ten years old. As a kid, taking long drives with my folks along New Hampshire's scenic coast, I'd stare in awe at the turn of the century hotel. As the years passed, I saw the Wentworth fall into disrepair and it weighed heavy on my heart. I always wondered what she had been like in her heyday and wished the building would be saved. The Wentworth with its tumultuous history, elegant architecture, and grand setting is one incredible source of inspiration I had to write about. Giving my characters Harmony Parker and her relatives a connection to the Wentworth's history helped fuel this series. I used the hotel's tragic event in 1989 when eighty percent of it was torn down as a climactic scene in *The Rare Pearl*. I took the snapshot in the front of this book not long afterward the teardown, when only the original facade remained. Like many great stories with tales that rollercoaster from splendor to tragedies to happy endings—the same goes for the Wentworth-by-the-Sea. She was eventually purchased, refurbished and reopened in 2003. After the reopening I finally got my chance to step foot inside the building for the first time and stay as a guest—it left me giddy. The rooms, décor and service were top notch bringing her into a new era, but I found myself wondering about the days long ago and what kind of stories she could tell if her walls could talk.

I'm always happy to hear from my readers. I encourage you to leave me a message on my website www.jenniferwsmith.com. Please let others know how you liked the book by leaving a review on Amazon.com and/or Goodreads.com.

Follow:

Twitter.com/authorjenwsmith
Facebook.com/authorjenniferwsmith
Instagram.com/authorjenniferwsmith

Be sure to look for the release of book 2 in the Broken Water series, The Forsaken Pearl.

ABOUT THE AUTHOR

Jennifer W. Smith lives in a leafy New
Hampshire town with her husband, two children,
Balinese kitty, and Rough Collie. Jennifer's
passionate about travel and exploring her New
England surroundings. The New Hampshire
coastline inspired this Broken Water series.

Also by Jennifer W. Smith

Flying Backwards

Made in the USA
Middletown, DE
10 July 2016